PROLO

The crescent of the new moon slid from behind a cloud, casting a pale orange glow onto Tower Green. A furtive shadow slid to the cover of the nearest wall, and slowly crept towards the door behind which a guard was waiting with a pounding heart. The clink of coins in a bag was followed by the muted creaking of the opening woodwork, and Tyrrell slipped inside, commanding the guard to follow him as they took the stairs cautiously one at a time.

Inside the chamber, the two boys were snuffling and muttering in their uneasy slumber, each on a separate cot. Tyrrell tiptoed to the sleeping form of the older boy, who was lying face down, and forced his full body weight down on the unsuspecting head; there were a few choking noises, and it was done. The guard — a man named Dighton — found the younger boy lying on his side, his golden fair hair across his face. Dighton placed his mailed fist over the boy's mouth, and when his eyes opened in terror he gestured with his free hand for the nine-year-old to remain silent, then lifted him onto his shoulder.

Down the stairs, and through the shadows along the wall of the Inner Ward, the two men carried their bundles to the already opened gate and portcullis that gave access to the oily river, in which a waiting wherry was moored alongside. They stepped round the inert form of the gate guard, who had opened up to Tyrrell when shown the written authority under the seal of the Lord High Constable of England, and had then slid silently to the ground when a dagger had been inserted firmly and accurately between his ribs and into his heart. The two men lowered their bundles into the bottom of the boat, and the wherryman was ordered away from the landing steps.

Downstream an hour later, Tyrrell had completed the essential task of securing rocks around the body of the youth he had been carrying, and with a grunt he heaved it over the side and consigned it to the crabs. Then he ordered the wherryman to steer to the north bank, where he stepped over the gunnel and waded, thigh deep, to the grassy shore after delivering one last encouragement to his companion.

'Downstream to Gravesend, to the *Beau Marie*. She will take you to Calais, where you will receive more gold. Go now, without delay.'

The next morning it was discovered that the guard had abandoned his post, and that the royal prisoners were missing. In fear for his life, the constable, Sir Robert Brackenbury, remained silent, and an enduring mystery was born.

JUSTICE FOR THE CARDINAL

Published by Sapere Books.

20 Windermere Drive, Leeds, England, LS17 7UZ,
United Kingdom

saperebooks.com

ISBN: 978-1-913028-99-2

JUSTICE FOR THE CARDINAL

The Tudor Saga Series
Book Three

David Field

SAPERE
BOOKS

PART I

I

1536

As Thomas Cromwell approached Fyfield Manor down a long lane framed by two elderly oaks, he saw a young man throwing stones at the waterfowl that flapped and fussed in a large ornate pond.

Cromwell dismounted and waded through the long grass towards the pond, and the young man looked up to meet his stare.

'You must be Richard Gordon,' Cromwell announced.

'Depends who you ask,' Richard replied. 'My grandmother would have me addressed as such, but my step-grandfather insists that I answer to Richard Ashton, else I will be beaten. By his sons, no less.'

'But your grandmother is Lady Catherine Gordon?'

'She was once. Now she is merely Catherine Ashton. Before that she was Catherine Craddock, and before that who knows? Another question might be who cares.'

'If I follow this track, I will reach the manor house?' Cromwell asked.

'You will, and much luck may it bring you. It has brought me little enough. Who are you?'

'Master Thomas Cromwell, Chancellor of the Exchequer, Recorder of Bristol, Steward of the Abbey of Westminster, Master of the Rolls, Secretary to His Majesty and Visitor-General of the Monasteries, in which last capacity I am likely to be welcomed at the manor house. I go to bring your step-grandfather the good news that he will shortly be allowed to purchase the twelve hides of Abingdon Abbey that he has long coveted.'

'Many titles. You must in truth be very wealthy.'

'So it is rumoured by my enemies, of which I have many. But not as wealthy as your grandfather should have been.'

'My grandfather?'

'Yes. There is much to discuss, but first I must first seek confirmation of some further details from your grandmother.'

'She was put to bed some days ago. They say it is but an ague, but at her age who can tell?'

'Clearly I must delay no longer. Until the morrow, then.'

Cromwell remounted his gelding and nudged him up the track to the manor house, leaving Richard Ashton to re-engage the waterfowl.

Had Cromwell been the King himself, he could not have been treated with more deference, with excessive bowing and scraping once his identity and his business were announced. The Ashton sons were sharing the fireplace with their wives and offspring, and the old man himself was summoned from his aviary by a menial who came back armed with wine and wafers.

'You will stay for supper, and perhaps bide overnight?' Christopher Ashton enquired hopefully.

Cromwell nodded. 'You are one day's ride from Westminster, hidden away here in the Berkshire countryside, and not even Master Secretary would be safe from footpads on the night lanes around Windsor, so I thank you for your hospitality. I'm informed that your good wife has taken to her bed?'

'You obviously spoke with the manor idiot on your way in,' one of the Ashton sons observed, and his brother sniggered. 'His concern for our stepmother's health would be touching, were it genuine. He seeks only to be assured that he is rid of his duty to her, then he will no doubt ride away to seek his fortune in the town.'

'I must speak with your step-mother,' Cromwell told them.

'She was sleeping, when I was last up there,' one of the brother's wives replied. 'She took a draught not an hour ago, to ease the pain, and she would not thank you to wake her.'

'Not an ague, then?' Cromwell asked.

'A canker,' came the reply from one of the men in front of the fire.

An hour later, shortly before supper, Cromwell crept up the narrow staircase and eased his head round the half open door. There was a rustling movement in the bedding, then a sharp cry of pain, followed by the raising of a skeletal head from the bolster.

'Who's there?' Catherine Gordon called out.

Cromwell moved to the bed, sat down on the end of it and smiled reassuringly. 'Master Cromwell, Secretary to King Henry.'

'You bring me news of the Princess Mary?'

'The "Lady" Mary, as we are bidden to call her. But no, no news.'

'She must be mourning her mother's passing, the poor mite. What age will she be now?'

'She had her twentieth birthday just a few weeks past. A grown woman now, and much changed from when you were in command of her Privy Chamber.'

'She was but fourteen when I last saw her, but virtuous and beautiful in her own way,' Catherine reminisced sleepily. 'The King still intends to have her declared bastard?'

'The Queen, madam, not the King.'

Catherine made a noise in her throat as if expelling unwanted mucus. 'That whore belongs on a pyre.'

'With your assistance, she may shortly complete her reign on the scaffold.'

'Gladly. What may I do? Be brief, for I feel the pains returning.'

'Your first husband — the one they hanged as a traitor.'

'My only true love? Perkin of blessed memory?'

'He indeed. What became of his son? I believe you had a son and a daughter before Perkin was detained at the whim of the old Henry, and you went into the service of Queen Elizabeth of York?'

'Indeed. My daughter married a cloth merchant, and is now in Antwerp, no doubt scolding her own grandchildren.'

'Antwerp?' Cromwell repeated, looking up sharply. 'Has she made herself known to those who raised your first husband?'

'Not to my knowledge. And it would not be safe, with another Tudor on the throne.'

'Probably not. But your son?'

'Jamie died some years past. He fell from his horse. He had no children. Jamie had but one child — Richard.'

'So Richard is truly Perkin's grandson?'

'Yes. I left England after Perkin was hanged as a traitor, and after the death of the Queen Elizabeth, whose lady-in-waiting I had become. I was sent as a lady in attendance on the Princess Margaret upon her marriage to the King of Scotland, but after his war with King Henry that led to his death, my lady came back south to London, with me still in her train. A Gentleman Usher of the King's Chamber, James Strangeways, paid me court, and we were married. I took letters of denization to make me officially English, and was granted these estates in Fyfield in my own right, with a condition that I may never again return to Scotland. My Huntly entitlements have by this means eluded me, but my status as a comfortable widow has yielded me two more husbands since then.'

Her head fell back on the pillow after all the effort of speaking, and even more colour left her bony cheeks. Gazing down at her pure white hair and haggard face, it was difficult for Cromwell to recreate, even in the imagination, the beauty that had once been the talk of two nations, although her ocean-pure deep blue eyes had lost none of their lustre.

'I must take Richard back with me,' Cromwell told her gently.

'That he may be used like his grandfather?' Catherine wheezed back.

'No-one must know his true identity. Does he know of it himself?'

'He knows who he is, but he has never been told who, or what, he might have been.'

'It might be a kindness not to tell him, but I must if I am to give him the lust for revenge that will spur him on to greatness.'

'He is all I have left,' Catherine reminded Cromwell weakly. 'I would plead with you to let him remain here in ignorance, were I not marked for death within days.'

'Did you believe what your first husband claimed?'

'Why would I not? He was my husband, and I loved him dearly. Do *you* believe it?'

'I had occasion, during my time in the service of Cardinal Wolsey, to learn from him certain facts revealed in the confessional many years ago. If those facts be true, then there can be no doubt of who your late husband truly was. And they say that facts revealed in the final confession must be the truth, else the gates of Hell will open for the sinner.'

'You will take Richard to Court, say you? To what purpose will you put him?'

'He will be my eyes and ears. The presence of Master Secretary in any assembly, but most notably that of the Queen, closes mouths these days, I observe. But nothing is more likely than the presence of a handsome young Courtier, such as I will make Richard, to open the mouths of the Queen and her Ladies. They grow indiscreet in their belief that they can do and say anything and Henry will pardon it.'

'So Richard is to become your spy? But what is likely to be his fate, if he be discovered?'

'You speak as if I meant harm to the throne. I am no foreign assassin, madam.'

'But you mean the whore no good, as you said before?'

'I said that I mean no harm to the throne. Anne Boleyn's days, however, are only a little less limited than yours, madam. Henry grows tired of her tongue, and the bridle that she places on his pleasures.'

'I grow tired again,' Catherine all but whispered. 'When I am gone, please give my loving regards to the Princess Mary, and say that I hope she will remember me fondly.'

'I will certainly undertake that pleasant duty, but you should know that few are allowed to attend upon her these days. She currently abides in her father's house at Hunsdon, where she grieves for her mother and studies the scriptures.'

'Will you leave on the morrow? If so, please allow Richard time to say his farewells. He does not know that I am dying, and you must not tell him.'

'I will not, madam, on my oath. And now I make my own farewells.'

'God speed your enterprise. And so goodbye.'

Cromwell kissed her hand, and bowed backwards towards the door. His eye lit upon a goblet on a table beside her bed, which had no doubt contained her latest draught to ease the pain. Through a mist of tears the scene changed, and lying in the bed was an elderly man at death's door, his Cardinal's finery put off for the last time and draped over a chair. There was a wine goblet on the table, but this time it contained the draught that Cromwell had prepared for his master, which both of them had known would be fatal if swallowed.

It had been the Cardinal's final sin to take his own life in that way, but Thomas Cromwell's had been the hand that had made it possible. It had been in the Abbey at Leicester, on his way south to the Tower, where the Cardinal would doubtless have died anyway. But did that make what they had both done less of a sin? Cromwell did not believe that one could expiate sin by mumbling *pater nosters* and handing coins to priests; that was why he could bring himself to continue the work the Cardinal had begun, of bringing the so-called 'holy houses' to heel.

But without the intervention of the clergy, how did one make one's peace with God? Was it by direct communication, as the heretic Luther claimed? If so, then God must know how many nights Cromwell had spent on his knees, begging forgiveness for his one uncharacteristic act of weakness in helping an old man end his own bodily agony. Surely God would forgive that?

II

'Do you bring me the boy?' the Countess of Salisbury asked eagerly.

Cromwell nodded. 'Why would I be here, otherwise?'

'There is some truth in that, although on this occasion you are welcome.'

Margaret Pole, Countess of Salisbury, was now in her early sixties. The daughter of George, Duke of Clarence, niece of both the last Warwick-made Plantagenet monarch Edward IV and the man who had allegedly usurped his throne by foul means, Richard of Gloucester, she had somehow survived the Tudor whirlwind that had swept the nation following the battle of Bosworth Field. She held her title in her own right, but had taken to husband Sir Richard Pole, a staunch Lancastrian, whose mother had been the half-sister of the wily Margaret Beaufort, grandmother to the King.

Cromwell regarded the wily old Margaret as a fox in the henhouse; an adder lying curled in the long grass, ready to strike. Behind what should have been her gratitude and loyalty to the King lay two burning reasons for desiring revenge, one of them as old as history, and the other more recent.

Margaret had watched with sad disbelief when the Infanta Katherine of Aragon had been cast aside in favour of 'La Prostituta', as the Spanish called Anne. Margaret had defiantly worn mourning weeds for a fortnight when Katherine's death had been proclaimed throughout the nation. But her seething resentment of the newly installed Tudor dynasty went much deeper than that.

Margaret had seen Henry VII of Richmond as a usurper — stealing the throne from the Houses of York and spreading false rumours against her late uncle, Richard. The first was that Richard had ordered the murder of her own father George, Duke of Clarence. The second, and equally foul, had been that Richard had murdered the two heirs apparent to his dead brother Edward. They had been Edward, Prince of Wales and Richard, Duke of York.

'You call him a boy, my lady, but in truth he is a grown man, and a handsome one to boot.'

'Who does he resemble?'

'Forgive me, madam, but I never saw anyone with whom to compare him. All I have seen is a sketch of his grandfather, but I can confirm, from the mouth of the Lady Catherine Gordon, as was, that he is his true grandson. You must judge for yourself, although it will not suit my immediate purpose should he too closely resemble your long-lost kin. It is not my intention to reveal his true identity to anyone at Court. He would not survive long, were King Henry to hear of it. And, as I have already intimated in my conversations with your husband, he is to play a crucial role in the downfall of she whose ruination we all desire, albeit for different reasons.'

'There are new rumours at court about George Rochford, the Queen's brother. The tittle-tattle of the kitchens at Beaulieu is that George prefers boys. Or horses. Or dogs. Or anything with a hole other than Jane Parker, as was.'

'Forgive me if I blush, my lady. I spent some years in the service of a Cardinal of Rome.'

'A Cardinal with a mistress and two children? How did *that* serve to sharpen your sensitivities, Master Secretary?'

Cromwell's face darkened in the way that many under his interrogation had learned to fear as he glared back at the

Countess. 'Madam, if we are to continue in civil discourse, you would do well not to besmirch the memory of the man whose memory I most revere.'

'The man who made you what you are today, you mean?'

'The man who raised me to such eminence as I currently enjoy with King Henry. But it was the Cardinal who placed me in such a position that my talents might be noted, and employed in the royal service.'

'Yet you plot against Henry?'

'Not against Henry directly, madam. Against the whore alone.'

'And why she?'

'Because it was her vile tongue, at a time when Henry was lusting after her maidenhead, that blamed the Cardinal for the refusal of the Pope to grant the annulment of his marriage to Queen Katherine.'

'An annulment which you succeeded in securing?'

'No, madam, which Henry himself succeeded in securing when he threw the Pope out of the English Church. It was then a simple matter of granting himself his own annulment, as the new head of "the Church of England", as it is now to be known.'

'But in the eyes of God that was no annulment, surely?' the Countess argued.

'That is a matter for the theologians, madam. I am a mere common lawyer.'

'A *far* from common lawyer, if rumour be correct. But for all your skills, you could not break Sir Thomas More, whose eyes to the very end were raised to the *true* Church.'

'His eyes when I last saw them,' Cromwell replied with a slight shudder, 'were facing the ground below the scaffold, along with the rest of his head.'

'Is it true that his daughter has his head preserved?'

'So it is said. Now, the boy? He has been amusing himself with your kitchen staff ever since we arrived, and I do not wish him to form the belief that such is his natural level in life.'

'What do you wish me to tell him?'

'With all due respect, I propose that I be the one to tell him, and that you simply confirm it.'

'And how do you propose to use him, once he is thus advised?'

'As my messenger, in due course. I have noted, of late, that amidst the levity and lewd utterances of the Ladies attending on the Queen, there has crept in a note of contempt for His Majesty. Most recently, when I enter the Queen's Audience Chamber, it falls quiet and that idiot boy Smeaton is commanded to pluck more wildly at his instrument to mask the fact that no-one is talking. It is high time that I replaced my own ears in the royal presence with those of another, and a handsome young Courtier will be best placed to join in their ribaldry, perhaps persuading one of the Queen's Ladies to be more forthcoming while throwing up her skirts in a side chamber, and bringing me back intelligence that I may convey to the King through the mouths of others.'

'Not your own mouth?'

'Much though I would wish it so, therein lies a danger. The King is like one of those cushions on yon bench over there — he bears the mark of the last person who sat on him. It is possible for Henry to be persuaded, by the first sycophant through his door, that the Thames rises in Buckinghamshire, and then be converted to the belief that it does so in Oxfordshire by the next to attend upon him. He then blames the first courtier for leading him astray.'

'The moral of this amusing anecdote?'

'That King Henry has a mind like a weathervane in March. It blows first this way, then another. Should I be the one to convey to him tidings that his wife is capable of conversation heard only in the lowest whorehouse, he will not be best pleased, and he will go in search of more comforting counsel. To the man who assures him that Queen Anne is worthy of sainthood he will give a purse, while ordering the death of he who claimed otherwise. But if he hears the same from several of his chosen arse-lickers in harmony with the main tune, he will believe it. I, Thomas Cromwell, do not wish to be the one who goes to the scaffold.'

'So once the boy — young man, rather — brings you the gossip, you will pass it to others to deliver?'

'Precisely. But before that may happen, Richard Ashton must be grown into a Courtier. And that must be your task.'

'He is but a rough country boy at present, say you?'

'Little better, I fear. He has received an average education, and his manners are those of a well-established country squire, but at Court he would at present resemble an abbot in a brothel.'

'Not so unlikely a spectacle, since Henry became our gatekeeper to God,' Margaret observed sourly. 'But I fear that I am of late so long absent from Court that what I can teach him will be out of fashion.'

'Teach him merely how to bow, and not to scratch his arse in the royal presence, and leave the finer points to me,' Cromwell said. 'I can leave him with you for a month, then I need him back at Austin Friars. Should you run out of things to teach him, you might consider sending him to Beaulieu.'

'Where George Boleyn can teach him how to bend over with his hose at his ankles?' Margaret chortled back. 'Bring him in without delay, and let us see what we can make of him.'

III

After Cromwell had led in his charge, the Countess sank into her favourite chair and made the sign of the Cross as she stared in disbelief at a bewildered Richard.

'God preserve us — you are the living image of your grandfather!'

'So my grandmother tells me,' Richard confirmed. 'Is this something of which I should be proud?'

'You do not know who your grandfather was?' Margaret asked.

Richard shook his head in frustration.

Cromwell looked across at Margaret with eyebrows raised in enquiry, and she nodded.

'Tell the poor boy without further delay, Master Cromwell. But keep it brief.'

Cromwell led Richard to another of the chairs around the large table and pushed him gently into it before taking the chair next to his, leaving the Countess on her own on the other side. Then he looked into Richard's eyes. 'What history have you learned?'

'I know of Julius Caesar, and the Emperor Constantine, and Charlemagne the Great, and...'

'English history,' Cromwell insisted.

'The Battle of Hastings? The Roman conquest? The Black Death?'

'The Princes in the Tower?' Cromwell asked.

'Yes,' Richard replied eagerly. 'They were murdered by King Richard, who ruled England before the first Henry won his crown in battle.'

From across the table came an angry snort from Margaret Pole, and Cromwell smiled. 'Your tutor must have been a Lancastrian. And it's time that you learned the truth.'

'It's time *everyone* learned the truth,' Margaret added with considerable feeling.

'What has this to do with my grandfather?' Richard asked.

'Have patience, and learn the true history,' Cromwell replied as he shook his head in disbelief. 'I cannot believe that our modern youth are still fed the same lies. But then again, there can be very few of us left who know the truth, and even I only know it because of what the Cardinal told me.'

'You can blame Thomas More for that,' Margaret reminded him sourly.

Cromwell shot her a disapproving glance. 'Let's not dwell on that.' He turned back to Richard and continued, 'Some years ago, Edward IV of England died, leaving two sons. The first was the older of the two, and his heir, and he was known as Edward, Prince of Wales. He was twelve years old, and was lodged in the Tower of London, ahead of his coronation, by his uncle, Duke Richard of Gloucester. He grew lonely, and asked for the company of his younger brother, Richard, Duke of York, who was nine. Then both boys disappeared.'

'But one of them was due to be crowned King?' Richard reminded him.

Cromwell nodded. 'He was never crowned, and neither was his younger brother, who would have inherited the crown had aught befallen the older boy. By the time it was concluded that the two boys had been murdered, the crown had been claimed by the man who had originally consigned them to the Tower, Duke Richard of Gloucester, who became Richard III of England.'

'And the present King's father won the crown from him in battle, just as I said,' Richard replied.

'He did indeed. But do you not wish to know what happened to the two missing princes?'

'They were not murdered by Richard?'

'No — I said that this was the conclusion reached at the time. But one of them survived.'

'Then why did he not become King?'

'That is a question you may well ask yourself in a short while. I must digress for a moment. For some years I was in the employ of Cardinal Thomas Wolsey, Lord Chancellor of England, and Papal Legate to England. He enjoyed a long and varied career in the service of England, and one of his first positions was as Chaplain to the Deputy Governor of Calais. The Cardinal of whom I speak had occasion to confide in me that one day, while in the service of Calais, he was called upon to give the last rites and dying unction to a soldier in the garrison at Guines. He was an old man, and wished to make confession. He gave his name as John Dighton, and he confessed to the Cardinal that he had been present when the princes were removed from the Tower.'

'They were not murdered, then?'

'Not by that point. But at some stage the older of the two, the heir apparent to the throne of England, the boy named Edward, was killed by Dighton's companion, a man named James Tyrrell. Some years later Tyrrell confessed under torture, and on the orders of Henry Tudor, to having killed both boys, though, in my experience, a man under torture will confess to having gone to it with his own grandmother, should that be what is required of him by the torturer. The confirmation that both boys were dead suited what King Henry VII wanted to hear, and that was deemed to be the end of the matter. But the

Cardinal sought admission to Tyrrell's chamber the night before his execution, to hear his confession, during which Tyrell confirmed what Dighton had already told the Cardinal.'

'That only one boy had been murdered?' Richard asked.

'Correct. Dighton was paid to take the younger boy, still alive, across to Calais, where he — Dighton — was richly rewarded, and lived out the rest of his days as a hired sword in the English garrison at Guines.'

'Rewarded by whom?' the Countess asked.

Cromwell opted to reply with a question of his own. 'That depends, does it not, upon who employed Tyrrell and Dighton in the first place?'

'It is popularly believed that it was my uncle,' Margaret muttered. 'I hope that you are about to reveal otherwise.'

'Your uncle?' Richard repeated, open-mouthed.

'My uncle was Richard of Gloucester,' the old lady replied proudly.

Richard's mouth remained open as Cromwell continued.

'You are correct that Richard of Gloucester has long been accused of the murder of both princes. In fact, only one of them died, and Gloucester was no more guilty of those disappearances than you or I, even though he stood to gain from them by being given a clear path to the throne.'

'But if not Richard, then who?' Richard asked.

Cromwell smiled his conspiratorial smile, and again answered with a question of his own. 'Who else might have benefitted, at that time, from a clear path to the throne?'

Richard knitted his brows as he sought for the answer out loud. 'All the sons of Richard of York were dead. There was the royal widow Elizabeth Woodville, and the royal princesses.'

'And to whom was one of those royal princesses already spoken for in marriage?' Cromwell prompted him, as his face lit up in realisation.

'Henry Tudor!'

Cromwell nodded.

'This is a serious accusation,' Richard replied uneasily.

'The Cardinal took with him to his grave the certain knowledge that the princes were removed from the Tower, and one of them killed, if not on the direct order of Margaret Beaufort, the current King's grandmother, at least with her money. The entire Tudor line that has followed has depended upon that information being kept from public knowledge.'

'But why was the younger boy allowed to live?' Richard asked.

'I believe that he was a hostage to fortune,' Cromwell explained. 'Buckingham had it in mind that if Henry became King, he — Buckingham — would use the existence of the surviving boy, who had been taken to live with a family in Antwerp, either to secure a powerful position of his own alongside the throne, or use it to topple Henry from power. But of course he was able to do neither, since he was executed by Richard of Gloucester, and very few people remained who knew of the boy's existence.'

'So what happened to the boy?' Richard asked, suddenly alert with expectation.

Cromwell smiled. 'I see by your face that you anticipate the next part of the tale. When no further news came from England of what the family in Antwerp — a family named "Warbeck" in our tongue — was to do with the boy, he was raised by them as one of their own. They seem to have forgotten who he really was, and he never knew until he was apprenticed to a silk merchant who travelled to Ireland, where the likeness of the boy to Edward Plantagenet — the dead Edward IV — was noted by some nobles who had no love for the Tudors who were seeking to strip them of their independence. He was crowned by them as "Richard IV of England", and then travelled to Scotland, where he fell in love with the daughter of the Earl of Huntly.'

'Huntly?' Richard echoed.

'You see where this is leading, young man?'

'The boy of whom you speak. He was my ... my...?'

'Your grandfather. You even bear his true name of Richard, and you are the rightful Duke of York by descent.'

'And you are the living image of my Uncle Edward,' Margaret added, almost in veneration.

'If the older boy was killed, am I not the rightful King of England?' Richard asked.

Cromwell smiled kindly across at him. 'That would depend upon many factors, but given a tail wind in your favour, you are correct.'

'What happened to the boy? My grandfather? According to my grandmother he was executed for treason.'

'That much is true. He made the fatal error of landing in England with a pathetically small army, in the belief that the people would rally to his cause, as they had done to Henry Tudor, who by then had lost his popularity with the people, due to his heavy taxation of them. The boy was captured and put on show, allowed briefly to live in Courtly splendour as a pathetic pretender called "Perkin Warbeck" — his name from his Antwerp days — and then executed in punishment for an escape bid that he was tricked into by one of Henry's more devious ministers.'

'Did Henry Tudor know that Perkin was really the lost Prince?' Richard asked.

Cromwell shrugged his shoulders. 'That we do not know, but his Queen, Elizabeth, never resiled from her belief that he was her younger brother, and she took his wife — your grandmother — under her wing as a lady-in-waiting to her. But of course the Cardinal knew the truth, and it weighed heavily on his conscience when circumstances required him to assist the now King Henry to take his place on the throne when Henry Tudor died. The Cardinal was hounded to his death on the urging of Queen Anne, for different reasons, but we cannot be sure that it did not also suit the present King Henry when the Cardinal died, taking his secret with him.'

'Such a tale of treachery makes my own family seem normal by comparison,' Richard observed, 'but what is it that you seek of me? To lead another rebellion, and finish up on Tower Hill like my grandfather?'

'Do you currently command ten thousand men?' Cromwell asked sarcastically.

'Of course not, and neither am I trained to fight with sword or lance,' Richard replied with resignation. 'I cannot even joust.'

'Neither may Henry, thanks to his wife,' Cromwell grinned back at him, 'and therein lies your opportunity for revenge.'

'How?'

'The King grows cold towards the Queen, who senses her own sunset, and becomes more shrewish in consequence. She gives the outward appearance of confidence, and she bullies her Ladies and other attendants as she ever did, hoping upon hope that the child currently hosted by her belly will be a boy.

If she gives Henry a son, her arse may remain securely on the throne. The Tudors must have a male heir to continue their ill-gotten line, and we must ensure that this does not come about.'

'Why is it "we"?' Richard asked suspiciously. 'What interest have you in this matter?'

Cromwell's face darkened in reply. 'I am base-born, the son of a brawling Putney innkeeper, and could not have expected to rise to my current position in life were it not for the kindliness of another who was also base-born. I refer of course to Thomas Wolsey, whose father was a butcher, but who rose by sheer ability to be the second most powerful man in the England of his day. He took me into his service, and here I am today. But the Cardinal made many enemies among the old families. They conspired to bring down this commoner who outran them all in wits and oratory, and they took their chances when they arose. One in particular, Thomas Howard, Duke of Norfolk, saw his opportunity when his Boleyn nieces returned from France. King Henry bedded the first without difficulty — the older girl, Mary. Then when Anne held out for her honour, Henry saw a need to rid himself of the then Queen, Katherine.'

'God rest her blessed soul,' Margaret muttered as she crossed herself again.

'What has this to do with the Cardinal?' Richard persisted, as Cromwell appeared to look at the far wall for his next words.

'The Cardinal and Norfolk were old enemies, from their boyhood days in Suffolk. Anne was anxious for the old Queen to be put aside in favour of her, while Norfolk was chafing at the bit to see Wolsey humbled. Their interests were joined in the matter of the removal of Katherine, and Henry looked to the Cardinal to bring this about.'

'And he failed?' Richard asked.

'No, he did *not*,' Cromwell insisted vehemently. 'The Pope failed. Henry sought to have Katherine put aside on the ground that she had previously been bedded by Henry's older brother Arthur, who was heir to the throne until he died, leaving Henry to pick up both his crown and his bride. This was obviously a religious point, and since Wolsey was by then one of the Pope's two Legates in this country, the question was passed to them by Henry, who believed that he had my master firmly in his tunic pocket. But when Wolsey was obliged to refer the matter back to the Pope, the time was inauspicious. His Holiness was by then in thrall to the Emperor Charles of Spain, and in all but name was his prisoner. Charles was Katherine's nephew, and the Pope was easily persuaded to play for time in the matter. Time that the Cardinal did not have.'

'It was spoken abroad at the time that Wolsey was a friend to Katherine himself,' Margaret reminded him.

'Sympathetic, certainly,' Cromwell confirmed, 'since under his robes of office beat a heart that retained common humanity. But Norfolk and his faction let it be popularly believed that Wolsey was against any annulment of the royal marriage, and used the now Queen Anne as the worm in the bud. She persuaded Henry that my master was deliberately delaying the matter, and furthermore that he was in league with Charles, who was also the Holy Roman Emperor, on the promise that he would become the next Pope. Norfolk had papers forged to support that wicked slander, and my master fell rapidly from grace.'

'It is said that he died of a broken heart,' Margaret mused out loud.

'He died of a canker, in great agony,' Cromwell told her, 'and to my eternal shame I assisted him to a merciful end by his own hand. But his heart was broken, certainly, and in my grief I rashly made a solemn vow to be revenged on Anne Boleyn, who of course became Queen shortly thereafter, when Henry turned the Church upside down, with himself at its head, and perfectly positioned to grant himself his own annulment of his marriage to Katherine.'

'For which he will roast in the fires of Hell,' Margaret hissed.

Richard remained puzzled. 'You seek only to bring down the Queen? Not the King?'

'That may be your ambition, after what I have this day disclosed to you of your own family history, but I am sworn simply to bring down his queen.'

'And I may assist in that?' Richard asked, still puzzled. 'Why should I, since she has done me no ill?'

'She has a womb,' Cromwell reminded him, 'and one, moreover, that may yet yield a male heir that will perpetuate the House of Tudor that has usurped the throne from your own House of York. Is that not motive enough?'

'Surely my grievance lies directly with the King himself?'

'His father, perhaps, but not Henry himself. In the same way that you had no command over who your grandfather was, and what he did, how might King Henry be held to account for the deviousness and treachery of *his* grandmother?'

'But why should I aid you in the matter of the Queen alone?' Richard persisted.

Cromwell shook his head in exasperation. 'Think, boy! I have already demonstrated how the absence of any womb to generate further Tudors will have grave consequences for the line. Further to that, will you not be bringing the King great heaviness of heart when his queen is removed? If you play chess, you must realise the seriousness of losing a queen.'

'The King will surely marry again?' Margaret argued. 'The whore has only thus far given him a girl — who is to say she cannot bear a boy? Perhaps the child currently inside her? And if she does not deliver herself of a boy, and Henry puts Anne aside for another, how long before that results in the birth of a boy? And you forget the bastard Fitzroy. You are surely blinded by your passion for revenge against the Boleyn woman.'

'*And* Norfolk, by your own words,' Richard added.

Cromwell's face twisted in anger. 'Oh yes — and Norfolk too, the double-dyed son of Satan! He will fall by my hand, just as Thomas Wolsey fell by his.'

'And why should I join my head to all this, which could easily end on the scaffold?' Richard persisted.

Cromwell regained his composure, and his wily smile returned. 'If the reasons I have already given are not sufficient, here are two more. You have the opportunity to rise from your unhappy existence on an obscure estate in Berkshire, where you were described, in my hearing, as the resident idiot. I offer you a place in my service, where you may rise to prominence as I once rose through the patronage of the Cardinal. In that service you will attend Court, where your undoubted good looks will render you many a roll between the sheets of a fine lady, one of whom may take your lusty cock to be her lawful wedded husband.'

Margaret coughed her embarrassment, but Cromwell was unmoved.

'We deal with realities here, madam. Let us not obscure the raw truth of life at Court with the tattered veil of propriety.

The nation is driven by diverse forms of lust, and that which occurs between the sheets is one of them. Do you think King Henry sought to take Anne to his bed in order that they might converse on the constellation of the stars in the firmament?'

'Be that as it may,' Margaret countered, 'it is not seemly to discuss such matters so openly. Nor, I am emboldened to say, so crudely.'

'This is nothing compared with what the lad will hear in the Queen's Chamber, even from the Queen herself, who speaks the language of the whorehouse as fluently as her Ladies. She was raised in France, remember, where they fuck on the staircases.'

Margaret tutted, but remained silent. However, Richard had not finished.

'And what if I choose not to leave my country estate and join in this uncertain enterprise? What if I report your treasonous words?'

Cromwell's smile became more of a threat as he supplied the answer. 'You speak to the Master of the Rolls, remember. A man whose word would be preferred to that of a young idiot from an estate so impoverished that its head deems it a great reward to be allowed to expand it with a mere twelve hides of land from a local monastery. And even were the matter to come to court, there would be no-one to support your story, and once I revealed your own sickness of mind that causes you to believe that you are the rightful heir to the throne of England, where would lie your case?'

'I would have the evidence of this lady,' Richard argued, pointing at Margaret, who shook her head vigorously.

'See, you are wrong even in that,' Cromwell gloated. 'And why do you speak of "evidence"? Of what use is that in our courts? Take it from this experienced and weary common lawyer that what rules the day in our courts is not evidence, but expediency. The King would not wish to lose the services of his loyal, efficient bringer-in of wealth from the dissolved monasteries on the word of an adjudged idiot.'

'I would seem to have little choice,' Richard conceded, 'but I fail to see what role this "idiot" can play in your angry schemes.'

'Once you are suitably prepared for Court, you will go where I once went,' Cromwell told him. 'Namely, into the presence of the Queen and her Ladies. You will join all those other popinjays who sniff around the cunnies of the Queen's Ladies and you will bring back word to me of how things sit. Who is enamoured of who, who intrigues with who, who is in the royal favour, and who not. Unless I miss my mark, there is scandal enough there to remove a queen from her throne, and an eager womb from the royal bed.'

'And how will I prepare myself to play the peacock, and from whence will come my fine feathers?' Richard asked.

'You see how your tongue becomes more filed even after an hour in my company? Leave the fine words for me to pour into your ear when you join my household at Austin Friars. As for Courtly manners, and I suspect less coarseness of language, I leave you in the willing hands of this good lady, to whom you have not formally been introduced. She is, as you will have deduced for yourself, distantly related to you and is best thought of as an elderly aunt. She is the Countess of Salisbury in her own right, and she can be your guiding light as to how gentlemen behave in the presence of the King. You may leave it to me to advise you on how to behave in the Queen's presence. I shall return a month from now to collect my new Senior Clerk.'

IV

'Welcome back to Court, Thomas,' King Henry smiled benevolently. 'Do you bring me more monasteries in your saddlebags?'

Cromwell had only been required to walk up one floor to the King's Audience Chamber from his apartments of convenience on the ground floor of Whitehall Palace. It had previously been occupied by the Cardinal, in his role as Archbishop of York, before it had been seized by Henry on Wolsey's downfall. Henry now resided here with his Queen, while extensions to the old Palace were under construction.

Cromwell adopted a doleful look for his reply. 'I thought I had witnessed all the depravity and blasphemy that the Church of Rome had hitherto tolerated in these houses of idle iniquity, but still I encounter more. I have confiscated enough pieces of the alleged "True Cross" to account for half the forests in Germany, and enough teeth of Saint Anthony to fill the mouths of your entire royal bodyguard. In Glastonbury I was offered part of Christ's burial shroud, which is alleged to ooze with blood each Passion Sunday. It is a simple trick with a vegetable dye that reacts to strong sunlight.'

'A matter of considerable regret, clearly,' Henry replied, 'but how much have we generated in our passion to restore order to these unholy houses?'

'Abingdon will bring in several thousand, Your Majesty. And even now there is a caravan of wagons under armed escort returning from parts of Wiltshire and Dorset loaded with false idols, gold plate, damask altar cloths and alleged holy relics that will fetch a fine price among the gullible across the sea in Ireland. I estimate another twenty thousand, in all.'

'This is good,' Henry acknowledged as he waved Cromwell to a seat. 'Speaking of Passion Sunday, you presumably heard what the Queen ordered her Almoner to preach at us?'

Cromwell was confident that the man would either be burned as a heretic or demoted to the position of parish priest somewhere in darkest Northumbria. 'Indeed, Highness. He claimed that the revenues from the dissolved so-called holy houses should be distributed among the poor. I am surprised that he still retains his bollocks, if either Norfolk or Suffolk were in attendance.'

Henry laughed. 'Norfolk was all for throwing him from a window, and had his hand on his collar before the man threatened him with excommunication. I ordered Norfolk to back away, under promise that the man should attend before Council and show cause why he should not be either hung drawn and quartered for treason, or burned for heresy. The Queen was not pleased.'

'She *will* be pleased, however, with what Parliament achieved in my absence, in the matter of the succession?'

Henry nodded with some sadness. 'Indeed, the Lady Mary is now out of contention, and is officially a bastard. It goes hard on a father to do that to his own daughter, but we must think of Elizabeth.'

'I trust she thrives?'

'So her nurse advises me.'

'And you, Majesty?' Cromwell enquired solicitously, nodding at the ominous bulge formed by the tight bandaging beneath Henry's hose just above thigh level, and only partly hidden by the loose jerkin.

Henry sighed. 'The poison will not retreat, despite the many leechings and other dreadful ministrations of those horse doctors who pose as royal physicians. Anne insists that I never joust again, and that is perhaps as well, given that I might be unhorsed for once if I did. But I can no longer dance properly either — not that the Queen forbids that, although her condition is such that she will only sit and watch while I attempt to cavort around with her Ladies.'

'Some of whom are probably glad to be led gently,' Cromwell grinned.

'There is one in particular who has caught my eye,' Henry told him confidentially, with a facial expression that Cromwell had not seen since the heady days of Hever Castle, and Henry's ardent pursuit of 'the Lady Anne', as she been then. 'Little Jane Seymour, daughter of old Sir John, of Wulfhall in Wiltshire,' Henry continued to ramble. 'She was lady-in-waiting to the Lady Katherine in the days when she was Queen, and she has remained to serve Anne. We were down there some months ago, during the progress, and although she was then in residence, she was seen only behind her book, or bent over her needlework, in which she excels.'

'I cannot bring her to mind,' Cromwell lied in an effort to sniff the wind.

Henry was only too eager to oblige. 'She is no great beauty, yet such a sweet docility flows from her countenance, like spring sunshine. She does not strut and flounce, like so many of the Queen's Ladies, nor does she have an edge to her tongue, like the bites I so often seem to receive from Anne these days. She has no suitors, of whom I am aware anyway, but you might like to make enquiry on that matter, Thomas, since such a sweet creature must be betrothed to the gentlest of men, that her fragile grace be not flattened beneath coarse flesh. See to it, Thomas.'

'Without delay, Majesty.'

'Pray God she is not already spoken for to some ruffian with more breeding than manners.'

'So it is to be hoped, Your Highness. The papers containing a full account of the latest holy houses we have ordered closed will be brought to you by a new Senior Clerk I have engaged. Name of Ashton. Richard Ashton.'

'Whatever,' Henry responded with a dismissive wave of his hand. 'To Wiltshire, Thomas.'

'Without delay, Majesty, as I promised,' Cromwell replied as he bowed from the presence.

V

Richard Ashton took a deep breath and walked up to the two guards who stood with crossed halberds at the entrance doors to the Audience Chamber on the first floor, clutching the two copies of the list he had been handed minutes earlier by his new employer Thomas Cromwell. He was conscious of the richness of his dark brown velvet doublet with matching hose and shoes, with a bonnet of light green perched on his neatly shorn golden-red locks.

'Is the King in there?' Richard asked timorously.

The guards sniggered, and the one on the left answered for them both.

'No, boy — we always stand here of an afternoon.'

'We likes ter look alert, in case there are ladies passin', then we slips our cocks out when they draw level,' the other replied, and they both burst out laughing.

Richard sighed and began to walk away, before one of them called him back.

'Is it important, lad?'

'I have no idea. Master Cromwell asked me to deliver a list to His Majesty.'

'Master *Secretary* Cromwell?'

'Yes.'

'Why the fuck didn't yer say so ter begin with? In yer go, lad, and sorry for the cheek.'

The two guards uncrossed their halberds, leaving Richard with a full view of the closed doors. He stepped forward and knocked as hard as he could. When there was no response he knocked again, even harder.

'Stand back, boy,' one of the guards ordered him as he rammed one of the closed doors hard with the butt of his halberd. There was a brief silence, then the doors were opened from inside, and the face of an usher in full Tudor livery came into view.

'You are?' Richard was asked.

'Master Richard Ashton, Senior Clerk to Master Secretary Cromwell, with some papers for His Majesty.'

'Wait there,' Richard was instructed, and the door was closed in his face.

'Master Secretary normally just barges in without waiting fer an invitation,' Richard was advised by one of the guards as he waited.

'I saw 'im *kick* the door open, one time,' the other added, just as the doors opened again and the usher reappeared, this time with a smile.

'Come in,' Richard was instructed, and with another deep breath he walked through the open doors and into the presence.

King Henry was studying some parchment or other, his head bent over the vellum as he sat resting his left leg on a footstool to one side of the padded chair that Richard took to be the throne. He looked up as Richard approached, made a sweeping bow and went down on one knee.

'I wish I could still do that,' Henry muttered with a smile. 'Take my advice, boy, and stay away from the tiltyard.'

'Yes, Your Majesty,' Richard replied dutifully.

Henry held out his hand. 'You are Cromwell's man?'

'Yes, Your Majesty.'

'And the paper you have in your hand is the list of monastic resumptions that he promised me?'

'Yes, Your Majesty.'

'Very well, young man. Without saying "Yes, Your Majesty" yet again, hand me the list.'

Richard kept his lips tightly gripped together as he leaned forward and handed the list across the few feet between them, Henry grunting with the effort of having to double over to take them. Then Henry looked more intently at what remained in Richard's hand.

'What are those other papers? Are they for me?'

'No, Your ... no, Sire. They are for the Queen.'

'And what are they?'

'A copy of the list that I just handed to you, according to my master.'

'Anne requires a list of those monasteries we are closing down?'

'So I am instructed, Your Majesty. I have no idea why she requires such a list, merely that I am to deliver it once you have your copy.'

'Very well, you'll find her down the hallway in her own Audience Chamber, surrounded by her twittering coven. If you emerge with your tackle intact, send me a message to that effect. It will be the first such event.'

'Yes, Your Majesty,' Richard replied, then cursed inwardly as he remembered the earlier instruction. He began to bow from the presence, until Henry raised his hand for him to remain for a moment.

'You are new to the Court?'

'I am, Sire.'

'Two things. The first is that I was jesting regarding your likely fate among the Queen's Ladies. They only go to it in private, and your tackle will remain safe as long as you only ever approach them in a group, and in daylight. The second —

tell that cretin on the door not to attack it with his halberd in future. Cedar is expensive these days.'

'Certainly, Sire,' Richard replied as he made it to the entrance door on his fifth bow, and slipped happily behind it into the safety of the hallway. He nodded at the guards as he began to walk away, before one of them called after him.

'How did you go in there?'

Richard stopped and turned. 'Very well, thank you. And I have a message for you from the King.'

'What's that?'

'He says to stick your halberds up your arses. Sharp end first.'

Then he set off at a trot towards his second audience of the day. The more important one, according to his instructions.

'This one's very pretty,' remarked the dark-haired matron as she looked up from where she was seated beside the Queen. 'I didn't realise it was Christmas already.'

'You must forgive my sister-in-law Lady Rochford,' said the woman in the centre of the group, who Richard took to be the Queen herself. She reached out a languid hand for the papers that Richard was carrying. 'How nice of Master Secretary to send such a pleasing substitute, instead of depressing us all with his usual miserable presence. Mind you, after the way he spoke to my Almoner at the Council meeting, little wonder that he dares not show his face in here. You have the list he promised?'

'I do, My Lady,' Richard replied with a slight bow.

'*Your Majesty*,' Anne corrected him with a flash of black eyes that put Richard in mind of a hawk snapping at its prey. Were she not seated in the centre of the group, the obvious focus of everyone's attention, he would not have taken her to be the

Queen of England. There was little evidence of her famed beauty, and even less indication of the child she was known to be carrying. Her frame was light and bony, and not covered by any of the fashionable padding worn by her surrounding Ladies, while her haughty face seemed stretched across the bony structure of her head. Only her dark eyes seemed vibrant and alive, as they darted this way and that down the list, occasionally glancing up at him with looks that could kill. Eventually, she handed the list to another woman on her right with a disdainful snort.

'Take that, Mistress Shelton. I doubt I will need it again.' She looked more carefully at Richard. 'Who are you, and where are you from?'

'Richard Ashton of Fyfield, Your Majesty. I serve Master Secretary Cromwell.'

'In what capacity? Do you procure him more boys for his household, to pose as musicians?'

'No, Your Majesty. I am one of his senior clerks.'

'So you are not a musician?'

'No, Your Majesty.'

'Master Smeaton, over in the corner there, is a musician. Play something, Mark.'

A young man with a baby face and a mop of unruly black hair sticking out from under a red velvet bonnet looked lovingly back at the Queen as he picked up his lute from the cushion on which it had been resting.

'What shall I be playing?' he asked in heavily accented English.

Anne smiled at him coquettishly. 'Do you love me, Mark?'

'With all my heart, dearest lady.'

'You see?' Anne smirked triumphantly at Richard. 'He loves me, and will do my every bidding. If you are to join our daily company, as I am sure every woman here wishes you to do, you must first appreciate that every man who joins us eventually loses his heart to me. Play something merry, Mark.'

Mark began to coax a lively tune of some sort from his instrument, and Anne smiled at Richard, then nodded to the far corner of the chamber.

'There is a seat remaining, on the other side of Mistress Seymour. The gentleman next to her is Sir Francis Weston, one of the few Courtiers allowed to beat my husband at tennis. He also outranks him in other matters, about which it is perhaps better that nothing more be said, but I feel sure he would welcome your company, if only to share with him the tedium of wringing conversation from that pale little violet Jane Seymour. You need not fear any inroads into your honour from her.' She raised her voice to be heard in the corner of the chamber above the rhythmic lilt of the music from the lute. 'Make way, Jane. Here comes a worthy contender for your maidenhead.'

It went on like this for the best part of an hour, after which Richard felt that perhaps he should take his leave, since he was getting nowhere in his gallant efforts to engage Mistress Seymour in conversation. Her eyes would only rise from her needlework when she felt obliged to reply to a direct question from Richard, while the Courtier on her other side, Francis Weston, clearly had eyes only for the rest of the company, and most obviously the Queen herself, who would occasionally reward his dedicated gaze with a smile or a gentle wave of the hand.

Jane Seymour seemed to Richard to be a strange contrast in this chamber full of high-born courtesans. She was pale of countenance, with fair hair that showed modestly from under her hood in the French style that the Queen had made so popular, and — some said — compulsory. Her eyes were either blue or green, depending upon the light, and exuded a demure serenity that seemed like an island of modesty in the midst of all the bawdy innuendo being exchanged by the remainder of the Queen's Ladies, who seemed almost to be competing with each other in ribaldry.

He gave up the effort of engaging Jane in conversation, rose, and walked over to where the Queen was playing cards with Mistress Shelton while Lady Rochford looked on with barely concealed boredom. He bowed, and sought leave to withdraw about his business.

'More scribbling for Master Secretary?' Anne asked. 'Or has he saved you a randy abbess from one of the holy houses that he plunders for my husband?'

'No, just routine copying from the Chancery Court that my master presides over. As for abbesses, *are* there any randy ones?'

'Ask your master,' Anne replied curtly. 'According to him, the holy houses are a hotbed of lust, with monks going to it with monks, and nuns likewise. It is one of his excuses for closing them down.'

'You do not agree that they deserve to be closed down, Your Majesty?'

'That is one question. Another is what should be done with the wealth they yield. My Almoner says that it should be distributed among the poor, but the King my husband would add it to his coffers in order to further enrich his palaces.'

'Such as this one, Your Majesty?' Richard could not stop himself replying before Anne's black eyes flashed once again with the anger of being gainsaid.

'Show him out, Jane,' she instructed the older woman behind her, and Lady Rochford stepped lightly from the low rostrum on which the Queen's chair was mounted, took Richard daintily by the arm and paraded him proudly to the door. Instead of leaving him to go through it alone, she closed it gently behind her and led Richard down the hallway, then stopped abruptly and leaned in towards him so closely that he could smell the cloves on her breath.

'You must think nought of all the ribaldry you heard in there, Master Ashton. They are, in the main, but young chicks that have yet to be plucked, and they only go to it in their imaginations. As for the Queen, her mind is fed on memories of former days, and she imagines all men to be in love with her, as indeed she fondly imagines that the King still is. If you should be seeking bed exercise, my advice to you would be to seek it with an older woman, and one who knows what goes where, and how to pleasure it when it does.'

'I thank you for that advice, Lady Rochford, but I saw no older women in that company. One alone, that is, whose beauty deepens with experience,' Richard flattered her as he felt her full breasts pressed against his arm.

'Have a care how you flatter, Master Ashton,' she breathed softly, 'else I may put you to the test. Perhaps one night next week, when I have use of the adjoining bedchamber to the Queen's? Attend upon us before then, and we shall see what assignation may be made.'

'I swear she was seducing me!' Richard declared in faint disbelief as he reported back to Cromwell, who smiled.

'Why should she not? Her own husband has not lain with her since their wedding night, or so it is rumoured.'

'But she is most alluring — how can he not want her?'

'Do you lust after boys, or perhaps very young girls who have yet to see any monthly flow?'

'Of course not!'

'Your taste is for women slightly past their youth, as with Lady Rochford?'

'Yes, I suppose so. Why?'

'Because every man is aroused by something different. With you it is mature matrons — for George Boleyn it is boys and little girls. In the same way that you would not be drawn into sexual congress with a boy, George cannot be teased into it by his own wife.'

'Then why did he marry her, if he found her not comely?'

'He is a Boleyn, and they marry where they are told by their father, who has risen from very little to become Earl of Wiltshire and Lord Privy Seal through the marriage of Anne to King Henry. His son was ordered to marry Jane Parker, the daughter of Baron Morley, a distant relative by marriage of the Countess of Salisbury who made such a commendable Courtier out of you.'

'He would not have been obliged so to order *me*,' Richard replied. 'As you say, her husband clearly has no eye for mature beauty.'

Cromwell smiled. 'There is said to be a particular reason why George was ordered to marry, once his sister Anne was clearly headed for the throne. It is mere rumour, of course, but one that I hope to be able to give more reliable form on our next visit to Beaulieu.'

'*Our* next visit?'

'Your *first* visit, of course. By then you may be closer to Lady Rochford anyway, and it will be easy to secure your invitation. As for me, no one ever closes the door of hospitality on Master Secretary.'

'You wish me to encourage Lady Rochford?'

'I wish you to bed her,' Cromwell replied.

Richard's face lit up. 'And to think that you once warned me that my duties under you would be onerous! When shall I set about this most pleasant of tasks?'

'It is more a question of "where",' Cromwell replied. When Richard looked confused, Cromwell revealed more information regarding arrangements inside Whitehall Palace. 'For some time now, it has been the custom for one of the Queen's Ladies to sleep on a pallet at the foot of her bed. It is said to be for the Queen's added protection, since an incident some time in the past when an unextinguished candle caused a fire in the draperies festooned around the walls. Less kindly rumour has it that it is to ensure that the Queen remains faithful. Whatever the reason, the custom has been somewhat modified, unknown to Henry who first ordained it. A side chamber has been created to the Queen's bedroom, and has been equipped with a bed, on which her ladies take it in turn to sleep every night for a week, with the dividing door kept open. It is an equally open secret that on some nights that door is closed, whether to allow the lady to be visited, or the Queen herself, is subject to speculation.'

'But whoever visits the lady in the side chamber must tiptoe past the sleeping Queen?'

'You are assuming that the Queen sleeps on such occasions. The side chamber may be entered through a secret door from the hallway, hidden behind a hanging depicting the Martyrdom of Saint Anthony.'

'How do you come to know of such things?' Richard asked in open-mouthed respect.

Cromwell smiled. 'One of the advantages of being base-born is the ability to speak with others of like origin. In Courtly company I can play Cromwell the Master Secretary, while in the kitchens and guardrooms I can revert to being Cromwell the offspring of the Putney alehouse.'

'So that is what Lady Rochford meant when she suggested one night next week,' Richard mused out loud. 'Next week must be her week to lie in the side chamber.'

'This is excellent, and well to my purpose,' Cromwell grinned and clapped his hands. 'Let me know which night, and I may lay my plans.'

'What have you in mind?'

'That is for me to know, and for you to conjecture. But when you hear disturbance from the Queen's bedchamber, be sure to make yourself a mere interrupted memory in the adjoining chamber. Now, tell me of other conversations you overheard during your audience with Anne.'

Richard knitted his brows in disapproval. 'I had never expected to hear such open lewdness between ladies of such high birth. Rarely did the conversation rise above the cods, and it was as if all the ladies were competing to seem the lustier bawd. Chief among them Anne herself, who spoke as if she were a prize bitch on heat, surrounded by panting dogs.'

'It is her manner, of late,' Cromwell reassured him. 'She fears that her beauty is fading, and with it her allure for Henry. Now that she is with child, they have withdrawn from nightly congress, and Henry goes to it with royal whores, some of whom she fears that he prefers. But most of all she fears that unless she whelps a son, she will be out of the royal favour, out of his bed, and off the throne. He grows daily more anxious over the succession, and begins to look for another who can land him a boy onto the childbed sheets. He knows that the fault does not lie with him, because of the daily reminder of Henry Fitzroy, who can occasionally be seen wafting around the royal corridors like the smell from an ill-kept drain.'

'There were some very embarrassing references to His Majesty's alleged lack of sexual prowess, even in the presence of a stranger such as myself,' Richard told Cromwell. 'Merely to have heard them makes me feel tainted with treason.'

Cromwell chortled quietly and patted Richard reassuringly on the back. 'You may rest easy. Such slights are by no means restricted to the Queen's chamber, and half of England believes Henry to be one hundred and eighty pounds of siege powder with only a three inch fuse. There are currently broadsheet ballads in circulation through the alehouses along the wharfs describing the failures of "King Littleprick". If Henry were to learn of their existence, and were he to hunt down their printer, he would have him boiled alive.'

'But does Henry himself fear that his manhood is waning?'

'Perhaps, but do you imagine that he is about to admit it openly around the Court? No — instead he blames Anne, hinting that she has become such a shrew and a nag that his manhood flags at the mere sight of her disapproving countenance. He clings to his memories of lustier days, as of course does Anne herself, and each of them strives to reawaken what has died with fresh liaisons. Unfortunately for Anne, there is only one of them who can convert the thought into deed. If she is unfaithful, she will be for the Tower or one of the few remaining convents. For him it is easy — find another royal bride and hope that his member rises to the challenge.'

'But what ground will he cite for putting Anne aside? Will it be as it was with the former Queen Katherine?'

'That will be for the theologians such as Archbishop Cranmer, and the lawyers such as myself, to determine. But the signs are there already, and I must shortly ride to Wulfhall in Wiltshire.

'Why, and what is at Wulfhall?'

'Your second question first. Wulfhall is the family seat of the Seymours.'

'I met a Seymour only this afternoon. A whey-faced mute with all the vitality of an alabaster virgin on a cathedral wall.'

'*Jane* Seymour?'

'Such was her name, as I recall. Why should you be riding to visit with her family? Are you seeking a second wife among the Queen's Ladies?'

'The grief I experienced on the death of my first is not something I would wish to repeat. As for matrimony, it is not I who seeks the limp hand of the daughter of old Sir John.'

'Who then?' Richard asked. When Cromwell smiled and raised his eyebrows in an invitation to Richard to work it out for himself, Richard's eyes opened wide in disbelief. 'You cannot surely be serious? Henry himself?'

'I go simply to confirm that she is in no way spoken for, in order that Henry may thereafter lay siege to her virtue.'

'The only way she could be spoken for is as a novitiate in a nunnery, but you have left precious few of those, as I learn daily. Surely Henry cannot find her comely? She is as cold as the frost on February grass, and as lively as goats' cheese. Come to think of it, that is much like her complexion. I own that Anne herself wants some more flesh on her bones, and would be best advised to smile with more warmth than venom, but it is difficult to imagine two more contrasting women.'

'I am minded of two old adages,' Cromwell replied. 'The first is that a change is as good as a holiday. And the second is that he who is busy poking the fire into life is not fixated on the mantelpiece above it.'

Richard chuckled, and Cromwell opted to move the conversation sideways.

'How did you enjoy your first audience with Henry?'

Richard's brow knitted at the memory. 'It was not as I expected. Before I entered the presence, I was burning with resentment regarding how the Tudors had stolen my birthright, and imagining how I might myself have been enjoying all the luxuries of Whitehall Palace. But when I actually came face to face with King Henry, I found myself tongue-tied — almost afraid. He has a most commanding presence, and I would die rather than let him suspect my true identity for one moment.'

'He has that effect on most people,' Cromwell reassured him, 'so you need not feel in any way inadequate. Should it transpire, when I speak with Sir John Seymour, that the Lady Jane has another suitor, Henry will surely blow him away like a field cannon, in the same way that he put Harry Percy to flight over a suggestion of his prior understanding with Anne Boleyn. But no time must be lost in discovering the true state of things.'

'When do we leave?' Richard asked.

Cromwell frowned. 'For the moment, it will be me alone. You stay here and light the fire inside Lady Rochford. But do not poke around in her hearth until my return.'

VI

Cromwell handed his bridle to the stable groom and strode towards the front door, from which emerged a scuttling Steward, all elbows and knees as his gown fluttered in the late April breeze.

'I am advised that you are Master Secretary Cromwell,' the Steward stuttered.

'So am I,' Cromwell replied kindly. 'I was not among the King's party when he was here on the progress last year, but he speaks highly of your hospitality. Is Sir John at home?'

'He is in the Long Gallery, sir, with the Mistress and Master Edward. If you would care to follow me, I will announce your attendance.'

'We are not a monastery, Cromwell, so piss off and close somewhere else down,' Sir John Seymour grinned as he rose from his chair at the table by the window and grasped Cromwell warmly in a handshake. 'It's been many years, by my reckoning. I have a memory of you as a fresh-faced boy in the service of the Cardinal at "the Field of the Cloth of Gold", as it was called.'

'And I have a memory of you being carried, puking, from the banqueting hall into the fresh air,' Cromwell smiled.

'Blame Harry Tudor for that — he was the one who ordered the fountains to run with mulled claret.'

'And he has changed little,' came a pleasant cultured voice from another seat at the table from which Sir John had risen.

Sir John smiled amiably, and indicated the source of the voice with an almost regal gesture. 'My wife, Lady Margery. The third member of our family group is my oldest son,

51

Edward. Our second son, Thomas, is out somewhere, getting up to the sort of mischief that is the birthright of every second son. I was a first-born, let it be noted. Ah, here comes Ralph with more wine.'

'So to what do we owe the honour, Master Secretary?' Edward enquired as the wine was served, and Cromwell took the seat indicated.

'Before that, I must advise the cook and the housekeeper if you intend to stay overnight,' Lady Margery interceded.

'So I had hoped,' Cromwell replied with a smile, 'and I thank you for your generosity. But the nature of my business must remain undisclosed until your return, since it concerns something which only the mother of a daughter would know.'

'Is Jane in the Queen's black books?' Margery asked, a hand to her mouth. 'I hear that Anne can take skittish moods against some of her Ladies, and dear Jane confides in me that she much preferred her time of service with the old Queen.'

'I think that she shares that preference with all those who also attended on Queen Katherine,' Cromwell replied with an encouraging smile. 'Do not fret that I come with sad intelligence — quite the reverse, in fact. What I have to tell you is in the strictest confidence, but I come with King Henry's blessing, seeking further information.'

'We are not hiding any emissaries of the Pope,' Sir John joked, but his wife tutted.

'It is not safe even to joke of such matters in these uncertain times, John,' she reminded him.

'Sir John may rest assured that I will not report him to Henry for his wit,' Cromwell said. 'But he does wish me to report back to him on a matter close to his heart.'

'Which is?' Lady Margery enquired, still with a look of concern.

'Your daughter Jane. Is she spoken for, or does she have any understanding with any young man? Or any old man, for that matter?'

Edward Seymour burst out laughing. 'What, "Plain Jane?" The only understanding she has with men is that she does not care for their coarse ways. She cares for her horse, and her dogs, and perhaps her family at a push, but men? If you had left us any convents, Master Secretary, I doubt not that she would run, head bowed and hair neatly shorn, to one of those ere she would contemplate having to do with any man.'

'A simple "no" would have sufficed, Edward,' his father chided him, 'for it is the plain truth, and plain truth should never be hidden inside a parcel of words.'

'Unless one is an envoy in the royal service,' Cromwell replied. 'But that simple "no" completes my mission, unless there are any words such as "unless" or "perhaps" that you might wish to add?'

'You have surely not ridden this distance for that simple answer?' Sir John asked suspiciously, while his wife's face lit up like a brushwood beacon on a dry night.

'The King has some husband in mind for her, does he not? *Do* please tell further, Master Cromwell, for my heart already beats faster at the prospect of a good match for such an awkward daughter. "Awkward" in the sense that she is almost nun-like in her manner, and no man has ever before admired her gentle, docile, loving, tender, generous, kind nature. She is now approaching thirty, and well past the age when we could reasonably have hoped to marry her off. We are not blessed with great wealth, as you must know, and...'

Sir John reached out and patted her hand, before smiling back at Cromwell. 'You will perhaps have surmised that my wife is excited at the prospect that our oldest daughter might even yet become a wife and mother. But I will suspend my excitement until you advise me who Henry has in mind. Not some reprobate like Sir Francis Bryan, I hope?'

'The Vicar of Hell?' Cromwell laughed out loud. 'Trust me, Sir John, I would not have dared travel in person with such dire tidings, had that been the case.'

'Who, then?'

'I realise that I am in company that values the blunt truth, but it would come as too great a shock were I to tell you outright. Let us first consider the state of the nation.'

'We may consider the state of the *weather*, if you insist,' Sir John replied with a piercing stare into Cromwell's eyes, 'but you will tell me who the King has in mind for Jane before you will be allowed to rise from that chair.'

'Very well,' Cromwell continued, undeterred. 'You will have heard that Queen Anne is again with child?'

'Yes, so what?' Sir John continued as the family spokesman.

'It may not be a boy.'

'There will be an even chance, surely?'

'The previous child was the Princess Elizabeth. Before that the Lady Mary. Both girls. Henry wants a boy. The nation *needs* a boy. And — please regard this as being in the strictest confidence — the King and Queen Anne are not at present as close as they once were.'

'Only appropriate,' Lady Margery pointed out. 'During pregnancy there should be no congress, and the best way of preventing that is for the couple to sleep separately.'

'I'm afraid it goes much deeper than that, Lady Margery,' Cromwell explained. 'The Queen grows shrill and critical of Henry, and he expresses to me his discomfort at being so closely confined by Anne's tongue regarding those things he is allowed to do, and those things he is forbidden from doing, in which he once took such delight.'

'Whoring?' Lady Margery snorted.

'As I have, I believe, indicated, the royal marriage seems destined for the midden, and with only a less than average chance that the royal child will be a boy. If so, then all might be preserved, but if not ... well, not to put too fine a point on it, the King is looking elsewhere.'

'God's tits, not Jane?' Sir John thundered, as his wife and son settled for dropped jaws.

Cromwell nodded, relieved that he had got the point over without anyone either running him through or having a seizure, although Sir John gave the appearance of someone working up to one.

'This is not something we can decide on immediately,' Sir John finally stuttered.

'But surely,' Lady Margery urged him, 'it is the greatest advancement any young woman could wish for!'

'No doubt someone once said the same thing to Katherine and Anne,' Edward reminded her.

The Steward appeared to announce that the trestle had been laid for supper, and Cromwell took his opportunity. 'Since I am kindly invited to bide the night here, why don't we postpone discussion of this until the morning?'

'I think we require more than one night before deciding whether or not to commit our oldest, and gentlest, daughter to that fat old whoremaster,' Sir John muttered, and nobody argued with him.

VII

The following morning Cromwell stood alone at the edge of the lawn that led to a much neglected and reed-strewn fishpond, watching the early smoke rising from the cottage chimneys of the local land labourers and trying to put himself inside the heads of the Seymours. They were impoverished gentry who had seen better days, with two sons who had no prospects of advancement in public life without either a great influx of money or better connections at Court. Their sister was no great beauty, and not given to the sort of flirtatious harlotry that might normally be employed as a substitute for comeliness. One could forgive any family in such circumstances for throwing up their hands in joy upon being advised that 'Plain Jane' had caught the King's eye.

But it was obvious from what Cromwell had carefully observed the previous evening that they deeply loved their oldest daughter, and Sir John had been around royal circles for long enough to know what sort of fate might befall a young woman as open and trusting as Jane.

If Henry did have his heart set upon Jane, she would not have to simulate shy virginity, as Anne had done under the guidance of 'Uncle Norfolk', her father, and her worldly sister Mary, who had opened her legs to Henry when they had barely been introduced. No, the task this time would be persuading Jane — if that was the proper course to pursue — that Henry was not as bad as he was sometimes decried, would make a loving and supportive husband, and would not treat her like a brood mare at the mercy of an over-eager stallion.

It was unlikely that being Queen of England would be a sufficient attraction to poor simple Jane, as it had been for Anne. Jane wanted a gentle loving husband, and if Cromwell was to complete the humiliating downfall of 'the concubine' by slipping one of her ladies into the King's bed as her successor, he would need to do so by somehow converting Henry into the sort of man that would appeal to Jane even if stripped of all his royal rank. There would, of course, be a delicious irony in the fact that Anne herself had made the same transition from Queen's Lady to Queen. But she had played her cards wrongly thereafter, and the marriage that Anne had obtained over the disgraced and exhausted corpse of the Cardinal would, if circumstances played into Cromwell's devious hands, be brought to an end by the man who the Cardinal had inspired to be his avenger.

Cromwell heard a footfall behind him, and turned quickly, reaching instinctively for the dagger at his belt, then smiling apologetically when his supposed assassin proved to be Sir John.

'You spent too long in Italy, Thomas,' Sir John grinned at him. 'There is bread and cold meat in the buttery, should you be hungry. For myself I cannot eat, any more than I could sleep last night.'

'I must speak frankly and openly with you, Sir John,' Cromwell replied. 'I am certain in my mind that Queen Anne will be shown the whore's exit from the Palace ere long, and I have reasons of my own to rejoice when that happens. But happen it will — it is only a matter of time, even if she gives Henry a boy.'

'How say you?' Sir John queried. 'From your words before supper yesterday, I took the case to rest upon the lack of a male heir.'

'That is indeed part of the matter,' Cromwell conceded, 'and it may be that if Anne can whelp a boy, and it looks like Henry, she may survive on the throne for another year or two.'

'Why might it not look like the King?' Sir John demanded, aghast. 'Say you that the Queen has entertained others in her bed?'

'Almost certainly she has,' Cromwell assured him, 'and it becomes a matter of who, how often, and how energetically. It is a matter I am currently investigating with some dedication, although Henry does not know of it. But the rot has set in far more deeply than that. Anne grows haughty and arrogant in her belief that she can snap her fingers and bring any man to their knees. While she may retain the power and influence to secure sycophantic sighs from boys of no consequence such as her musician Smeaton, and old lechers in search of younger flesh such as Norris or Weston, her dominant and strident nature of late has robbed Henry of his self-respect, and shamed him in his manhood. One does not do that to a Tudor and expect to retain one's head.'

'Think you that Henry will take her head?'

'With a little encouragement from me, that is precisely what he will do. But being Henry, and being ashamed to admit that the woman he put his previous wife aside for, and who has caused us such difficulty with the Emperor, has diminished his prowess between the sheets, and treats him like an errant schoolboy, he will be seeking other grounds than adultery. Since he fears that the woman merely scorned and put aside will employ heralds to proclaim all over Europe that the King of England has a cloth cock, he must have her head. However, he has not yet reached the point at which he knows that to be his only course. To make him see that must be my loyal task.'

'Your *gleeful* task, as I judge,' Sir John replied.

'There are times when being in the royal service allows one to see justice done. In my case, justice for the old Cardinal.'

'You loved him so deeply?'

'I respected him for his wisdom, his grace, his charity and his loyalty. To be a friend of Thomas Wolsey was to be blessed in this life; to be his enemy meant certain damnation in the next.'

'A pretty speech that you have rehearsed?' Sir John asked.

'In my head, every day since the Cardinal was taken from us.'

'But how does all this sit for our dear Jane?'

Cromwell chose his words carefully. 'When we spoke yesterday, I may have inadvertently given the impression that I had been sent down here to seek Jane's hand for the King. I did not have that intention, and I do not have that authority. Furthermore, should Henry seek Jane's hand, he will do so for himself. I merely intended to alert you to the fact that Anne is on her way out, and that Jane has caught Henry's eye, mainly for all the virtues that Anne lacks.'

'How can one man have passion for such strongly contrasting women?'

'If you are hungry, do you not eat? If thirsty, do you not crave water, or perhaps wine?'

'You have also been a lawyer for too long, Thomas. Speak more plainly.'

'When Henry was first attracted to Anne, it was not simply for her looks. Had he simply wanted a comely whore, there are many to be had with the jingle of a coin bag in and around the Palaces. And one has to own that Anne has not gained beauty at the same pace that she has passed into motherhood and almost matronly maturity. She is now even more angular, and her duckies, having swollen to suckle the Princess Elizabeth, fell back inside her chest as if embarrassed to be there. So it was not for her beauty then, and even less so is it now.'

'What, then?'

'She made Henry feel comfortable, loved, cherished, respected, even adored. She rarely questioned his judgment or opposed his will. Those days have passed. She now tells him that he may not joust, she chooses with whom he may dance, and she reminds him that he has put on so much weight since his accident took him from daily exercise that there is now a substantial portion of him to which she was never lawfully married.'

'The Lady Margery is similarly humoured,' Sir John grinned. 'Must I therefore put her aside?'

'That depends where lies your determination, not only to be seen to be the master in your own household, but also to feel within yourself that you are. Much more the case if you are in command, not simply of a modest estate in Wiltshire, but an entire nation.'

'And Jane attracts the King because she is meek, submissive, dutiful and largely silent?'

'Basically, yes. But should matters progress between she and Henry, she must not lose those attributes in the excitement and reflected glow of being Queen of England, as Anne has done.'

'So how lies the matter at present?'

'She has caught Henry's eye, that is all. Knowing this, I regarded it as my duty to alert you to that fact, and ensure that there were no emotional encumbrances or distractions of the heart that might prevent matters progressing from there.'

'And think you that they will?'

'The King will be without a wife in the very near future, Sir John, on that you may rely. Beyond that it depends upon the inclination of Jane's heart, the depth of Henry's desire for a wife who treats him as a husband should be treated, and the speed with which the whore currently in the Palace is transferred to the Tower.'

'God help anyone who falls foul of Thomas Cromwell,' Sir John muttered.

'Or who drove the Cardinal to his death,' Cromwell added. 'And now I think I could summon up an appetite before I return to Court.'

VIII

The news reached Cromwell by a fast messenger who intercepted him in Reading during his return to London. Queen Anne had, two afternoons previously, withdrawn unexpectedly from the company in her Audience Chamber and hastened to her bed, accompanied only by Lady Rochford. Physicians had been summoned, along with priests and women skilled in childbirth, and it had been one of those who had confided in Lady Rochford that Anne had miscarried, and that the child had appeared to have most resembled a boy.

It had been left to Henry's old childhood companion, and former brother-in-law, Charles Brandon, Duke of Suffolk, to break the news. Henry had immediately asked for Cromwell to attend him, but had been advised that Cromwell was believed to have journeyed to Wiltshire. Henry had demanded that Cromwell be located and ordered to return immediately.

Cromwell had barely dismounted outside the royal stables when he was all but bowled over by a bustling mountain whose every nerve and sinew, including his unkempt and unbarbered long black beard, seemed to quiver in the midday sun.

'Thank God you are returned, Thomas!' Suffolk proclaimed. 'Harry calls for you at every hour of the day. He will see no-one else, not even his jester Sommers, who can usually be relied upon to lift his spirits. The only one allowed into the presence is myself, and the urge to bat his ear when he bombards me with endless self-pity is such that I fear the axe if I have to go in there again. For mercy's sake, lose no more time.'

'At last!' Henry bellowed as Cromwell bowed into the presence. 'Where in fuck's name have you been?'

'In Wiltshire, Sire, as you commanded.'

'Ah yes, I recall that now. What of the Lady Jane?'

'She has no suitor, Sire, and no prior engagement of the heart.'

'Is she still a maid?'

'I believe so, Sire, but it would take the skills of a physician to deliver certainty on that point.'

'Hmm, it may come to that. You have heard the news of the Queen's misfortune?'

'Indeed, Sire, and may I express my...'

'Fuck that, Thomas. Just get me out of this mess. I begin to think that your former master knew more than he was telling when he stood in the way of the annulment from Katherine.'

'It was not the Cardinal who delayed, Sire, but the Pope.'

'Perhaps it was, but I paid them *both* out. I have lately thought that perhaps I misjudged Thomas Wolsey.'

'In fairness to yourself, Sire, you were grievously misled by others.'

'You refer to the Queen?'

'Not her alone, Sire. Her uncle, Norfolk, and her father, Thomas Boleyn.'

'But her hand was in it more than those two. Had she not bewitched me, her family would have had no means by which to ingratiate themselves into my favour.'

'Perhaps "bewitched" is too strong a condemnation, Sire.'

'How else to explain how she led a king from the path he trod to secure the nation's peaceful future? I shall be into my forty-fifth year come June, and still no royal heir.'

'The royal daughters, Sire?'

'Do not talk such shit, Thomas. England will never accept a woman on the throne, and in any case Mary is bastardised, while Elizabeth still totters on child legs. Perhaps I should bastardise her, too, but what am I to do with her mother?'

'Sire?'

'Do not dissemble, Thomas, I am not in the mood. I am in sore need of the guile that you learned in the service of the Cardinal. He would have known the best way forward.'

'Forward to what exactly, Sire?'

'God's prick, Thomas! If you do not cease this pretence I shall have you carted through the city streets with a sign upon your back inviting pisspots to be emptied on your head! You know of what I speak!'

'The future of the Queen?'

'Of *course* the future of the Queen! I must be rid of her, Thomas, and I care not how. I must be free to marry again, this time to a douce maid who loves me for myself, who does not set her cunny at me in order to win a throne, and who may bear me sons.'

'The Lady Jane?'

'Who else? There is no other who so fills my thoughts of late. Who smiles so serenely in my face while Anne spits venom in my ear. The lovely, graceful and swanlike Jane, whose sweet face puts me in mind of summer days spent by cool fountains.'

'How shall we bring this about, Sire?'

'If I knew that, I would not be seeking your counsel, Thomas. You have grown wealthy through my preferment, and while I ignore the murmurings of those who seek to persuade me that you rob me right and left, you must realise that your continued prosperity depends upon your value to me at times such as these.'

'I think we are at one in realising that Norfolk is not to be trusted, Sire. He helped bring down the Cardinal, and he has ever after sought to lay me alongside him in the same tomb in Leicester. In the matter of his niece Anne, he would be even less worthy of trust.'

'I do not need your counsel on that point, Thomas, and you will know that your final day has come when you find armed men at your door, led by Norfolk.'

Cromwell suppressed a shudder as he recalled that dreadful day when he arrived for work at York Palace to find Norfolk screaming for the return of the Cardinal's seal of office as Chancellor of England, and the pile of furniture, hangings and plate in the centre of the Great Hall that the Cardinal's servants had been obliged to bring out ahead of their return to Henry. No, indeed, he had no wish to be thus visited by Norfolk, and the time for diplomatic evasion was over. Cromwell's cause had become Henry's cause and wanted only the veneer of justification.

'With your leave, Sire, I shall meet with Archbishop Cranmer and Lord Chancellor Audley, to determine the best way of securing the lawful justification for another divorce.'

'Do that, Thomas. Do it quickly, and do not return until you have the answer to hand.'

Cromwell bowed out but kept the smirk from his face until he was back in the hallway. He left his horse where it was and took the barge downstream to Austin Friars. In the Great Hall he found Richard Ashton arm-wrestling with his son Gregory. Although only sixteen years old, Gregory Cromwell was an energetic and combative youth, much given to fighting with the younger sons of neighbours, who he normally defeated. He and Richard had become natural rivals in almost everything, and although Gregory had the greater justification, given the way in which his father had slipped Richard into the household like an older son, Richard found Gregory's assumption that he would inherit his father's wealth and position irritating, and rarely missed an opportunity to remind him that in order to make best use of those advantages, he would require more ability than he currently demonstrated.

'Off the table, you two,' Cromwell ordered. 'It must be set for an early supper, and we shall have important visitors. I meet this night with the Archbishop of Canterbury and the Lord Chancellor.'

'You have delayed the Pope until dinner tomorrow?' Gregory asked cheekily.

Cromwell frowned. 'Guard your tongue and respect your elders, young Gregory. Richard here knows the value of a sheathed tongue on certain occasions.'

'Mainly because he does not know how to employ it properly when unsheathed,' Gregory retorted, ducking to avoid a swipe to the side of the head from Richard.

'Enough!' Cromwell ordered them both. 'Since you must needs be separated as usual, if only to preserve the furnishings, come with me to my upstairs study, Richard, and bring me the most recent news from Court. Have John bring us wine, Gregory.'

'Well?' Cromwell demanded as they sat on adjacent chairs in front of Cromwell's document-strewn table.

Richard shrugged. 'Since the misfortune of the Queen's miscarriage there is little to report, since we do not always gather daily, as we were disposed to do previously.'

'They have accepted you as one of their company?'

'Indeed,' Richard said proudly. 'I think that may have been assisted by Jane Rochford, who is forever drawing me into their conversation.'

'How go things between you?'

Richard blushed. 'I feel like a virgin under siege by a randy suitor. She makes hints that perhaps we should be better acquainted, and there is almost daily reference to her duties in the ante-chamber to Anne's bed chamber.'

'She is still occupying that side chamber?'

'So she is at pains to establish, on pretence of making the other Ladies jealous, but always with an eye in my direction. If you wish me to "poke her hearth", as you put it, I cannot delay much longer. Nor, I must own, do I wish to. She is quite comely in that way of mature matrons.'

'You shall shortly have the opportunity to unleash your cock in that direction,' Cromwell reassured him, 'but I must know of ought else that has transpired, and of conversations that have passed.'

'The Queen was most anxious to learn why you had journeyed to Wiltshire, and I was fortunately able to dissemble on that point, assuring Her Majesty that I was simply your Senior Clerk, and not your Steward.'

'Was she convinced, think you?'

'I would have said yes to that, were it not for Anne's rude behaviour towards Mistress Seymour.'

'More, please.'

'Well, we sat one afternoon as usual, with Harry Norris and Francis Weston making up a group in the corner with Jane Seymour and Lady Worcester. Jane had a locket on a chain around her neck, which was one of those that often contain love tokens or miniatures. Jane was ever opening and closing it, admiring its contents, and eventually Anne bid her come and sit by her. Then she demanded that Jane lean forward and display the inside of the locket, which Jane seemed reluctant to do. Eventually Anne commanded her, as her Queen, to do her bidding, and Jane did as commanded. Anne opened the locket, looked inside, then gave out a loud scream and ripped the locket from Jane's neck, hurling it into a corner.'

'Did you see what was in the locket?'

'No, but Jane Rochford has let it be believed that inside it was a lock of Henry's hair. She even alluded that it might not have come from his head.'

'Did ought transpire after Anne treated Jane thus?'

'Jane Seymour rose swiftly from her chair and rushed, in floods of tears, to the corner of the room where Mark Seaton sat playing his lute. He ceased playing, and was in the act of giving Jane such comfort as he could when Harry Norris chided him for giving solace to someone who had angered the Queen. When Mark sought to protest that he was only acting out of gentle kindness to a lady in distress, Norris rose angrily from where he was seated and rushed across the chamber, knocking poor Mark, and his instrument, clean off his chair.'

Cromwell chuckled. 'I would wish to have been there to witness that. But is there more?'

'Not of that nature. It was but the following day when the Queen rushed from the chamber, calling Jane Rochford out with her, and the next we heard she had miscarried of her child. We have only lately resumed our afternoon meetings, and even then not every day.'

'The Queen is fully restored to her former self?'

'As far as can be judged from a distance. She is obviously much distressed by her recent loss, and her brother is said to be lodging elsewhere in the Palace, having travelled from his estate for the purpose of bringing her comfort. If he conjoins nightly with Lady Jane in the ante-chamber, I fear that my opportunity may have been lost.'

'Be of good cheer, Richard. If rumour be truth, there will be no husbandly queue for Jane Rochford's open legs. But what of Jane Seymour?'

'She has pleaded illness for the past few days, and I have seen nothing of her in the Queen's company. It is even rumoured that she may have returned to Wiltshire.'

'This is to the good, Richard. You must now make your assignation with Jane Rochford in the side chamber, but be certain to advise me when it is to occur.'

'You wish to watch?' Richard asked with a smirk.

'God forbid. I doubt which I wish to see less of — your tackle or Jane's greying quim. But I will be there, in another guise. Now leave me to make inroads into this tedious pile of Chancery writs.'

Two hours later, Cromwell pushed aside his platter of fish and looked at each of Thomas Cranmer and Thomas Audley.

'You will have surmised that I have hosted this humble meal with a purpose in mind?'

'It is said that an invitation to Austin Friars augers that Thomas Cromwell wants something,' Audley said, while Cranmer looked uncomfortable.

'Not to dissemble, gentlemen, Henry wants a divorce, and it is down to us to devise the grounds.'

Cranmer all but choked on a fish bone, spat it out, and fingered the jewelled cross around his neck. 'I have barely squared my account with God in respect of the last one,' he protested.

'I certainly look forward to hearing you explaining to Council how you were sorely mistaken in your belief that the marriage between Henry and Katherine had been unlawful, that Henry was free to marry, and that his betrothal to Anne was legitimate,' Cromwell replied with a smile. 'Although considering that by that stage she was preceded everywhere she went by a distended belly containing the Princess Elizabeth, it was perhaps a wise pronouncement. And one that justified your elevation to your current office.'

'He cannot plead consanguinity this time,' Cranmer moaned.

'There was the matter of Mary Boleyn,' Audley pointed out. 'Henry had her long before Anne, and they are sisters.'

'The Bible condemns only brothers' wives, if read literally,' Cranmer explained. 'That fitted the case regarding Katherine and Prince Arthur, but would hardly suffice here. In any case, Henry married Anne in full knowledge that he had previously had knowledge of her sister, thereby condoning any sin that might flow from it.'

'So you can find nothing in your scripture that makes the marriage between Henry and Anne illicit?'

'No. Unwise, certainly. Appalling, certainly. Lustful, no doubt. Tasteless and with unseemly haste, without question. But forbidden in the eyes of God, most certainly not.'

'And of course,' Audley commented sourly, 'God has grown more tolerant since He became an Englishman, has he not?'

'Please, Thomas,' Cromwell intervened, 'this is no time to be provoking his Grace. Perhaps you would be better employed coming up with some ground upon which the Queen may be impeached in law.'

'She is said to be a witch,' Audley offered, then withered under Cromwell's glare.

'She is also said to go to it with ten men and a goat on a nightly basis, if one is to believe the broadsheets in circulation around the city taverns,' Cromwell reminded him. 'We need more than scurrilous rumour that owes much to overheated imagination and little to fact.'

'If it were true, it might be adjudged treason,' Audley suggested. 'It is believed in our courts that for a queen to commit adultery is an act of treason against her husband the King. Of course, there are no precedents on the point, as yet.'

'I always thought that it was only treason to attempt the life of a king,' Cranmer chimed in.

'Then it is perhaps best that you are Archbishop of Canterbury, while I am Lord Chancellor of England. The two positions clearly call for different talents.'

'They were once combined,' Cromwell reminded them sadly, 'most recently in the hands of Thomas Wolsey, as Archbishop of York. But if you are correct, Thomas, then we need show only one act of adultery and Anne will be minus her head.'

'The punishment for treason by a woman is burning at the stake,' Audley told them, as Cranmer shuddered, 'but you are correct. Do we have evidence of such?'

'Not yet. You may leave that to me.'

'Is that not a matter for the Attorney-General?' Audley queried. 'It is no business of the Master of the Rolls to be procuring witnesses in a common law court.'

'It is for *this* Master of the Rolls,' Cromwell replied with a smile. 'Now, would either of you wish to sample one of my cook's excellent jellies? We recently acquired a mould of Windsor Castle, and the crenulations have been sculpted in marchpane.'

IX

Two evenings later, as the guards in the corridor were completing their midnight duty changes, Richard Ashton stood contemplating the somewhat overdone depiction of St Anthony being ripped apart by devouring demons that hid from view the secret door to the side room occupied by Jane Rochford, in official night attendance on the Queen.

A hand came from behind the tapestry, followed by the smiling eager face of Jane Rochford. Needing no further invitation, Richard slipped through the door, which Jane closed gently behind them as she took Richard by the hand, and led him inside the bedchamber, where they eagerly got down to what each of them had been anticipating for some time.

Meanwhile, Cromwell was at work. Satisfied that Richard was about his long-awaited joyful business, he had approached the guards outside the alcove further down the hallway that led, by way of a side door, to the Queen's Audience Chamber from which one might, via the Withdrawing Chamber, gain access to the Bedchamber itself. Breathlessly he expressed his fear that he had just spotted an intruder in the Queen's quarters.

'Go no further than the Withdrawing Chamber,' he instructed them, 'and I will wait by this door you were guarding. I have my dagger, and will acquit myself accordingly should anyone be flushed out by your actions.'

Once the guards disappeared around the corner, Cromwell raced to the grace and favour chamber granted to Mark Smeaton a few yards in the other direction. It was little regarded by other Courtiers, due to the constant noise from the adjacent staircase, but it was deemed good enough for a mere Palace servant, and Cromwell rushed in without knocking, to find Mark dressed only in his shirt and hose.

'Come quickly!' Cromwell urged him. 'There is another fire in the Queen's Bedchamber, and we need many hands to extinguish it. Waste no time getting dressed — the Queen is in danger!'

The unsophisticated boy with his imperfect grasp of English fell for the ruse without demure, and raced down the hallway half dressed.

'This way!' Cromwell urged him, as he threw open the now unguarded side door that led to the Queen's Bedchamber, and Mark raced in without hesitation. Then Cromwell pulled the door shut and held the handle firmly in his grip as he heard the screams of Queen Anne and her demands for an explanation for Mark's intrusion dressed as if for seduction. Then he prayed hard for the return of the guards.

It seemed an eternity before one of them returned, red-faced and breathless.

'We have the man trapped inside the Queen's Bedchamber!' he told Cromwell as he brushed past him and threw open the door. All three men then hastened through the Withdrawing Chamber into the Queen's bedroom.

The sight that greeted them might have been comical in another context. Mark was on his knees in his hose and shirt, and Anne was hurling bedding at him, calling him a filthy intruder and a pathetic wretch with no respect for her royal dignity and privacy.

Cromwell grinned and slipped back outside, in time to see Richard's retreating figure halfway down the hall. His grin deepened as he reached behind the hanging and quietly closed the door that Richard had left open in his eagerness to depart the scene.

The following morning the Tower guard unlocked the door, then stood respectfully to one side as Cromwell took a deep breath in precaution against whatever smells of fear and worse he might encounter, then stepped through the open doorway into the gloom of the first-floor cell in the Bell Tower.

Mark Smeaton lay curled in a foetal position in the far corner, and flinched as he looked up and saw Cromwell standing over him. Then he began to cry, and plead in his broken English. 'You are here to be torturing me?'

'No, Mark, there may be no need for torture, if you tell me freely what I need to hear.'

'You were tricking me when I am going to where the Queen she sleeps.'

'That is of no matter, Mark. You were found in the Queen's Bedchamber in a state of undress. You are believed to have been about to engage with her in carnal behaviour.'

'What is being this thing — "carnal"?'

'Sex?'

'No, never — she is my Queen! They say they will break my fingers if I do not say things that are not true. You must tell them what is the truth!'

'I may be able to do that if you tell me things that I need to know.'

'Please ask, and then I will be let go from here?'

'That will depend upon what I hear you say,' Cromwell replied as he squatted down on the floor to better hear what the terrified boy might be prepared to tell him. 'First of all, Mark, it has been noted that you dress very well, and that you have several good horses which you keep hidden in a stables in King Street. Where does your money come from? You receive but a hundred pounds a year from playing music for the

Queen, and when you were in the Cardinal's household you were known to dress poorly. Whence comes your wealth?'

'The Ladies,' Mark admitted with a downcast look of embarrassment and shame.

'What ladies? And why do they pay you?'

'For — for — for you know, the sexing?'

'They pay you money to fuck them?' Cromwell insisted, trying to keep the grin from his face, since the intimidation was clearly producing results. When Mark nodded, Cromwell persisted. 'Which Ladies?'

'Must I say?'

'You must if you wish to continue playing the lute. I am no musician myself, but I would imagine that broken fingers would not assist my efforts. The names — *now!*'

'There is Bess Holland. She was first.'

'Elizabeth Holland, Norfolk's mistress?'

'He grows tired of her, so she comes to me for comfort.'

A wonderful start, Cromwell told himself, *and who knows where this might lead?* 'There were others?'

Mark nodded, and looked up hopefully. 'If I tell you them all, you will give orders for me to keep my fingers, yes?'

'Just keep talking. Who else?'

'Mary Shelton.'

'The Queen's aunt, Mary Shelton? But she is ancient!'

'No, the other Mary — the young one who is the Queen's cousin.'

'Any more?'

'Just one. There is also Lady Worcester. She pays the most.'

'She is also with child, Mark. Is it yours?'

'So she is saying, but we must keep silent.'

'But you will tell all, if asked?'

'Will I keep my fingers?'

'That will depend. You must now tell me about the night you were found in the Queen's Bedchamber.'

'You tricked me.'

'I know that, and you know that. But it will be my word against yours, unless...'

'Please, what must I say?'

Cromwell sat back on his haunches and deliberately gave the impression that he was thinking deeply, although the version of events he was about to give Mark had been authored some days ago, before he dispatched Richard to give Lady Rochford a seeing to.

'If you were to say that you heard a noise from the Queen's Bedchamber while you were on your way to the closed stool further down — you know the one?'

'Yes. I sometimes use it, and it is necessary that you pass the chamber on the way.'

'Good. Now, if you could say that when you entered the chamber, a man jumped from the Queen's bed and ran into the chamber next to it, reserved for the Queen's lady?'

'I would be not to blame for being in the chamber?'

'No, because you would have a good reason for being there. You believed that the Queen was being attacked.'

'This is good, yes?'

'It is if you could give me a name.'

'I am not understanding.'

'Who was the man you saw going from the Queen's bed to the adjoining chamber?'

'I must think of a man, yes? But that man, he would be killed by the King?'

'Probably. Who do you hate most, Mark? Who has recently done you wrong?'

'Harry Norris!' Mark said without hesitation, and Cromwell's intuition had been correct. The morning had not been wasted.

'You would say that, to save your fingers?'

'Of course — where is the paper on which I must write?'

'It will be brought to you in a day or two. You have just preserved your future as a musician, Mark. As a prostitute, perhaps not. But as a musician, yes.'

Mark began to cry tears of relief and gratitude, and Cromwell made his way down to the private quarters of Sir William Kingston, Constable of the Tower, with a brief set of instructions.

'The boy Mark Smeaton — he is to be fed regularly, and in no way harmed, unless and until I say so. And you might wish to give instructions for your best chamber to be cleaned and suitably equipped to host a very royal prisoner.'

X

'Why am I here,' Sir Henry Norris demanded, 'and since when did the Master of the Rolls have the authority to order the arrest of the Groom of the Stool?'

Cromwell nodded for the armed escort to withdraw, and invited Norris to take the vacant seat in front of his table in the inner chamber of the Chancery Suite. Then he adopted a pained expression. 'It was either me, and this place, or Norfolk and the Tower.'

'On what grounds could the Earl Marshall of England — or you, for that matter — have me treated so grossly? The King shall hear of this.'

'Indeed he shall, Sir Henry, in due course. But then he will learn, no doubt to his considerable anger, that the man who wipes his arse so gently also applies his gentle touch to various parts of the Queen.'

'Outrageous! Unworthy! A disgraceful accusation!'

'I could not agree more, which is why it pains me to have to accuse you of it. In deference to your closeness with His Majesty, I have kept your apprehension as discreet as possible, but whether you leave here to return to your royal duties, or are conveyed to the Tower, will depend on how you acquit yourself during the next few minutes. Although I have the entire morning free, should that be necessary.'

'Of what am I being accused? Did I hear you aright? Having to do with the Queen?'

'I have a witness.'

'A witness to *what*, pray?'

'To your sliding guiltily from the Queen's bed into the adjoining chamber occupied by Lady Rochford.'

'That scheming whore? She has no love for me or the Queen, and would say anything to bring down a Boleyn. Her husband prefers boys, did you know that? And not just boys, if the rumours be true.'

'What rumours, Sir Henry?'

'No more of that. She is your witness?'

'No doubt she will confirm what Mark Smeaton told me barely an hour ago.'

'That peasant who is fit only to strangle noises from a lute? Why would you believe anything he says?'

'Because he has two strong reasons for telling the truth. For one, he wishes to retain the use of his fingers. Secondly, you recently humiliated him in the Queen's presence.'

'Is that all the evidence you have for this scandalous allegation? The lies of a low-born musician under torture?'

'I did not say he had been tortured, Sir Henry. Simply that he fears to be.'

'It's the same thing. Why would you condemn a man on mere lies?'

'It would not be the first occasion, in your lengthy experience. May I ask you to cast your mind back to a windy evening some years ago, when you were dispatched to meet my late master the Cardinal on his first journey from York Palace, as it then was, to a more humble lodging across the river?'

'I was bearing him a token of good will from King Henry.'

'Indeed you were. And did you not occasion him to kneel in the mud at your feet in order to receive it? The Cardinal Legate of Rome, the former Chancellor of England, the Archbishop of York?'

'He chose to kneel, from sheer joy!' Norris protested.

'That is not how I heard it,' Cromwell glowered back at him. 'I was not there on that occasion, but his Steward, George Cavendish, told me a different story. He was distressed by it for days.'

'So this is what this is all about? Vengeance for Wolsey? His downfall was ordered by King Henry, remember — have a care how you take your revenge.'

'He was not alone, and he was not the one most guilty. Your partner in lust must bear the lion's share.'

'You accuse an innocent man in order to be avenged of Queen Anne? You have fired your arrow of accusation at the wrong target, Cromwell. I can give you a far better one.'

'That person being?'

'Weston. That drivelling old tosspot Sir Francis hangs on her every word, her every gesture in his direction, her assurance that were she free to marry again, he would be her choice. It is a constant source of merriment amongst her gathering how he seems to glow every time she favours him with so much as a smile in his direction.'

'She speaks out loud of being free to marry again?'

'Regularly. She has left none of us in any doubt that Harry Tudor can't get it up any more, and that even if he did, it would get lost somewhere inside her, it is so small.'

'You would be prepared to say so publicly?'

'Certainly. *And* her promise to Weston that he would be next between her shrivelled thighs.'

'Have a care, Sir Henry. How could you know the state of her thighs?'

'A figure of speech only.'

'Do you have another moment of indiscretion available in order to name others to whom she might have promised carnal favour?'

'Brereton.'

'Sir William? He is barely capable of tottering around the Palace these days, surely?'

'They say there's no fool like an old fool. The Queen delights in promising Brereton one day and Weston the next. There are also hints that they may each have done the deed with her, and that she looks forward to their next encounters.'

'Again, you would be prepared to say such things to persons other than me?'

'If it leads to the removal of your baseless lies against me, most certainly.'

'Thank you, Sir Henry,' Cromwell smiled back appreciatively. 'You are free to wipe Henry's arse. Although, given your position at present, you might be better advised to *lick* it clean.'

'Lady Worcester, what a pleasant surprise.'

'Pray dispense with the mealy-mouthed shit, Cromwell. You asked to see me.'

'And how does your Ladyship? The child sits easily inside you?'

'Why am I here? And why is Mark Smeaton in the Tower?'

'I may conveniently answer both of your questions at once, may I not?'

'Your meaning, if there is one?'

'The child you are carrying may well prove to have musical talent just like Master Smeaton's?'

The arrogance slid from her face as if a veil had been lowered, and her skin turned the colour of the vellum rolls on Cromwell's table. 'Who told you? The Queen?'

'I have it on better authority than that, Lady Worcester. But, purely out of interest, how would the Queen know?'

'I owe her money, and being the mean, spiteful, two-faced, evilly-disposed whore that she is, she demanded to know the reason for my debt.'

'I feel sure that Her Majesty would speak more highly of you than you do of her,' Cromwell chuckled, 'but may I assume that the money was for the Queen's musician to finger a more mature instrument?'

'You're enjoying this, aren't you? But you are in no position to pass moral judgements, Cromwell. It is common knowledge that you once went to it with your wife's sister, but days after your wife had been laid in her grave.'

Cromwell took several deep breaths to control his anger. 'You would do better than to listen to the drivel of those dismissed from my service for stealing wine and selling it to a local alehouse keeper, whose premises, incidentally, I caused to have shut down. But then, you are more comfortable in lowly circles, are you not? Could you have caught that disease from your husband Henry Somerset, who prefers to fuck kitchen wenches up the arse?'

Lady Worcester grimaced her displeasure. 'We could spend an unpleasant morning exchanging insults, Cromwell, or we may cut to the chase. What is the price of your silence — some of what Mark Smeaton enjoys?'

'I do not recall him saying that he had enjoyed it, merely that you were the main source of his revenue. Not the sole source, but an important one. As for the offer to buy your way out of trouble on your back, you must be advised that while I enjoy my meat well flamed, I could not bring myself to consume it so well done.'

'Enough of this dissemblance, Master Secretary. What do you seek?'

'The Queen's darkest secrets.'

'How dark do you want them? Her flirtations with the gentlemen of her Courtly circle? Her promise to Mark Smeaton — purely, I am sure, in order to cause me pain — that if the King were dead she would like nothing more than to lie on her bed and enjoy "such music as he could produce with his urgent fingers"? Those were her exact words.'

'They would certainly be worth recording. But my interest was tweaked by the other thing you said — she actually spoke of her desires if the King were dead?'

'She most certainly did. She often holds the randy old goats with whom she surrounds herself in thrall with her fantasies about who might have her next, like a bitch on heat waving its cunny into the breeze to attract a mate.'

'You obviously missed your true vocation as a writer of bawdy verse,' Cromwell grinned, 'and I thank you for your candour, as also for your most descriptive way of conveying it.'

'There's more — the blackest yet.'

'Go on,' Cromwell encouraged her, barely able to conceal his excitement.

'The main reason for her dislike of me. The reason why she fears me so much that she must hold me down with threats and slights. I caught her going to it with her brother.'

'Lord Rochford? Good Christ Almighty, can you tell of that?'

'With considerable satisfaction. I was one night established in the side chamber to her own bed chamber. You know of the arrangement?'

'Indeed I do, but to forestall any further speculation, I have never taken advantage of the fact that the dividing door is invariably kept closed.'

'There is good reason for that. If asked, Anne will tell you that it is in order that her ladies may be attended during the night by their husbands, or whoever. But it is well known that the true reason is that she may admit her own chosen cocks through the side door to the hallway. Then, there was this one night ... may I have some refreshment for my throat?'

Cromwell reached for the unused goblet to the side and poured a generous measure of best Burgundy into it, handing it over with a smile. 'Pray do not delay, now that we have reached the nub of it.'

'Well, as I was saying, there was this night when I awoke and heard what I thought were cries of pain from the Queen's chamber. Fearing that Anne was ill, I opened the door between us, and there she stood with her brother. They were leaning back on one of the posts that surround her bed, and he was rubbing his fingers into her cunny while she was frigging his cock. They did not seem to be aware of me, but the next morning I made the mistake of telling Anne what I had seen, and promising never to divulge it to a soul. Nor have I done, until today, but she has persecuted me for that knowledge ever since.'

'I thank you most sincerely for that, Lady Worcester, and I apologise if my manner toward you earlier was less than gallant. But you gave as good as you got, as I recall. I bid you good day, with the assurance that Mark Smeaton will shortly be back inside you, and that your debt to the Queen will expire in the near future.'

'By a lawful process?'

'Most certainly, my lady. It will, like all debts, expire on the death of the creditor.'

'Richard told you what we had been up to?' Lady Rochford asked nervously as she took the seat not long vacated by Lady Worcester.

'Not the precise details, no, but I am a man not unfamiliar with these things. Between a man and a mature woman, that is. Not something that Lord Rochford would be all that familiar with, however. Would I be correct?'

Jane Rochford turned bright scarlet. 'What passes between my husband and myself is no business of yours, Master Secretary.'

'Until it *becomes* my business. I am not so much concerned with what passes between you and your husband as what passes between him and his sister.'

Her jaw dropped. 'What are you suggesting?'

'That he prefers flesh closer to his own, that he prefers small boys and girls, and has even been known to cast lascivious eyes on his own horse.'

'That is quite disgusting! I was warned that your mood today was one that properly belongs in a brothel or the Paris Garden, but really, this is beyond any justification!'

'But like any man who leaves his wife as unsatisfied as you, he must realise that you take your pleasures elsewhere?'

'If you intend by this means to threaten me into disclosing matters regarding the lady whom I serve, then you have misjudged the situation,' Jane said. 'My husband could not care less if I fuck his groom of the stable, provided that I make no such demands of him.'

'But while you are taking your pleasures in the adjoining chamber, you are not guarding your Queen, as your duties require?'

'And why would he care about that?'

'His own sister? And, if the truth be known, the woman he prefers in his bed to you? How can you bear to spend each day being commanded by she who is preferred over you, contrary to the laws of God and mankind? Surely you would wish revenge for that cruellest of slights?'

'I have long resigned myself to what passes between the two of them.'

'But you do not rush to deny it, even though the truth casts shame on both of you?'

'Get to the point, Master Cromwell.'

'My point is that should the King hear that you leave the Queen unguarded in order to pursue your own pleasures, and keep your door shut in order not to see what the Queen does in there, sometimes with her own brother, would he not regard that as bordering upon the treasonous?'

'You cannot prove any of that.'

'No, but I can call upon two Palace guards who will testify, if required, that on the night when the Queen was "entertaining", shall we say, the door between you was closed.'

'You know *why* it was closed, and I do not care if you tell my husband.'

'Do you care if I tell the King? They tell me that women burn for treason.'

'This becomes tedious. What is it you wish to me say, if questioned?'

'That on the night that Mark Smeaton entered the Queen's bedchamber in the erroneous belief that she was in danger, a man slipped quickly from the Queen's bed, came into your bedchamber, and closed the door before making good his escape behind St Anthony.'

'And that is all?'

'Do you not wish to learn who it was?'

'Richard Ashton? I'm sure that the Queen would have wished it were him. Or did you mean my husband, her brother? If so, then I cannot oblige you.'

'I speak of Sir Henry Norris.'

'And if I concur in this lie?'

'The Queen will go to the Tower, along with her brother, Gentle Norris and several more Gentlemen of the Privy Chamber, Mark Smeaton will survive to service half the Queen's former Ladies, while you will remain in this world, and will be free to marry again — possibly Richard Ashton, if your father will consent.'

'You are assured that Anne will die, and her disgusting brother along with her?'

'As assured as I have ever been of anything.'

'Then we have an agreement. Tell Richard that we have business to complete whenever he feels so inclined.'

'I will if you will do one further thing.'

'And what is that?'

'You retrieved the locket belonging to Jane Seymour that Anne threw into the corner?'

'Of course.'

'You may complete your business with Richard in my private chamber here in the Palace this afternoon, and I will leave word that you are not to be disturbed. Bring the locket with you by way of payment of the hire fee, and leave it with Richard.'

Henry was unsure whether to smile or burst into tears of self-pity. He had ordered the information, but now that he had it he wished that he could travel back to the days of the Cardinal.

'Her own brother, say you?' he croaked in shattered disbelief.

'Regrettably yes, Sire,' Cromwell confirmed.

'And you say that this is treason enough to have her dispatched?'

'So I am informed by Audley, Sire, and he should know best regarding these matters. But should that be too moot a point of law, there is another alleged ground of treason.'

'Other than the blade that she rams through my heart as truly as if it were an assassin's dagger?'

'Truly, Sire. But perhaps another day might be more conducive to further ill tidings. I am myself overcome with sorrow at having to so burden you on this occasion.'

'No, it were best done all at once. Are they all in the Tower?'

'All but the Queen, her brother Rochford and Henry Norris. I am advised that Norris intends to enter the lists at the May Day tournament, and it may be that you would wish to challenge him on the matter, although clearly not during a joust. I must, in all deference, ask that you be the one to order that the Queen be conveyed to the Tower, where I have already discreetly arranged for Lady Kingston to receive her in special lodgings. As for her brother Rochford, he may be scooped up whenever Anne is taken in, since he is still residing in the Palace, to which he came in order to comfort Anne following her miscarriage. Or so he claimed.'

'What is this other treasonous matter of which you spoke?'

'It seems that on more than one occasion the Queen spoke of who she might take up with were you no longer alive.'

'Idle fantasy, surely?'

'It constitutes "imagining the King's death", strictly interpreted. That is one of the well-established grounds of treason. And in this instance it is more treasonous than what the Cardinal was accused of, namely wishing to become Pope.'

'I went deeper than that, as you well know, Thomas. There were papers said to reveal his invitation to the Emperor Charles to invade.'

'They were forgeries, Sire, as I subsequently proved. Not soon enough to save poor Thomas Wolsey, unfortunately.'

'And this evidence you have against the Queen? Not more forgeries?'

'I have the sworn testimonies, Sire.'

'That may prove to be forgeries, or at least obtained under torture, long after those they condemn have paid the price?'

'There has been no torture, and those whose testimonies I have are in the main not those accused.'

'And there can be no doubt?'

'None, Sire.'

'Adultery with Norris, Weston and Brereton, and incest with Rochford?'

'Yes, Sire.'

'And treason on two separate grounds?'

'Regrettably, that also.'

'Very well. It shall proceed as you advise. Find Lady Jane Seymour and ask her to attend me, that I may break to her gently the news of her mistress's downfall.'

'She is believed to be with her family in Wiltshire, Sire. Do you wish me to travel down there and bring her safely back to Court?'

'Yes, please do that, Thomas. After you have seen to the arrangements in the Tower.'

XI

'I still don't understand why you need me,' Richard complained as he and Cromwell trotted side by side through Hungerford on the final stage of their journey to Wulfhall. 'After all, the woman hardly spoke a word to me in all the times that we were in attendance on the Queen.'

'According to you, she hardly spoke a word to anyone,' Cromwell reminded him, 'and your face will be a more familiar one than mine, so as to put her at her ease.'

'If we wish to put her at her ease,' Richard countered, 'why are there four armed Royal Yeomen riding behind us?'

'Because she may be our next Queen,' Cromwell replied. 'And even if she is not, she is important to Henry. But well minded — we shall need to find somewhere to billet them overnight. You can no doubt be found accommodation in the main house, but do not be offended if it turns out to be above the stable. We should in any case only be there for one night.'

They were met at the front door by a beaming Sir John, who shook Cromwell firmly by the hand, and bowed briefly towards Richard when advised that he was Senior Clerk of Chancery, and had ridden with Cromwell in order to assure 'the Lady Jane' that she had not incurred the Queen's displeasure by departing so abruptly from Court without leave.

'You have heard that Edward has been appointed a Gentleman of the Privy Chamber?' Sir John enquired with a broad smile.

'I had not,' Cromwell replied, 'although I have been somewhat distracted of late by matters pertaining to the

Queen's honour. She will shortly be committed to the Tower on charges of treason.'

Sir John took the news calmly, but seemed somewhat distracted as he asked, 'You are here to take Jane back to Court, by my guess. Is she implicated in the Queen's downfall?'

'Only in the best of ways,' Cromwell assured him. 'I am here mainly to return an item taken from her by the Queen in a moment of anger, but while here I might, with your leave, enquire of her whether or not she might look kindly on King Henry at this time of considerable distress to him.'

'You will find her in the rear garden,' Sir John told him, 'but be sure to approach her kindly, and set her mind at rest regarding the Queen's anger.'

Jane looked up from her needlework as they approached where she was seated in the shade of a massive elm tree.

'You are here to drag me back to face the Queen's fury? If so, might I first be permitted to complete this altar cloth for the family chapel? It wants but two days' more work.'

'You need not fear the Queen's wrath any longer, gentle Jane,' Cromwell assured her. 'She is taken up on charges of treason, and will, by the time of our return to Court, be lodged in the Tower.'

'Are any of her Ladies implicated?' Jane asked, ashen-faced. 'Lady Rochford, for example? Or Lady Worcester?'

'Should they be?' Cromwell replied. 'In truth, it was largely their words that led to the bringing of the charges.'

'I have nothing of which I could speak,' Jane replied fearfully. 'Please give His Majesty my best regards, and say that I expressed my sorrow that things should have come to this sorry pass.'

'My Senior Clerk, Master Ashton here, put me in possession of information regarding an exchange of words between you and Anne that led to the loss of a locket from around your neck. Would I be correct in surmising that King Henry would be sad to learn of its loss?'

'Indeed he will,' Jane replied sadly. 'Please give him my heartfelt apologies, and ensure that he is well advised that its loss was due in no part to a lack of care on my part.'

'In truth, it is not lost.' Cromwell reached inside his tunic and held his hand out towards her. 'Would I be exceeding my place if I were to enquire if the letters "H" and "J" inscribed inside each half are meant to represent "Henry" and "Jane"?'

'You were able to retrieve it?' Jane asked, almost in tears. 'I thank you for your kindness, Master Secretary. It was within my possession for such a short while, yet it had become very precious to me. How did you obtain it?'

'That is of no consequence. What *is* of considerable consequence is what those letters signify. Has Henry given any sign that you might occupy a very important place in his affections?'

'Indeed he has,' Jane murmured, 'but I gave him no cause to believe that such feelings might be matched by mine. After all, the Queen...'

'There will soon be no Queen, Jane,' Cromwell told her in his softest voice. 'Is it your wish to be Henry's wife? Or do you fear that he will prove brutal and unfaithful? Because if so...'

'It is not that,' Jane whispered, her head down over her needlework. 'Henry has shown me nothing but kindness and affection. I have seen a loving and caring side to his nature that others have probably not had occasion to experience. Were he not King...'

'Yes?' Cromwell urged her.

'Were he simply lord of an estate, such as my father's, I would gladly become his wife. But he is King, and obliged to show his power and strength to the entire world.'

'All the more reason why he should have opportunity to be kind and gentle at home, particularly should he have children by his next wife.'

'Why should he need to marry, in order to have children? And in what ways has he shown his loving nature as a father? He has declared his precious, and most gracious, daughter Mary to be no daughter of his.'

'He has declared her bastard, certainly,' Cromwell conceded, 'but that was only because he was driven to it by the wicked Anne. And Elizabeth remains in favour.'

'By the same token, because she is Anne's daughter,' Jane argued, 'will he not bastardise her when Anne is gone?'

Cromwell took the seat next to her and took her hand in his. 'I had two daughters of my own, Jane. Sadly, they passed in the same sweating sickness that took their mother, but were I in your father's position, and seeking future happiness and prosperity for one of my daughters, I should not stand in the way of a match with Henry. You forget that I see him daily, and I know his true nature. Because of that, I would have had no fear were either of my daughters, Anne or Grace, to have become Henry's bride.'

'But if I were to marry Henry, I would have to become Queen, would I not?'

Cromwell could not hold back the laughter. 'You would regard that as a disadvantage? There would be an endless queue of women for Henry's hand, were he to send heralds abroad in search of a replacement for Anne. But they would be seeking merely the crown, as was the wicked Anne. Do you not think that Henry deeply craves the companionship of a woman who truly loves him for himself, rather than the title that Fate has burdened him with? Think you that he is not, under all that finery, a normal man with a normal man's hopes and dreams?'

A tear rolled down Jane's cheek as she looked hopefully, first at Richard, then at Cromwell. 'Think you that Henry would have me on those terms?'

'I *know* he would, Jane.'

'Then let us join my brother Edward in London, and see what transpires.'

As they walked back towards the house, Cromwell was chuckling. 'The most reluctant Queen of England that ever was. And the first woman to marry Henry for love.'

'I have never heard her speak so much,' Richard whispered, awe-stricken. 'It is like she has become a new woman at the mere prospect of marriage to Henry. I hope that some woman shows me that much natural devotion one day.'

'A new woman indeed,' Cromwell said. 'And soon to become yet another woman — Queen of England. When we meet with her tomorrow, remember this time to bow in her presence. We may as well get used to it.'

XII

The following morning Richard walked from the stables in which he had been accommodated overnight and wandered through the back door of the manor house into the kitchen, in search of something to eat. A young woman with long flowing auburn hair was at the table in the centre, on which the cook had placed the first bake of the day, and she was tapping each loaf in turn with her knuckle. She turned as she heard Richard enter the kitchen, and the smile she gave him made his heart lurch.

'You are in search of breakfast?' she enquired.

'Indeed, and it will be none the less appetising to know that it has been touched by such a fair hand. Does the cook instruct you to test each loaf for its freshness?'

'No, she does not. But these are required for the journey to London by those who have been residing here overnight, in addition to the soldiers who will be accompanying them. They must be fresh, if they are to last beyond Reading.'

'I am one of those who will be savouring them, so my grateful thanks. My name is Richard, and I serve Master Secretary Cromwell.'

'Bess,' the young woman replied with lowered eyes. 'I do not envy you your return to Court.'

'You have served there?' Richard asked.

She nodded. 'Some years ago, before my marriage, I was in the service of Queen Anne.'

'As her seamstress, or perhaps in her kitchen?'

'No, as one of her Ladies, along with my sister Jane. Then I married and went to Jersey with my husband. He was Governor there, until his death last year.'

'You are Jane Seymour's sister?' Richard enquired unnecessarily, as he asked himself how someone so naturally beautiful could come from the same loins as her somewhat plain older sister.

'Did I not just say so? Or did you perhaps mistake me for a kitchen wench?'

'At first I did, I must own, mainly because of your fresh country complexion and natural beauty. It is a refreshing contrast to the painted whores at Court.'

'I was a Queen's Lady once, remember,' Bess grinned back at him mischievously. 'No doubt, had you seen me then, you would have accounted me one such.'

'No, never!' Richard blundered in his embarrassment. 'But how does one so young as you come to be already a widow?'

'I was but thirteen when I married Sir Anthony Oughtred, and fifteen when I bore him my son Henry, who remains in Jersey. I plan to return to our estate in Yorkshire, to give birth to the child that is currently in my womb.'

'Where exactly in Yorkshire?

'Kexby, on the outskirts of York. You have heard of it?'

'York, certainly. They say it is very wild and lawless.'

Bess laughed lightly. 'They say that also of London, and from what I recall they are correct. Yet you would drag my sister back there?'

'We accompany her at her request. You surely know that she may become our next Queen?'

Bess's face fell. 'It is to be hoped that Henry treats Anne mercifully when she is adjudged guilty. She was very kind to both myself and Jane when we were younger, and it was through her influence that my late husband received his rich office.'

'You seem certain that the Queen will be found guilty,' Richard commented.

Bess screwed up her pretty mouth in distaste. 'Henry wants rid of her, does he not? Why he should want my sister instead remains a mystery within this family.'

'Perhaps love?'

'And what would a young gallant such as yourself know about *true* love? You chase the ladies, and you fill their heads with fancy promises and protestations, thereby overcoming their natural modesty, then you move on to the next conquest.'

'I pity you, should that have been your experience of affairs of the heart thus far,' Richard replied.

Bess challenged him with a look as she threw back her head. 'Admit that when you came across me here in the kitchen you took me for a serving girl, and entertained thoughts of testing my virtue.'

'I did no such thing!' Richard protested. 'I was certainly taken by your natural beauty, and I certainly mistook you for a servant, given that you had not wasted your looks with guile and paste, like the women I encounter daily at the Court. But I had no designs on your virtue, I swear.'

'Then perhaps you lack imagination — or even manliness,' Bess replied with a coquettish grin, just as the cook entered the kitchen and demanded that the loaves be removed from the table to make room for the morning milk.

Three hours later the returning party crossed the Thames at Wallingford, and took advantage of the shade afforded by a copse of yew trees to dismount and eat the bread and cheese supplied on their departure from Wulfhall, which they washed down with clear water from the river.

Jane smiled across at Richard. 'My sister was much taken with the handsome young clerk she encountered in the kitchen this morning.'

'Bess?' Richard asked with a returning smile.

'How many more of my sisters were in the kitchen?' Jane teased him.

Richard blushed. 'She is quite one of the most naturally beautiful women I have ever encountered,' he mumbled, but Jane was still in a playful mood.

'You must wonder how she ever came to have a sister as plain as me.'

'A sister who has caught the King's eye,' he reminded her, and her face reflected her uncertainty.

'Do you *really* believe that he has an eye for me with a view to marriage, or simply as another of his mistresses?'

'The King does not confide in me on such matters, my lady, or indeed any matters at all. You must ask my master that question, although I do not believe that even Master Secretary is privy to his infidelities.'

'I do not think I could bear it if he were to prove unfaithful,' Jane mumbled as she looked down at the grass.

'You are minded to marry him, then?' Richard pressed her.

She nodded. 'Would you be prepared to do me the kindness to attend upon me in the afternoons, when I am Queen? I so enjoyed your visits when I served Anne, and few Courtiers other than you regarded me as suitable for conversation.'

'As I recall, those conversations consisted largely of me trying to coax you into saying something. You were very shy in those days.'

'In truth, some of us dared not so much as open our mouths in that company, since we knew not what humour the Queen was in from day to day, or indeed from hour to hour. Then, when she began to suspect that Henry had an eye for me, she took every opportunity to belittle and demean me in the eyes of her hangers-on. There was only Lady Rochford who dared stand up to her. It was being rumoured, ere I departed the Court, that you and she have — well, shall we say, an "understanding"?'

'If we do, then it is all in her imagination,' Richard protested in his own defence, horrified in case Jane Rochford had boasted of their antics, both in the side bed chamber and in Cromwell's private quarters.

'She would not be the only one with fantasies in your direction,' Jane told him, then blushed. 'I do not, of course, refer to myself, but there were other comments passed on those days when you had been in our company and departed that suggested that more than one lady would welcome the opportunity. Even Anne, in my hearing, on one occasion.'

'Do not add me to the list of those condemned to the Tower!' Richard replied in mock horror. Then it occurred to him that a change of subject might be in order. 'Is it true that we journey, not to Whitehall, but to Placentia Palace at Greenwich?'

'Yes. Word came from Edward just before we left this morning. He and his wife have been allocated a suite of rooms there that will be large enough to accommodate me as well. He added that they were convenient for Henry to visit us all.'

'I suspect that the main object of Henry's visits will be you, My Lady.'

'You are probably correct in that. Isn't it all so romantic? But I shall hold you to your promise to make frequent visits also.'

XIII

In the absence of the Master Secretary and his Senior Clerk, much had been happening. Those accused and marked for trial were already lodged in the Tower, and there was a message awaiting Cromwell that his attendance was urgently sought there by Sir William Kingston, its Constable.

'I require you to accompany me at all times, from now on,' Cromwell insisted to Richard over breakfast on the morning after their return from Wulfhall. 'There is much clerking to be done, and I believe that it would be expedient to have a witness to my every conversation as the matter proceeds to its conclusion.'

'Its *foregone* conclusion?' Richard asked cynically, but Cromwell's only response was a hard stare.

'Smeaton is still here,' Kingston told them an hour later over wine and wafers, 'since I have been advised that a charge of treason has been added to his account.'

'By whom?' Cromwell demanded.

'By whom was I advised, or by whom has he been accused?'

'Both, although I'd wager that Norris was the one who paid him back with the treason charge.'

'You are correct in that. But it was my lord of Norfolk who conveyed the instruction to keep him close confined. He also wished him tortured, but I declined to do so, and advised him of your instruction to me.'

'How did Norfolk take that?' Cromwell enquired with a grin.

'He blasphemed horribly, and all but demolished yon door on his hasty departure.'

'Little wonder,' Cromwell gloated. 'He must be shitting himself copiously with the fall of his queen piece on the chessboard of Court politics.'

'He treated her very roughly when they brought her downriver, and we were receiving her at the river steps,' Kingston told them both. 'As she set foot on land, she fell to her knees. At first we thought she had merely lost her footing after being on water all the way down from Whitehall, but then she threw herself flat on her face, and began such a wailing and kicking that I feared that she had lost her wits. Norfolk grabbed her by the back of her neck, hauled her to her feet, slapped her around the head and told her that she was no niece of his. She fell silent after that.'

'Who wouldn't?' Cromwell replied. 'Norfolk has the capacity to silence thunder when the fancy so takes him. How has Anne been since?'

Kingston shook his head from side to side in a gesture of uncertainty. 'She behaves like someone who cannot believe what has happened, then at other times she seems resigned to her fate. My wife attends her, as you commanded, but she is constantly demanding the attendance of her other Ladies, who she asserts must be concerned for her welfare.'

'If only she knew,' Cromwell replied with a grimace. 'There is not one of them left who would wish to be associated with her — except perhaps Lady Rochford, and then only to gloat.'

'But Lady Kingston cannot shoulder the burden of her company for twenty-four hours in every day. Anne must have other Ladies attend her.'

'Perhaps Lady Shelton? The aunt, that is, not the cousin.'

'As you command,' Kingston confirmed.

'The boy Smeaton — has he asked to see me?' Cromwell enquired.

Kingston nodded. 'Every hour of every day.'

'Tell him I am dead,' Cromwell replied as he made to leave, gesturing for Richard to follow him. 'As indeed I am, to him.'

The trials began less than a week later, and Cromwell and Richard were forced to take men with halberds with them to fight their way through the multitude clamouring for admission to Westminster Hall, many of whom had been queuing since noon the previous day. It was almost as chaotic inside, as the cream of England's nobility mingled uneasily with the senior judges of the King's Bench to form the most unlikely, and certainly the largest, jury that English common law had ever known.

Norfolk glowered as he came over. 'Was it *really* necessary to have me as senior judge?' he thundered.

'Did you wish someone else to take from you the baton of Lord High Steward, or are you fearful that the substitute thus chosen might prove more worthy than you? I could understand why being bested by a goat-herd might prove galling.'

'Fuck off, Cromwell.'

'He is to sit in judgement over his own niece?' Richard asked, horror-stricken, as Norfolk stormed away in a cloud of blasphemy.

Cromwell grinned. 'The jury will have the yes or no of the matter. As for any family sentiment that Norfolk might retain for his errant niece, that came apart when her legs did. She has let down the Howards and the Boleyns, whose titles and preferments will now take off like startled crows.'

'But the Queen is not for trial today?'

'No. Today we fry the first dish. Smeaton and the non-ennobled.'

'How are they pleading to the charges?'

'They haven't heard them yet. They will be read out, and then they will be asked how they plead.'

'Then the court adjourns while they prepare their defences?'

'No, we proceed straight into our accusations.'

'In what order will you call the witnesses?'

'No need. We have their sworn statements.'

'But defence witnesses?'

'If they have any, they will be heard.'

'Is this how the common law courts normally conduct their business?'

'Of course not. If they did, there would be popular clamour and allegations of breach of Magna Carta. But for the trial of a Queen and her alleged conspirators on charges of treason there is no procedural precedent.'

'So you are making it up as you go along?'

'Precisely. That is why I was asked to prosecute. As the man at the head of the Court of Chancery, I am accustomed to being inventive.'

By the end of the day's proceedings, as the condemned men were escorted back outside to the waiting barge that would return them to the Tower, and whatever form of death awaited them, Richard had abandoned any belief he might have harboured regarding justice in any cause that involved a monarch. Smeaton had pleaded guilty, with many tearful pleas that he might be dispatched quickly and mercifully, while the remainder had defiantly denied any guilt, but then steadfastly refrained from offering any evidence in their defence.

Cromwell, in his role as prosecutor in the King's name, had solemnly read out, without any trace of hesitation, embarrassment or shame, all the accusations that he had spent days carefully wording, and Smeaton, Norris, Brereton and Weston had bowed their heads when Norfolk had thundered out their death sentences above the boos, hisses and catcalls of the mob that heaved and pressed around the public spaces below the special platforms constructed for the occasion for the comfort and safety of the jury.

'Why did they not defend themselves?' Richard asked in shaking tones of disbelief as the Hall slowly cleared of ghoulish spectators, and Cromwell rolled up his vellums with a satisfied smile.

Cromwell looked sideways at Richard as he explained. 'They were doomed to conviction anyway, as they all knew — with the possible exception of poor Smeaton. The only remaining question in each of their minds was the manner of their deaths, and the possibility of the attainder of their estates. Henry enjoys absolute power over both, and had they sought to justify their actions, or denied in any way what it suited Henry to have proved against them, they faced the gruesome end awaiting all traitors — hanging, drawing and quartering. But the King has the power to order a more merciful death by axe on the block, and may even decree that it be done privately on Tower Green, rather than in front of a screaming mob on Tower Hill. Remember that lesson, should you still entertain any wild dreams of asserting your title to Henry's throne.'

'And their estates?' Richard enquired in a voice all but stilled by the horror of what he had just learned.

'Likewise,' Cromwell replied as he tucked the scrolls under his arm and prepared to depart. 'The King may, in his mercy, allow something for the families they leave behind, who will starve otherwise. Poor Mark Smeaton has nothing to lose in that, of course, but Norris leaves three children and a vast estate, Weston has a wife and child, and Brereton has much land on the Welsh Marches that he must preserve for his wife and two sons.'

'So they will plead guilty to something they have not done, rather than hazard all by defying the allegations?'

'They were to all intents guilty once charged,' Cromwell explained with a quizzical stare at Richard. 'Do you not yet understand how these things are done?'

'God forbid that I ever displease Henry,' Richard shuddered. 'But what of the Queen and Viscount Rochford? Surely they will make a braver display of proving their innocence?'

'The higher they come, the harder they fall,' Cromwell muttered as he began to make his way through the almost deserted Hall. He stopped and turned back to address Richard. 'Are you coming with me, or will you remain here and pray for the lives of those who are effectively dead already?'

Richard stepped down the Hall behind him, sick to the stomach.

Three days later Richard followed Cromwell with considerable dread and foreboding into the Great Hall of the Tower, where the jury of twenty-seven peers of the realm awaited their instructions from Norfolk, who — with apparent enthusiasm, as he demonstrated once the proceedings commenced — was to preside over the trial, first of Anne herself, and then her brother. Since they were of noble birth, they could not have been tried alongside the commoners who had preceded them, but the evidence that had already been heard in the previous trial, and most notably the lack of any defence offered by any of them to charges that directly implicated Anne, would not do Anne's cause any good.

Anne appeared regally defiant until the very end. She had taken considerable care over her appearance, as if fully aware that her final public performance would be far less romantic, and her scarlet and black gown was topped off with a black and white feathered hat that wavered slightly in the breeze.

Norfolk maintained order in the only manner of which he was capable, namely yelling at anyone who made a noise that was not part of the proceedings. His face became more and more murderous as the disgraceful, unedifying, and at times disgusting allegations were put to Anne, specifying dates, times and bodily actions that owed more to the latent playwright that lurked inside Cromwell than any vestige of truth. She denied each and every vile charge, but like those who had gone before her, she offered no defence, either in the form of witnesses or by way of testimony of her own. When asked if she had anything to say she shook her head, and when advised by her uncle Norfolk that her response was required in verbal form, she shouted, 'No! None of it! I have more self-respect than to do any of that!', then fell silent.

Richard almost fainted when, following the guilty finding against her, it was announced grimly by Norfolk that she would be taken to Smithfield and burned at the stake, as the only prescribed penalty for a female adjudged to have committed treason. Cromwell saw the colour draining from Richard's face, and reached out to pinch his wrist. The sudden pain seemed to prevent him from passing out, but the reassurance from Cromwell that the lady would almost certainly be spared the flames sounded as if it was coming from a great distance away.

'When will they try her brother?' Richard asked, ashen-faced.

'Once they have taken Anne out,' Cromwell replied. 'It would not do for them to collide in the doorway.'

The afternoon's proceedings were far more entertaining.

Rochford had accepted that he was as good as dead, and being the flamboyant show-off that he was, he milked every opportunity to play to the crowd. He was not concerned to preserve his estate for any family, since he had never had any regard for the wife his father had bought for him, he was being brought down simply because he was a Boleyn, and his uncle on the Howard side of the family was determined to see him to the scaffold. He could therefore have this last bit of fun.

He laughed when it was put to him that he had carnally known his sister, adding for good measure: 'Since she has been found guilty of going to it with so many others, when would she have found the time for me?' Norfolk then asked him if he knew of any reason why Anne would engage with so many men, and he replied jocularly, 'Why should she not, if they were available? It is well known that Harry Tudor can't get it up any more.'

'He just lost any chance of a merciful end,' Cromwell said with a sideways smirk at Richard.

As the sun began to sink towards the river at far distant Mortlake, it was all over, and George Boleyn's name had been added to William Kingston's 'to do' list.

'You seem to have lost your appetite,' Cromwell observed over the meats that evening, as Richard stared at the roast that was still oozing some blood onto the salver, converting itself in his imagination into the severed head of a disgraced queen.

'I wonder that you can eat,' Richard countered. 'At the risk of being accused of treason, as is everyone who displeases you, it would seem, I am bound to observe that when you first approached me, at Fyfield, with the promise of righting an injustice, and the prospect of claiming my rightful place on the throne of England, you were as guilty of as much falsehood and guile as when drawing up those false charges regarding the Queen and her alleged lovers.'

'Have a care, boy,' Cromwell growled. 'I have a knife in my hand, remember.'

'Then plunge it into my heart, just as readily as you have used me to gain revenge for the Cardinal. It was my work that led to your knowing where to strike, and with what. Even my few moments of pleasure with Lady Rochford were allowed me solely in order that you might further your schemes to bring down half the nobility of England. Have you done yet?'

'Such ingratitude does you no credit,' Cromwell muttered as he excised a slice from the pork. 'When we first met, you were the resident failure of an impoverished estate whose only friend was a dying grandmother. Through me you have enjoyed the life of well-fed Courtier, surrounded by high-born ladies who lusted after your loins, one of whom has sampled them. You have also learned a few invaluable lessons in Statecraft.'

'What I have learned,' Richard replied in mounting anger, 'is that to perform any act that displeases the Tudor usurper of a throne that will never be mine is to sign one's own death warrant. You filled me with hopes and aspirations that can never be fulfilled, and now that you have fully drained me of such value as I represented towards the achievement of your venomous ambitions, you will no doubt show me the door, leaving me much worse off than I began. At least before I met you I had no awareness of how fully Fate has shat on me.'

'Self-pity doesn't become you,' Cromwell replied quietly, 'but did you really believe that I would abandon you now? You are welcome to remain as my Senior Clerk for as long as it suits you — and never lose sight of the fact that for all I may have used you, you never foreswore to take all the advantages I placed at your disposal. I might equally argue that you saw your main chance with me, and exploited my good nature.'

'The good nature that has led three nobles of the realm, a talented young musician and a Queen of England to the scaffold! Who's next? No, let me hazard a guess: Norfolk.'

'Norfolk swims too deeply for the line that I threw out to catch the Boleyn whore. I doubt that her father will remain Lord Privy Seal for much longer, but Norfolk will no doubt retain his titles as a reward for ridding Henry of the niece he threw at him in the first place. If I am to be revenged on Norfolk, I have much work yet to do.'

'Which is no doubt why you seek to retain my services?' Richard asked, still angry but slightly mollified. 'Forget such an idea — my conscience has suffered enough already.'

'But you will remain in my service? I must own that your hand is neater than most of my clerks.'

'If I do, to what may I look forward?'

'Who knows? You seem to enjoy a natural friendship with our next Queen, not to mention her younger sister, by all accounts, and then there is still Lady Rochford.'

'What will happen to her?'

'Who is to know, at this stage? She will of course be seeking a new husband, and her father Lord Morley still has the wealth to acquire her another one. If she is allowed by what remains of the Boleyns to retain her title, she will be a reasonable prospect until her looks fade. In the meantime, you may no doubt continue to take your pleasures there. You might even persuade her into marriage.'

'I have no remaining interest in her,' Richard asserted with more volume than conviction.

'She has a cunny, and she is eager,' Cromwell observed unfeelingly. 'Should you continue to have to do with her, you will have no need to engage whores — at least, not common ones — and there will be no risk of disease.'

'You disgust me!' Richard spat as he rose from the table. 'Even women exist in your rancid mind simply in order to be of service in your perception of life. There is one I would know better, and it is not Jane Rochford. But I will not name her, since your response to that disclosure might be such that I would be obliged to strike you at your own table!'

'Assuming that you can do so before I slit your throat, or ram this knife into your unarmoured gut? I fought in France and Italy, remember.'

'Did you stab your foes in the back?' Richard demanded, before storming off to his chamber.

Cromwell followed his retreating figure with his eyes, and shook his head. 'He has much yet to learn,' he muttered to himself. 'Still, he has a worthy tutor.'

XIV

'I would really rather be somewhere else,' Cromwell told William Kingston as he sat sharing an excellent Burgundy in the main hall of Kingston's grace and favour residence at the Tower. In the corner sat Kingston's wife with her needlework, while from the room beyond could be heard the occasional shriek among the loudly intoned prayers.

'I would not have called upon you otherwise,' Kingston replied, 'but I need to know what are the King's intentions towards our very special prisoner next door. Do I prepare the usual scaffold, and if so is it to be on the Green out there, or on Tower Hill? Or, God forbid, does he intend to have her dragged to Smithfield for the pyre to be lit under her? The local populace complain of the smell every time we do a burning.'

'Rest easy, Master Constable,' Cromwell assured him. 'It will be here on the Green, but you will need no block.'

'She is to be hanged like a common criminal?'

'No, beheaded. But with a sword, not the axe. That was the King's instruction to me but an hour ago.'

'Have we such a swordsman, and how is it done?'

'Henry has sent to Calais for a specialist in such matters. The lady will kneel upright, and he will take her head with one swift sweep of the blade — it is to be hoped.'

'And the others — they are not to be quartered?"

'No, since they were all in the royal service at the time that they serviced the Queen.'

'Your black humour will be your downfall one day, Master Cromwell. So, the axe?'

'Yes, but on the Hill, not the Green. The public must have their entertainment.'

'Will you speak with the prisoner next door?'

'If I must. But leave the door open. I do not wish to be added to the list of those who are accused of having seen what Henry no longer desires.'

'Will Henry be merciful?' Anne asked pleadingly before Cromwell was barely through the door to the chamber that served as both her living quarters and her chapel.

'You have not been informed?'

'Of what?'

'It will take place outside on the Green, and Henry has sent for a swordsman from France specially skilled in such matters. There will be no axe, no block, and very few in attendance.'

Anne placed her hands around her own throat. 'I should supply him with little difficulty, since I have such a small neck. Will you be there?'

'The King commands it, madam.'

With terrifying suddenness, Anne's mood changed as her black eyes flashed. 'This is all about that wretched Cardinal, isn't it?'

'Madam?'

'Wolsey, that fat, self-satisfied friend of Katherine's who would not let Henry marry me.'

'There was rather more to it than that, madam,' Cromwell bristled. 'For one thing, it was the Pope who stood out against the annulment of the Kings' marriage to Queen Katherine that stood in the way of your ambition.'

'I had no ambition but my love for Henry, but Wolsey was the Pope's man, and hoped, by ingratiating himself with

Katherine's nephew Charles of Spain, to become Pope himself.'

'You believe that it was within my master's power to move the Pope? He did all within his power to fulfil Henry's wishes. As for the lie that he was in league with Emperor Charles, you can thank your uncle Norfolk for that; I found the forged papers, but it was too late for the Cardinal, whose heart was broken.'

'Is Uncle Norfolk on your list as well?'

'What list, madam?'

'Spare me the shit, Master Cromwell. You and I both know that I am to die because you blame me for the Cardinal's disgrace and death, when in truth he brought about his own downfall. It is only to be regretted that others will also die as the result of the tissue of lies that you wove concerning my alleged adulteries with men who I would not tolerate to even touch me, let alone paw my body. But from what you say, you hold Uncle Norfolk equally to blame for the Cardinal's downfall, and you are probably correct. The two of them were enemies from childhood, whereas I came only recently from my existence in France. Would that I had never left, but as for my uncle, he is too powerful even for your lies to bring down.'

'I know not to what you allude, madam, but it would be my best wager that he will bring himself down by his own arrogance. He believes himself to be beyond any possible disfavour of Henry's, as you once did, but he will learn in the fullness of time that there are some actions that cannot withstand a king's ire.'

'You are wrong on both counts, Master Cromwell. Henry will quickly realise that despite what I am alleged to have done, he still loves me. Then I will be freed from here, and God help you when I take *my* revenge! Now leave me!'

'Madam,' Cromwell muttered as he gave a barely perceptible bow in Anne's direction and moved towards the door.

'*Your Majesty!*' she screamed after him. 'When I am freed from here I will force you to crawl naked across the floor of my Presence Chamber, in front of the entire Court, and lick my feet! Liar! Perjurer! Spawn of Satan! When next we meet it shall be *your* head that is in peril!'

She was still screaming at the top of her lungs as Cromwell closed the door to her incarceration chamber and looked across at Lady Kingston, who had put down her needlepoint in anticipation.

'See to your prisoner,' he instructed her as he nodded his farewell to Sir William and hurried outside, slightly paler in the face than when he had arrived.

XV

Cromwell deemed it unsafe to attend the executions of the lesser nobles accused of adultery with Anne when they were dispatched by the axeman — with varying degrees of competence — on Tower Hill on the morning of 17 May 1536. It was unsafe, not because of the risk that the intrigue in which he had engaged would somehow come unravelled, but because the mob that always gathered to scream their appreciation of such entertainment had a tendency to get out of hand and seek further bloodshed.

There would be no-one more appropriate to pick on than the King's most senior officer, and the person blamed for bringing God's wrath down on the nation in the form of successive poor harvests, occasional outbreaks of the Plague, and worsening trading terms with the Low Countries. It was either Cromwell or the Boleyn witch, or possibly both, and since the former Queen was already marked for death in two days' time — in comparative privacy on Tower Green — Cromwell would have to do instead. But they were denied this pleasure when the man himself made an excuse of religious ordinances over which he was labouring with Archbishop Cranmer and stayed closely confined in Chancery until it was all over bar the removal of the remains to within the Tower precincts.

But Cromwell was ordered by Henry to attend two days later when it was the turn of Anne to meet her end on Tower Green.

Cromwell returned from the event whistling softly to himself, to be met by the disapproving face of Richard Ashton as he breezed into the Great Hall of Austin Friars and ordered that wine be brought in.

'You found the morning's entertainment to your liking?' Richard sneered. 'Did she plead for mercy, call down a blessing on Henry's head, or curse you to your grave?'

'The Bible says "Judge not, less ye be judged", and I was simply obeying a royal command to attend, in order to see the sentence carried out as the final act in a process that I had co-ordinated.'

'A process that you invented!' Richard reminded him in a voice rising in anger. 'An innocent woman went to her death in order that you might avenge another death that you allege was also unjust. Is this what our nation has become? A land in which big dogs eat little dogs?'

'It was never any different,' Cromwell argued, 'and have a care how you employ your tongue, young man. I am not in the mood for a moral lecture from someone who fornicates with the wife of a man who fucked his own sister, contrary to God's law.'

'And how dare you cite religion at me?' Richard continued, uncaring of what might follow. 'You are a heretic!'

'Enough, if you are to avoid being run through where you sit in the shit of your pious hypocrisy! You believe that by mumbling a few "Hail Marys" and donating money to be passed on by your confessor to his next whore, you will somehow be afforded a seat in Heaven? If you had followed me around some of the so-called "holy houses", and learned of the wickedness that they practised in there, you would have no lingering faith in the grace allegedly granted to those ordained to intercede between you and God. How can the sin of, say, pride, be expiated through the agency of a man who fucks his fellow man up the arse in the dormitory, drinks until he pukes, eats until his stomach is like to explode in gluttony, and sells pieces of wood from the local forest as relics of the Cross on which Christ died?'

'All creatures of God have their weaknesses, it is true,' Richard conceded, 'but that is merely to demonstrate how we are less perfect than God. Those whom God has ordained to intercede on our behalf when we seek forgiveness for our sins are, thanks to you and your conspirators, being cast out into the hedgerows and moorlands simply in order that King Henry may add another wing to this palace or that.'

'If I were to report those words,' Cromwell replied, 'I would soon be in need of a new Senior Clerk. Even Anne believed that the time had come to listen to the condemnation of preachers such as Luther, regarding the cesspit into which the Christian faith has fallen thanks to the influence of Rome. We seek to hear the word of God more directly, and what is more, in English, and not that hocus pocus mumbo jumbo they call Latin. There was no great demand for the Latin and Greek where I grew up in Putney — would you therefore argue that we were less deserving of God's grace?'

'I know not how matters lie in Putney,' Richard acknowledged, 'but it is said that you learned your Statecraft in Italy, where even an invitation to dinner may conceal the risk of death by poison. But tell me, how went the death of your queenly victim?'

'Middling well,' Cromwell replied. 'She made no great speech that could be heard, due to the clamour of the small crowd, the incessant wind blowing across Tower Green, and the fear in her tiny voice. The swordsman earned his fee without any botch, and Sir William suffered a moment of discomfort when he realised that he had not ordered a coffin. But an arrow casket proved a suitable alternative, and she lies now in the

117

chapel of St Peter ad Vincula, inside the Tower keep. England shall shortly have a new Queen, and tomorrow we are invited to the betrothal of Henry to Jane Seymour in her quarters at Greenwich.'

'We?'

'Well, me anyway. But "the Queen that soon will be" asked that you be invited along also, since for some reason or other she seems to regard you as a friend.'

'I talked to her when others would not, that is all,' Richard explained. 'On those afternoons when I attended upon the Queen whom you executed but a few hours since.'

'Will you come with me?'

'Who else will be attending?'

'Her brother and sister, obviously. Edward because they are his apartments also, and Bess because she is breaking her journey back north to Yorkshire, and will probably delay here until the wedding, which will be by the end of this month, as I calculate. Henry is eager to test his new seed bed.'

'If Bess will be there, then I shall attend.'

'You have taken quite a shine to her, have you not? But she is perhaps somewhat above your station in life, remember, should you be entertaining thoughts of marriage to her.'

'I merely, at this stage, admire her natural beauty, and would get to know her better,' Richard explained, 'but since we live in an age in which the son of an Ipswich butcher can become Chancellor of England, while a blacksmith and publican's son from Putney can rise to become Master of the Rolls, there may yet be hope for me. And do not forget that, as you yourself advised me, I am the rightful King of England.'

Cromwell burst out laughing. 'Shall I so advise Henry, or shall I leave that task to you while he is in such a mood for removing the heads of traitors?

'I was referring to my lineage, rather than my immediate prospects,' Richard explained angrily. 'And most days I wish you had left me alone in my ignorance.'

'We have recently had a similar conversation,' Cromwell reminded him, 'and I demonstrated to you how much you had gained from being in my service. Tomorrow you will have that further demonstrated when you attend upon Henry of England, whose arse is so firmly on the throne you covet that not even one of his jousting horses could remove him.'

'I may not always choose to remain in your service,' Richard warned him, to which Cromwell smiled in reply.

'The outside door lies but a few paces behind you, and you are not my prisoner. In the meantime, should you wish to earn your supper, Your Pretended Majesty will find papers on my study table that require to be copied.'

'It will not always be this way,' Richard threatened him as he walked towards the stairs in the corner.

XVI

'Why are there no guards on the door?' Cromwell asked Edward Seymour, the next morning, as they stood together with Edward's wife in the largest room of the Seymour quarters at Greenwich, awaiting Henry's arrival.

Edward smiled and nodded to a door cut into the wall adjacent to the fireplace.

'Henry comes to us through a private passage that leads from his Withdrawing Chamber. It is said that he has used it many times in the past.'

'I do not doubt it,' Cromwell smirked, 'in which case this room must have witnessed many a liaison.'

'Undoubtedly, but do not make reference to that, if you value your head. Even poor innocent Jane believes that it was constructed simply for her benefit. See how she blooms these days, even though she is currently engaged with your lackey.'

He nodded towards a group in the corner, consisting of Richard and the two Seymour sisters. Richard was making a considerable effort to engage Jane in conversation, while covertly admiring, at close quarters, the flawless simple beauty of her younger sister Bess, and hoping that she was interested in what he had to say.

'The Lady Mary has recently been sent to reside with her sister the Princess Elizabeth at Hatfield Palace,' Richard told them in the hope of conveying the impression to Bess that he was privy to great State secrets.

'It is so sad that Mary was declared a bastard and rejected by her father,' Jane chimed in. 'It must be a heartbreak for her —

I know how I would feel if my own father did that to me. I hope to prevail upon Henry to reconcile with her.'

'Have a care, madam,' Richard warned her. 'Henry does not like to be told what to do, as the death of Queen Anne demonstrated to the entire world. Rather move sideways to the point, and let the King believe that whatever you seek was his idea in the first place.'

'I did not realise that you had become the King's confidante,' Bess said sarcastically. 'I thought that dangerous task was allocated to your master.'

'Indeed,' Richard corrected himself, 'and it is from him that I learn of these matters.'

'Do you wish some day to be the master of your *own* destiny?' Bess asked, just as the door to the side of the fireplace opened to reveal a lone royal guard with a halberd who stood to one side as Henry bustled in, walked straight across to their group, took both of Jane's hands in his, kissed her chastely on the cheek and smiled.

'My dear, lovely Jane! Who are these good people who have kept you amused until my arrival on this happy occasion?'

Jane seemed to come alive as she replied, 'This lady is my younger sister Elizabeth, who once served as a Queen's Lady along with me. Then she married Sir Anthony Ughtred, who became Governor of Jersey. She is now a widow, and will shortly give birth to her second child in somewhat straightened circumstances on her modest estate in Yorkshire.'

'Would you wish her to be appointed as one of your Ladies upon your coronation?' Henry asked with a generous smile. 'You only have to ask, and it shall be done.'

'Perhaps later, once she has been delivered of her new child, and it is of an age to be left behind,' Jane suggested, then turned to Richard. 'This gentleman is Richard Ashton, Senior

Clerk to Master Secretary Cromwell. He was one of the few who showed me any kindness when I attended upon the late Queen; while she regarded me with contempt, and rarely spoke a civil word to me, Master Ashton was most attentive. Were it not for his good offices, I might have fled from the Court long ere I did, and then our love might perhaps not have blossomed as it did in more recent times. In some ways I feel that I have more to thank him for than most, excepting Your Majesty, of course.'

'That courtesy shall be well rewarded upon our marriage,' Henry told Jane with a smile towards Richard, who bowed his head in grateful acknowledgment. Then Henry raised his voice to be heard throughout the chamber. 'Come, friends, and let us about this most happy of ceremonies. Thomas, you shall be witness.'

Five minutes later Jane and Henry had become officially betrothed, and Richard reflected gloomily on the fluctuating winds of fortune in the court of Henry of England. The previous day had seen the execution of she whom Henry had, if anything, sought in marriage with far greater enthusiasm than this somewhat plain lady from a fading Wiltshire estate.

Anne had been beautiful in her day, the product of an upbringing in the household of a royal ambassador at the Court of France, but her remains now lay, with their head severed and tucked between her feet, in a converted arrow casket in a chapel in the Tower. It certainly did not pay dividends to betray the King of England, or even to lay oneself open to the accusation of having done so. It was to be hoped that this naive daughter of minor gentry would have better fortune.

The wedding took place ten days later, in the Queen's Chamber in Whitehall Palace, the service conducted by the Bishop of Winchester, Stephen Gardiner. Gardiner was definitely of the new school of English clergymen, whose academic grasp of matters ecclesiastical, and their ability to argue any point of holy scripture in a manner acceptable to Henry, rather than any inherent holiness, had brought them considerable preference. Gardiner had been Secretary to Cardinal Wolsey until his former master had found him too pedantic and boring by comparison with the darker and more charismatic Cromwell, and both men had hated the very ground that the other walked upon ever since.

Cromwell would have much preferred the ceremony to be conducted by Thomas Cranmer, Archbishop of Canterbury, whose clerical leanings were closer to those of the Protestant faith that was prevalent all over mainland Europe, and which Cromwell himself inclined towards. But it was, after all, merely one ceremony, and Cromwell clenched his teeth, smiled, and awaited the rewards that could be expected as one consequence of the generosity of which Henry was capable when he got what he wanted.

It came as no surprise when, shortly after the new marriage, Thomas Cromwell became Lord Privy Seal when the title was ripped away from Thomas Boleyn, Anne's father; Cromwell was happy to resign, in the same process, from his duties as Master of the Rolls, which had actually required him to engage in some work. A week after that he was elevated to the rank of Baron of England; he could not title himself 'of Putney' with a straight face when he remembered the squalid alleyways in which he had lurked, lurched, fornicated, fought, defecated and vomited in his wild youth, but 'Baron Cromwell of Wimbledon' seemed to have the right ring to it.

The Seymours themselves were far from overlooked, and Henry gave Jane over a hundred manors as a wedding present, one of which she hoped to be allowed to pass to Richard when, following her overtures during the actual honeymoon period, Henry instructed Cromwell to draw up the necessary papers.

By the middle of July of that year, Richard had become Sir Richard Ashton. This was nothing compared with the elevated fortunes of Jane's brother Edward, who became Viscount Beauchamp less than week after the marriage, and Earl of Hertford in October of that same year. At this stage, however, his younger brother Thomas received no such rewards, and experienced the first pang of jealousy against his older brother that was to dominate the rest of their lives together.

The wedding ceremony was followed by a magnificent banquet, to which all the principal players were invited. After the meal, Henry and Jane sat in splendour at the high table, smiling indulgently as the dancers bobbed and swirled before them. There were many French *courantes*, a slower dance in which the partners spent more time in actual physical contact at the arm and the waist, partly in diplomatic deference to Henry himself, whose mobility on the dance floor was restricted by his old jousting injury, and partly because it was the most popular with male courtiers seeking to interest a lady in an assignation once the music had ceased for the night.

Richard had been flattered by Bess's request that he accompany her onto the dance floor as often as he felt both able and inspired, since she was apprehensive of being either bruised or sexually mishandled by older courtiers with more enthusiasm than skill. He had not missed a single opportunity, and had spent a happy couple of hours almost overpowered by her rich, heady perfume, and the closeness of her full breasts as they pulled together for a swirling turn.

Their conversation had become less formal, and more personal, as the dancing wore on, and there came a point at which they agreed that they each preferred to spend the remainder of the festivities dancing together, to the exception of any other partner. After a while, it was Bess who steered the topic towards family matters.

'Jane tells me that you are now knighted.'

'That's so. You are now dancing with *Sir* Richard Ashton.'

'I danced for some years with another "Sir", although he had neither your youth nor your vigour.'

'He had enough to father two children though, did he not?' Richard replied. 'You were referring to your late husband?'

'I was indeed. Will you consider marriage yourself, now that you are knighted?'

'I have a certain lady in mind to whom I would wish to make my suit, certainly, but although I have the knighthood, I have no land to go with it, and my current duties are such that they do not generate much beyond my living-in keep.'

'If you love the lady enough, then you should not let anything on this earth prevent you from making your fortune by some means or other, then claiming her as yours.'

'You make it sound easy, but I have neither skill nor training for commerce, I know not how to wield a sword in battle, and I have no experience in diplomacy. What must I do — take to the life of a footpad?'

Bess laughed and kissed him gently on the cheek. 'Yet you will find a way, I feel sure. A handsome body like yours should not be allowed to go to waste.'

'Even were I to find the way to my fortune, how do I know that the lady who occupies my every waking thought would accept my suit?'

'That depends upon the lady, and how attractive she finds you, as well as your fortune.'

'Surely it is the fortune alone that attracts women to men in these times?' Richard argued cynically.

'Do you think so? I do not. Once the clothes are cast off in the bed chamber, any woman with capable eyesight looks for a firm muscular frame like yours, and a face as handsome.'

'So if, for the sake of example only,' Richard ventured, 'the object of my hopes were yourself, and I had a fortune, you would not reject my suit?'

Bess looked round quickly, then kissed Richard warmly on the mouth. 'Let us abandon the pretence. Come to me with your fortune and I will gladly accept your suit. But do not delay too long — having been exposed at an early age to the pleasures that await a man and a woman under the sheets, I am burning to re-engage in them.'

PART II

XVII

In July 1536 Cromwell had received yet another royal office, that of 'Vice-Regent in Spirituals', which made him second below Henry in the administration of the English Church. Given that Cromwell had never been ordained, this was the loudest message yet to the old order that religion in England was in the hands of the far from holy; even the old office of Archbishop of Canterbury no longer carried with it a direct line to Rome, and when Archbishop Cranmer began his series of collaborative meetings with Thomas Cromwell designed to flesh out the new order of religious observance that became known as 'The Ten Articles', he did so as an equal whose former high office as 'primus inter pares' of the Roman Catholic Church in England carried no additional weight.

The Holy Scriptures themselves, as the word of God, were to be given preference over any prelate's interpretation of them, while iconic images were not to be worshipped in themselves, and masses were not to be sung for the blessing of souls. When they were published and distributed in August, Cromwell had taken the opportunity to add the requirement for an English Bible to be made available in every parish church, and for some this was the final straw.

A rebellion began in Lincolnshire, when a local mob registered their protest at the planned stripping of its cathedral of all its icons and other items of wealth by surrounding the building and sealing its doors, bringing out the Great Cross that was its pride and joy, and gathering under it, defying anyone sent by Cromwell to loot so much as an altar candle holder. The local gentry had been obliged to pretend to join in the protest, on fear of death if they did not, but had ultimately convinced the rebels that a petition to the King would achieve their desired objective.

It did not, but a fervent Catholic of the old school, a lawyer called Robert Aske, had persuaded thousands of his fellow countrymen to rise up in opposition to recent unwanted changes to both law and religious practice. It was to be doubted whether the perceived grievances that were put into the mouths of farm labourers, stonemasons, brewers, blacksmiths and tilers were really their own, rather than that of their rural and urban overlords, but the final set of demands that the rebels listed as their price for handing back the towns of York and Pontefract that they had seized were very indicative of the recent upheavals in the way that life had been lived for centuries.

First and foremost, they wanted the Church in England to be returned to the ultimate control of Rome, with the Pope re-established over Henry as the apex of English Catholicism. Along with that came a call for the suppression of all heresies, and most notably those of Luther and Tyndale. Next, a reversal of the monastic policy, and the reinstatement of all monks and other holy men in their original houses. As if they had not already sufficiently affronted Henry, they also called for the re-legitimation of the Lady Mary, and for 'condign punishment' to be visited upon Thomas Cromwell as 'a subverter of the good laws of the realm' and a 'maintainer and inventor of heretics.'

Cromwell believed that the grievances listed by the rebels might well have been authored by Norfolk himself, and he suspected that his old enemy would be somewhat lacking in enthusiasm for bringing the rebels to heel. Then word came back south that the original rebel force had been joined by not only the Archbishop of York, but also Lord Thomas Darcy, who had handed Pontefract Castle over to Aske and his army when he should have been defending it for the King.

Cromwell saw his chance when word also came that Norfolk, instead of instigating the predictable orgy of slaughter, hanging rebels in rows from castle walls and putting their leaders to the sword, was negotiating with them for a peaceful resolution. One of their demands, apart from a general pardon for all their actions thus far, was that Henry journey north and hear their grievances in person in a special Council session to be held at Doncaster, and Cromwell seized upon this during his next audience with the King.

'I cannot believe that my lord of Norfolk would so belittle your authority that he could not only presume to offer a pardon in your name, not only even *consider* to dictate to you how you should act in the matter of your own daughter, but — and this grieves me most of all, Sire — command your presence in the north of the nation of which you are both the anointed sovereign by the hand of God, and the undisputed head of the Church that these presumptuous peasants are seeking to hand back to the anti-Christ in Rome.'

Henry smiled. 'I am warmed by your loyalty and concern for my royal dignity, Thomas, but I fear that you expect too much of Norfolk, whose forces are considerably outnumbered.'

'If Norfolk is no longer able to defend Your Majesty by force of arms, which in my lengthy experience has been all that he was ever fit for, then perhaps others should be sent north in his stead.'

'We have neither the men nor the finances, Thomas, as you yourself must surely be aware.'

'Then perhaps a more subtle approach, Sire?'

'What have you in mind?'

'That we pretend to negotiate, until we have their leaders in our grasp, then we deal with them as the traitors that they truly are. Once the head is cut from the beast, the arms and legs will follow as a natural course.'

'Would that not constitute low treachery?'

'One might say, instead, "inspired Statecraft", Sire. But should you shrink from such a course, lest it diminish your honour as King, let me do it for you, in my own name. I am already regarded as the blackest devil by those who seek to challenge your authority, and would lose little by simply playing the role that popular prejudice has ascribed to me.'

'What do we tell Norfolk?'

'Simply to agree that you will summon a Parliament in York, if the rebels will agree to disband. Then I will send separately to their leader, Aske, inviting him to London to meet with you privately and discuss those matters that are causing so much grievance. Once the rebels have disbanded, you order Norfolk to lay waste the countryside, hang such of the rebels as he can locate, and secure the royal strongholds. Then Aske can be tried for treason and executed — either down here, or in York.'

'You would incur that ignominy on my behalf?' Henry asked nervously. 'I cannot afford for my people to regard me as being so black-hearted.'

'Willingly, Sire, since you have done so much for me. Will you so instruct Norfolk?'

'I shall do so today, while you attend to your darker half of this stratagem.'

Cromwell was still chuckling as he re-entered his offices, explained the plan to Richard, and instructed him to send the invitation to Robert Aske.

Richard looked puzzled. 'Do you not fear that your name will become even blacker in the public estimation than it is at present?'

'Why should I?' Cromwell replied. 'Who is the person who offers peace terms to the sweaty mob up north? Who will be seen to be the one who restored the King's uneasy peace in Yorkshire? Robert Aske will know the truth of it, but Norfolk's is the name that will be remembered.'

Richard looked hard at Cromwell. 'There really is no end to your treachery, is there?'

'"Statecraft", Richard. As I explained to Henry, let us call it "Statecraft". Talking of which, it would seem that Lady Rochford is back in favour. At least, she is back at Court, and calling herself Viscountess Rochford. I am advised that her former father-in-law Wiltshire, who is now back to being merely Sir Thomas Boleyn, has allowed her one hundred pounds a year, and she has hopes of becoming a Lady to our new Queen. I promised to speak for her in Jane Seymour's ear, when it is free from Henry's mouth, and the Viscountess asked to be remembered fondly to you.'

'I have fond memories of her also,' Richard replied, 'but now my heart is committed elsewhere.'

'I rather imagine that Jane Rochford is more interested in where your cock will be committed,' Cromwell smirked, 'but if you are alluding to Bess Seymour, keep well in mind that she is now a royal sister. Others in her position in the past have been known to be traded off to foreign princes; she will be regarded as a fine catch for as long as Jane is in favour.'

'Think you that she will ever cease to be?' Richard asked.

Cromwell shrugged. 'If a man buys an expensive mare that will not foal, or which whelps only puny offspring, then in my experience it is either sold off or put to death. But while Jane is

Queen, Bess will exist in her reflected glow, and given her comeliness she will not be short of suitors.'

'During the wedding feast she gave me assurance that my suit would be welcomed, were it accompanied by a good estate,' Richard said.

'And you no doubt look to me to procure you one?' Cromwell asked with a quizzical stare. 'I can put you in possession of many a fine old abbey whose rental income might feed your horse for an entire year, but any land grant of appreciable size I shall reserve for Gregory.'

'Why would you favour your idle son over your loyal Senior Clerk?' Richard replied, only part in jest.

Cromwell smiled that infuriating smile of his. 'You have clearly not heard that popular expression regarding blood being thicker than water. And Gregory is *not* idle — he manages my several properties in and around the city with considerable skill.'

'He does not, however, labour long and hard to deal with the mountains of paper that keep you in your many offices,' Richard countered, but Cromwell even had an answer for that.

'Neither do you, while we sit here discussing your improbable dream of winning the hand of Bess Seymour. See to that letter for Robert Aske.'

XVIII

Shortly after the celebration of the New Year in 1537, the various royal palaces in and around London rang with the news that Queen Jane was with child. She had never been afforded any coronation ceremony, ostensibly because of the latest outbreak in London of the Plague that was currently holding the population in the grip of terrified anticipation. It appeared to be no respecter of rank, and it struck quickly.

'Fine at breakfast, dead by supper' was a popular way of describing the devastating speed with which the sickness could carry off someone who had become infected, and once the royal physicians had confirmed that Jane was indeed with child, there could be no suggestion of exposing her to the miasma of breaths from the London crowds that would line her coronation route. However, and as compensation once she began to swell visibly with the next royal offspring, Henry had Jane publicly proclaimed Queen. She was then confined to a special suite of rooms at Hampton Court Palace, where those allowed to come and go in and out of her presence were strictly vetted.

Richard was hoping that he would not be one of those, but his worst fears were realised when he was ordered by Cromwell to resume the same daily attendance upon the Queen that had first exposed him to the wiles of Jane Rochford, which he now wanted to avoid, and which he trusted he could resist if called upon. When he tried to protest, Cromwell proved adamant.

'There are some even yet who blame me for the downfall of the night crow, but it was the information that you brought back to me that enabled me to advise Henry of the sad state into which his marriage had fallen. So, in that sense, Anne's downfall was of your making.'

'Don't drop that shit on me,' Richard protested. 'I merely brought you the bricks upon which you built your house of lies. The finest pile of stone blocks still requires a skilled stonemason to convert it into a cathedral. Without you, those bricks I brought back with me would have remained simply a pile of unused masonry. But surely you do not apprehend that our new Queen keeps a similar menagerie of aging whore-masters about her?'

'Of course not. By all accounts her new afternoon gatherings are the height of decorum, and frequently graced with Henry's presence. However, I wish you to report back to me if there is any reference to the reinstatement of the Lady Mary into Henry's plans for the future of England. He constantly complains to me that Jane is ever in his ear, seeking to persuade him to reconcile with Mary, particularly now that Elizabeth has also been bastardised.'

'Have you succeeded in persuading Jane to take Lady Rochford into her service?'

'Yes, why?'

'Because I do not wish word to get back to Bess Seymour that I am intriguing with a Queen's Lady.'

'But you are not, are you?'

'Not yet, but I worry about my ability to resist, if she seeks to draw me back into her net.'

'A man who cannot keep his cock in his hose runs many risks at Court — not the least being that of disease — but why do you still cling to the pathetic hope of securing Bess Seymour's hand?'

'It is for a reason that probably does not exist in your view of the world, since it has to do with the heart.'

'Even more treacherous than the cock, in my experience. You may find this strange to your ears, but I once loved deeply and unconditionally. A wife and two daughters.'

'Not your son?'

'A different sort of love. But pray continue to search for a good reason why you should not take the daily barge upstream to Hampton.'

'The river is full of shit.'

'Less than an hour each way with your nose pinched and your breath drawn in will make you appreciate the perfumes of the Queen's Audience Chamber when you reach it. And remember that Jane Seymour once valued your conversation.'

'That was when she had none of her own. What makes you so confident that she will unburden herself to me regarding her innermost thoughts?'

'I am not, but if she is likely to confide in anyone in this unfamiliar world that she now inhabits, it will be you. And consider it this way — she is the sister of the woman whose heart you would besiege with protestations of love, and the more you ingratiate yourself with the older girl, the greater she may plead your cause with the younger.'

'I want but a sizeable estate, and she has already indicated that she will be mine, as I told you before.'

'Again, look to the Queen. She now has estates in abundance, and if she sees that the happiness of her adored sister depends upon it, she may well prevail upon Henry to let her assign some of them to you. Or she may persuade Henry to grant you a wealthy estate in your own right.'

'So I must revert to being your eyes and ears once again?'

'I'm glad you finally accept that.'

'How do you know that I will not play you false?'

'You have seen what happens to those who do, Richard, and I think that you possess more wisdom than to take that risk. Remember the fates of Norris, Weston and Brereton.'

'I do, almost daily. But you left out Mark Smeaton, who you betrayed most of all.'

'He was a youth of no account, seeking crumbs from the tables of the rich. A bit like yourself. Now go, if you are to catch the barge.'

Cromwell's scheming against Robert Aske came to fruition in March, when the undisputed leader of the northern rebels journeyed to London, and was received with politeness by Henry, who pretended to give weighty consideration to the list of grievances. Aske was then seized overnight at his temporary lodgings by men instructed by Cromwell and conveyed to the Tower on a charge of treason. By May he was facing trial by a Commission hand-picked by 'The Vice-Regent in Spirituals' and following his conviction he was sentenced to death.

A stately procession then wended its way north, with Aske paraded in a wagon, securely bound, for all to see. Darcy was also intercepted by Norfolk, acting on direct orders from Henry that had been drafted by Cromwell, and both men were hanged, drawn and quartered as traitors in full public view at York, on whose walls their heads were spiked.

Norfolk was then ordered to round up such of the now subdued rebels as he could find, and extract from each of them individually an oath of allegiance to King Henry, with sudden death as the alternative. Seventy-four executions later there was no more resistance, and although the less perceptive of those who had been thus suppressed could see only the hand of Norfolk in their downfall, Aske had left no-one in any doubt, in his execution speech, that the real villain behind the scenes had been Thomas Cromwell.

Bess Seymour, a widow left with two infant children, had been struggling for some time to manage the modest estate left by her late husband on the outskirts of York. After the disruption caused by The Pilgrimage of Grace, the task had become almost insurmountable, and she was in a perilous position financially.

She wrote to Cromwell seeking his support 'in whatever manner your Lordship shall see fit to grant me.' It seemed never to have occurred to her that, as a royal sister, she was a valuable asset in the marriage game, but the point was not lost on Cromwell. He wrote back with a proposition that she gratefully accepted.

XIX

With considerable reluctance and foreboding, Richard obeyed Cromwell's instruction and presented himself almost daily at Hampton Court, where Queen Jane held court with a small group of courtiers following her midday meal with Henry. But her group of friends was in marked contrast to the one that the former Queen Anne had assembled in order to pay homage to her beauty and status. This new inner circle owed much to Jane's serious attention to being a royal lady of learning and culture, and the topics of conversation rarely travelled beyond religious practice, the reformation of the Church, and the ongoing sensitive relations with France, Spain and Germany.

In regular attendance was Jane's brother Edward, now Viscount Beauchamp and a Gentleman of the King's Chamber. He was clearly high in the King's favour, and as if in recognition of the sister to whom he owed his preferment he was ever solicitous of Jane's health, and full of advice as to what she should eat, what exercise she should take, and what perils to avoid. Occasionally he was joined by his younger brother Thomas, who clearly regarded himself as something of a dandy and a gallant, seeking to impress those of the Queen's Ladies who were in attendance.

There was much competition to be a Lady-in-Waiting to the Queen, because of the opportunities that it brought to catch the eye of one of the King's Gentlemen of the Chamber. As a result, they tended to be hand-picked, and after her confronting experiences in the former Court of Queen Anne, Jane was determined that her Ladies should display far more modesty and grace, and engage in far less ribaldry. Lady

Rutland, Jane's Senior Lady, presided over younger, and less experienced, ladies such as Anne Basset and Mary Zouche, ensuring that their dress was appropriate and their behaviour the last word in decorum. The French fashions so favoured by Anne were now replaced by the older style gable hoods that had been introduced to the English Court by Katherine of Aragon, and woe betide any Lady who wore less than the prescribed number of pearls on her gown.

And then there was Jane Rochford, looking as if butter wouldn't melt in her mouth. The first time that Richard was announced into the presence by the usher, he was distracted by Queen Jane's delighted cry of welcome as she beckoned him over to a seat close to her.

'This is my true friend Sir Richard Ashton,' she announced to the assembled company, 'who was so solicitous for my happiness in those dark days when I was otherwise friendless in the afternoon audiences of the former Queen. Richard, who do you know here? My brother Edward, obviously, and perhaps you remember Viscountess Rochford from those days?'

'Indeed, we have met,' Richard conceded as he forced himself to gaze into the lustful eyes of the lady in question.

She nodded formally to him, and assured him, 'Your return to Court is most welcome, Sir Richard.'

The introductions complete, Jane confirmed, in response to Richard's polite enquiry, that she was as well as her condition allowed, but that she found the endless proddings and questioning of her physicians tedious in the extreme, and her confinement inside her own lodgings at Hampton 'most restrictive of my natural humour for the open countryside'. Then the conversation became more general, and Richard did his best to make polite contributions to it when appropriate, all the while attempting to avoid contact with Jane Rochford's burning looks in his direction as she undressed him with her eyes.

Then came an afternoon of events that Richard was obliged to report back to Cromwell in minute detail. Jane had indicated excitedly, as soon as the regular company had assembled, that she had been overcome with joy to be invited to dine, not just with Henry, but with 'the lovely Lady Mary, who he was most moved to be reunited with. It was such to make one's eyes flood with tears to see the love between the two of them, and it has quite made my day.' An hour later the chamber doors opened, and the usher announced the entry of 'His Majesty King Henry and the Lady Mary', and the entire company rose swiftly and bowed the knee.

It was Richard's first sight of the former royal princess, who was now officially a bastard and no longer heir to Henry's throne, any more than her half-sister Elizabeth. He was struck by Mary's general likeness to Henry, with dark red hair, a broad face and a stature tending towards the bulky. However, she had retained her late mother's lack of height and heaviness of facial features, coupled with a palely glowing complexion that most of the women at Court would have traded a ransom for. He watched, fascinated, as the royal daughter now in the fullness of womanhood all but raced across the chamber and grabbed the hand of Queen Jane.

'Dearest Mother,' she enthused, with what sounded like genuine affection, 'I must pay all honour to you for your tireless efforts in bringing about the joyful reunion between father and daughter. England is a much better place for having on its throne, alongside my honoured father, a lady of such grace and spirituality.'

In the somewhat embarrassed silence that followed, Henry cleared his throat and announced gruffly, 'The Lady Mary has been afforded accommodation here at Hampton, and she has graciously agreed to remain as a fitting companion to my dear wife as she approaches the time of her lying in.'

There were expressions of satisfaction and welcome all round, and as soon as he decently could Richard slipped away and took the barge back downstream on a rapidly ebbing tide, and broke the news to Cromwell when he found him in his study at Austin Friars.

'That should smooth matters a little with Spain,' Cromwell muttered with a smile. 'At least Ambassador Chapuys will now be obliged to find some other topic with which to make my ear ache. I can now also expect the French Ambassador to increase the size of his offered bribes. But I doubt that Henry will acknowledge Mary's title to the throne yet, if ever. At the very least he must wait to see if Jane gives him a son.'

'Can a queen be allowed to rule England?' Richard enquired.

'She can if the King decrees it so. He and I have lately been considering a new statute that will allow him to list the order of succession on his death, although that also must await the outcome from between Jane's legs. But the way it is currently drafted, Henry could lawfully declare one of his many dogs to be his successor.'

Richard grimaced. 'I pity you, and others like you, who are obliged to consider all such matters from the perspective of what they mean to the nation. What I witnessed this afternoon was a tear-wrenching reunion between a proud father and a doting daughter, brought about by a kindly and caring stepmother, and yet the way you describe its significance, it might just as well have been the trading of a mare at market.'

Cromwell looked up from his papers and studied Richard's face. 'You are learning, boy. But you have one more hard lesson to absorb before you fully appreciate how these things work. One more confirmation that in this world we inhabit there is no place for the weakness brought about by sentiment.'

'That I will *never* believe,' Richard insisted, and Cromwell's face set in a mask of determination.

'You will by the end of this week — no later.'

It was in fact only two days later when Richard's world fell apart, and his cobweb of vaguely formed romantic fantasies was blasted to shreds by the cold hard wind of material reality. He had barely entered the Queen's chambers for his usual afternoon of polite inconsequence when Jane beckoned him over with a worried frown, and signalled for Anne Basset to yield her seat to him as she leaned into him and kept her voice low.

'I wonder that you gave in so easily to the loss of the lady of your affections, Richard.'

'Your meaning, my Lady?'

'You entertained hopes for the hand of my sister Bess, did you not?'

'In truth I still do,' Richard confessed with a blush. 'Is there something I should know?'

Jane looked down uncomfortably at the carpet as she mumbled the awful tidings. 'She writes that she has accepted the hand of Gregory Cromwell. Did your master not tell you?'

Richard gripped the arm of his chair firmly as his vision of the Queen began to blur, and he feared that he was about to lose consciousness. He blinked, then looked blindly back at Jane in the vain hope that he had misheard, conscious of Jane Rochford's eyes burning into the back of his head.

'Did I hear you aright? She is betrothed to Gregory? But he is barely seventeen years old!'

'My sister is little older, remember,' Jane reminded him.

'How did this come about?' Richard demanded.

Jane shrugged. 'I know only what my sister writes. It seems that she is in some monetary straights, and wrote to your master seeking his assistance. It was he who put to her the suggestion that she marry his son, and failing any other alternative she accepted.'

'But she cannot love him, surely? Have they ever even met?'

'That I know not. But I know that her heart was inclined in your direction. It is to be regretted that you had no estate of your own.'

'And for that I must blame the man who has bought and sold her for his own devious purposes,' Richard replied as he tasted the angry bile rising in his throat. 'Would you excuse me from your presence?'

'Of course, and I shall advise Bess of your sorrow upon hearing the tidings.'

Four hours later, as the autumn sun sank behind the hills beyond Windsor, Richard could be seen walking morosely up and down the north bank of the Thames, tears streaming down his face and contemplating whether or not to cast himself into the oily waters upon which, even in the fading light, several turds could be seen defiantly floating. Night had fully descended before he was sufficiently calm to trust himself to limp exhaustedly through the postern gate that guarded the entrance to Austin Friars and walk back into its Great Hall, kicking the doorpost on his way in.

On the table lay a flagon of wine covered with a cloth, a goblet and a plate of bread and cold meats, presumably left out for him by the Steward. He threw himself down onto the bench at the table, uncovered the wine, drank two goblets without pausing for breath, then belched. He was staring at the candles burning on the far wall when he heard a soft voice from the dark corner of the room, from the man who had obviously been awaiting his return.

'I will not apologise for your grief, since it is of your own making, and I could hardly be expected not to give my own son such a wonderful opportunity to move so close to the throne. You will forgive me one day, if you resist the temptation to do away with yourself. And now I will withdraw, before you attempt to do away with me.'

Those in service at Austin Friars had no idea of the origin of the terrible atmosphere between 'the master' and his resident Senior Clerk, but they busied themselves with preparations for the wedding between Master Gregory and the Queen's sister, which was to take place at Mortlake, but which would be followed by a celebratory feast at Austin Friars.

Richard made a point of communicating with Cromwell by way of notes left on one of his desks, either in Whitehall Palace or in his home study. He refused to dine at the same table as either the father or the son, but would take such food as he required — which was very little — seated on a stool in the kitchen. The Cook reported to Cromwell that Master Richard was rapidly losing weight, but Cromwell's only reply was to the effect that it would do him no harm, since he had grown 'pudgy' during his time in clerical service, having rarely engaged in any physical exercise.

When not carrying out his duties for Cromwell with grim tight-lipped efficiency, Richard took to walking along the Thames west of Whitehall Palace, but deliberately avoided going so far upstream as to be able to view even the chimneys of Hampton Court that Henry had recently added to the original structure commissioned by Cardinal Wolsey. He was therefore barely aware of how Jane's pregnancy was proceeding, and such information as he had gleaned had come from conversations he overheard between junior clerks in his Whitehall office.

One morning, after completing yet another seemingly endless pile of copying for the Lord Privy Seal, who he would cheerfully have run through with a sword, if he possessed one, he was walking down a main corridor heading for the communal Buttery where minor Whitehall Palace staff would find plates of meats, bread, sometimes fish, and small beer, left out for them as their entitlement. As he passed the opening from a linen store, a hand shot out and grabbed the collar of his tunic, pulling him sideways and twisting his head until his lips were smothered by a mouth that had become a distant memory.

'Dear God, what that does to my cunny!' Jane Rochford leered at him as she released her grip. 'When can we fuck again? Name the time, and leave the place to me. In this cupboard behind me right now, if you're feeling as randy as me.'

The 'place' turned out to be Viscountess Rochford's quarters in Hampton Court, and the 'time' every night, as Richard angrily fornicated away his bitterness between thighs that never seemed to tire of him, whatever his motivation.

XX

Early in September of that year, Queen Jane withdrew to her lying-in chamber at Hampton Court, surrounded by fussing physicians and clucking midwives. Only a select handful of her Ladies were allowed access to her, and even then only after performing almost ritualistic cleansing actions designed to prevent any infection entering the chamber. Incense was burned in special holders, rifled during the emptying of the monasteries that was almost complete, pinecones were burned in fireplaces, and high-born ladies were required to rinse their hands in vinegar brought up from the Palace kitchens. All to ensure that nothing might hazard the royal birth, and hopefully the safe delivery of a son and heir to continue the Tudor dynasty.

Jane Rochford was among the select few, and she gleefully ignored the command from the King that the Queen's Ladies refrain from sexual activity, even with their husbands, in case they thereby incurred the risk of carrying infection into what had almost become a shrine to the impending birth. Night after night she and Richard went to it like parched travellers who had discovered a sweetly flowing stream, and Richard was able, by this means, to block out from his consciousness the celebrations that had attended the marriage of Gregory Cromwell to Elizabeth Seymour in August. Thereafter Bess was in attendance on her older sister Jane as a newly created Lady of the Queen's Chamber, and given that no-one other than those Ladies, and certainly not those men who had recently formed part of Jane's afternoon audiences, were allowed near the heavily pregnant Queen, Richard was spared the ordeal of seeing Bess in her new role as the wife of his master's young son.

Because of his nightly attendance on Jane Rochford, Richard was kept up to date with the details of the final days of confinement, which Cromwell demanded that he pass on to him. The two men were back to speaking to each other, but only in strained formal tones that were essential for the business that they had to conduct on behalf of Henry, and any warmth that might previously have crept into their daily discussions seemed to be lost forever. Cromwell refrained from making any reference to his son Gregory and his new bride, and Richard only grudgingly supplied a bare minimum of information from inside the birthing suite, most of it almost irrelevant to Cromwell's ambitions, such as the fact that Her Majesty had developed a craving for quail.

In the second week of September, Jane's waters broke, and she went into the first stages of labour. It was obvious from the outset that the baby was not well positioned inside her womb, and physicians came and went with remedies for lining it up with her pelvis. Some of these involved manual indignities that Jane bore with patience, but which did nothing to ease her discomfort, or provide the rest that she was destined to require as the labour went on through the second night, and into the third day.

Henry had obeyed his own stricture that no-one from the outside world be allowed inside the chamber in which Jane was sweating, screaming, cursing uncharacteristically, and yelling to her attendants to 'get on with what you are summoned to achieve,' as the Ladies took it in turn to wipe her brow and see to her more intimate needs. But the King was only down the corridor, and one floor below, and a chain of messengers had been established to pass on any information.

For most of those two days, Edward Seymour, the royal brother, closely attended Henry, and during that time he and the King grew closer as they discussed anything and everything that might take their minds off what was transpiring on the floor above. Then, at two o'clock in the morning of 12th October, Edward woke Henry where he was dozing in a chair with the joyous tidings that Jane had delivered herself of a boy.

Preparations for the christening had been well under way for some time, although they had been kept hidden from Henry, who was superstitious in such matters. Nevertheless he was delighted with what Cromwell had secretly planned in conjunction with appropriate members of the Household, and on 15th October, the three-day-old Edward was christened in the chapel at Hampton Court, in a ceremony that brought together all the Tudor offspring, with the twenty-one-year-old Mary acting as godmother, and four-year-old Elizabeth holding the 'chrisom' baptismal cloth in place while the holy water was sprinkled on Edward's head.

During the same ceremony the infant heir to the English throne was proclaimed Duke of Cornwall — the traditional title for a royal heir when born — and Earl of Chester. The closeness of other Seymours with the royal family was also acknowledged in the appointment of the royal uncle, Edward Seymour, as Earl of Hertford.

Queen Jane had not attended the christening of the child to which she had given birth. It was traditional for the royal mother to be absent on such occasions, but Jane would not have been capable, even had it been deemed appropriate. She had not risen from her bed since the birth, and although visited several times by a tearfully grateful and besotted Henry, her body appeared to have paid dearly for the delivery of the royal treasure.

The argumentative physicians who surrounded her bed ultimately agreed that she was suffering from 'child bed fever', which was their way of obscuring from general knowledge their inability to prevent infection of any afterbirth that had not been delivered along with the child.

A little over a week after the birth, Jane was dead, and the stunned Court lurched into mourning.

Henry was a pitiful sight as he sat slumped in his favourite chair, crying like a child for days at a time, dressed in funereal black and refusing to see anyone other than the menials who delivered his food and drink. Even that was frequently left unheeded as Henry sank deeper and deeper into his own misery, and the mounting conviction that God's curse had struck once again. He had defied God by bigamously marrying a whore who he had subsequently executed, and he had blasphemed against God's will when taking over his Church and removing England from the grace of Rome. Now God was repaying him by robbing him of the greatest love of his life, in exchange for grudgingly granting him the son he had so long craved. Was ever a man more cursed?

A month later, Henry made his first public appearance since Edward's birth when he forced himself, weeping openly, to attend Jane's funeral at St George's Chapel, Windsor Palace, where he let it be known that when his time came he wished to be buried alongside 'my true Jane'. The funeral procession was symbolically composed of twenty-nine people, one for each year of Jane's life, and it was headed, as chief mourner, by a genuinely grieving Lady Mary. The birth of her step-brother had finally blocked her path to the throne, but she had nothing but loving memories of the now lost step-mother who had brought her back into her father's bosom. She was seen to shed a tear in public on one of the few occasions in her life.

XXI

Jane Rochford shook Richard awake, and he screwed his eyes against the glare of the sun that streamed in through the window of the bedchamber as she pulled back the shutters.

'Wake up, lover man — we have a visitor.'

They were in their second week at Grimston Manor, on the outskirts of Lynn, in Norfolk. It was a modest estate that Henry had given to George Boleyn on his marriage to Jane Parker, as she had been in those days, and which he had either forgotten to seize back upon George's execution, or tactfully left unattainted as some sort of reward to Jane for her assistance in ridding him of her sister-in-law Anne Boleyn.

Following the funeral of Jane, the Court had been formally dismissed until resummoned, and Richard had informed Cromwell — rather than seek his permission, as protocol demanded — that he was taking a holiday. Cromwell had not demurred, principally because he was utterly weary of the long face and grim silent expressions of accusation that confronted him every time he gave instruction to the man who only remained in his service because he was reliable and, to a limited extent, talented.

'Whoever our visitor is, tell them to come back tomorrow,' Richard grumbled sleepily. 'Or, should that be too polite, tell them to go and piss in their bonnet.'

'One does not say that sort of thing to the Duke of Norfolk,' Jane grinned back at him. 'Now, get off your beautiful arse.'

'Norfolk?' Richard echoed with raised eyebrows. 'Why is *he* here?'

Jane inclined her head in a gesture of uncertainty. 'One might regard it as a family visit, I suppose, since he was uncle to my late husband. But Uncle Norfolk is not famed for his fondness for family — not since he threw his wife bodily from their house, anyway — so I suspect that he has business with you.'

'Does he know about us?'

'If he didn't before, he does now, but I hardly think he's here to give you a thrashing. Much though it pains me to say this, pull on your hose and hide that lovely cock, then go downstairs and be polite.'

Ten minutes later, Richard descended into the main hall, where Norfolk was pacing up and down impatiently, his dark ferrety face set in a mask of determination.

'About time,' he muttered. 'I set out from Norwich at daybreak, while you were presumably sleeping off your excesses of last night.'

'I assume that you are not here to chide me regarding either my drinking habits or my choice of bed partner,' Richard replied sarcastically.

Norfolk allowed himself a wry smile. 'Cromwell has taught you all he knows about politeness, clearly. How go matters between you?'

'Why should that be of any concern to you?'

'None whatsoever in the immediate future,' Norfolk replied, 'but I am advised that since he bought the Lady Elizabeth for his son, you and he have hardly been bosom companions.'

'You are well advised,' Richard replied coldly, 'but hardly worth a hard ride from Norwich to have confirmed, I would image. Since I place you in the same sack as my master, I can only assume that the purpose of this visit is one that suits a devious purpose of your own.'

The girl scuttled in with a tray of wine and wafers, followed in a more sedate fashion by Jane, who bowed formally in the direction of their guest.

'Uncle,' she murmured in acknowledgment.

Norfolk smiled. 'It is good to see that since the death of my almost totally useless nephew you do not lack for male company. Now, please leave us.'

With a puzzled expression, Jane left them alone, and Norfolk helped himself to wine, then grimaced. 'This local sheep's piss doesn't improve over the years.'

'Why did you dismiss Lady Jane?' Richard asked.

Norfolk gestured for him to take a seat as he stared unseeingly at the far wall and began to explain. 'My father and grandfather fought on the side of Richard of Gloucester against the usurper Richmond, who became Henry Tudor. That makes my family Yorkist, a fact I underlined by first marrying Anne of York, the daughter of Edward Plantagenet. She was your grandfather's sister, by my reckoning.'

Richard's mouth sagged open and he reached for the wine. 'Who told you this?'

'I was recently in the company of your great aunt, the Countess of Salisbury, Margaret Pole, who asked me to convey to you her best wishes for your future. But at present, you do not have one, do you?'

'I certainly do not, if you intend to make known to King Henry who my grandfather was,' Richard confirmed nervously. 'May I assume that the purpose of your visit is to bribe me into betraying my master?'

Norfolk smirked. 'Do not judge me by the low standards you have been taught. I am here to offer you the throne of England — if not for yourself, at least for your descendants.'

'At least now I understand why you dismissed Lady Jane from our conversation. You speak treason.'

'Fluently. But only if you believe the Tudors to be the rightful occupiers of the throne. We Howards have for generations supported in arms the true descendants of Edward III, by which I mean the House of York, of which you are the closest surviving member of true blood. The direct descendant of Richard, Duke of York, who was himself from the loins of Edward IV.'

'You are not here, I assume, to give me a history lesson? And you tell me nothing of which I was not already aware — at least Cromwell did not play me false on that score.'

Norfolk spat into the rushes before responding. 'Cromwell is typical of that tribe of low-born carrion who have fed off the rotting corpse of a family of usurpers. Before him there was Wolsey, the son of a butcher who I more than once dumped into the Ipswich mud when we were boys at school. Cromwell's father was a brewer, a publican, a blacksmith, a bully and a knave. Base-born, the lot of them, but gifted with a guile with which the Devil infected them, by which means they have blocked the fortunes of those of us who were born to rule this nation that has fallen into heresy and iniquitous practices. Babylon itself had nothing to compare with what was practised in Queen Anne's court, all because we have forsaken God as the result of Henry's desire to be rid of Katherine, that pious daughter of the true Church.'

'Hardly the way to remember your own niece,' Richard mocked him, provoking another spit aimed at the rushes.

'She was only my niece because my idiot sister married that weak, pathetic lump of goat's shit Thomas Boleyn,' he snarled. 'The only true Howards come from male loins like my own.'

'You clearly feel strongly regarding these matters,' Richard replied politely, beginning to doubt the man's mental stability, 'but apart from employing me as some sort of icon in an uprising, thereby imperilling my head when it comes to nought, how else may I assist? By betraying my master? Much though I feel he has deceived me in the matter of his son's marriage to the woman I loved, I still owe him my improved existence, since he plucked me from an uncertain future in a Wiltshire shithole, and I would be loath to repay him with treachery.'

'Your loyalty does you credit, and further underlines the purity of your Yorkist blood,' Norfolk replied, before taking another swig of wine. 'But if you have an infection of, say, an arm, as the result of a battle wound, how do you prevent that infection from spreading?'

'Clearly, you cut it off,' Richard replied with a faint grimace.

'Precisely. In just the same way, we need to cut off infectious limbs such as Cromwell and the fawning Seymours before we can remove the main canker and restore England to its former eminence, with you at its head.'

'You bring me an army?' Richard asked sarcastically.

'I bring you several armies,' Norfolk replied with a triumphant smile. 'And a royal bride, only slightly soiled by use, if at all.'

'Let's start with the armies,' Richard invited him, content to humour the man in order to bring the meeting to a close.

'There is, of course, my own,' Norfolk replied as he preened himself. 'That is to say, the army I command in the name of King Henry. But soldiers follow their immediate commanders, and for all that my loyal men care, I could be instructed by the Sultan of Turkey. They will serve any king who commands me, so long as they receive their sixpence a day, and their opportunities to loot houses and ravish women. Then there is the sizeable force that can be assembled by Geoffrey Pole, the Countess's son. He is in contact with disaffected Yorkists throughout England, and we calculate that between them they could raise another five thousand men. Finally, the Holy Roman Emperor himself, Charles of Spain.'

Richard could not restrain a sceptical guffaw. 'Our quarrel with Spain is long past! Queen Katherine has been dead for some years now, and the execution of your niece Anne was deemed to be sufficient penance, according to Ambassador Chapuys.'

'The Emperor speaks for the Pope, remember, and his Holiness would dearly wish to see England back under his wing with a devotee of the true Church at its secular head. Even Francis of France fears the Pope, despite all the support he secretly gives to heretics, and he and Charles would be delighted were the Tudor line that they so detest be cut down.'

'And the wife you promised me?' Richard prompted him.

'You have heard, of course, that Henry's bastard son Fitzroy died last year?'

'Yes, what of it?'

'He was married to my only daughter, the Lady Mary Howard. She is now the Dowager Duchess of Richmond and Somerset, and she is still a maid.'

'Yet she was married to a Tudor? How did that miracle come about?' Richard asked with a grin.

'King Henry ordered that they live apart. She is still barely eighteen, and a virgin, insofar as she assures me. She is part Howard and part Stafford, which latter bloodline gives her a further Plantagenet connection through her grandmother Katherine Woodville. She is not uncomely, and would make a perfect wife for one who might one day become King of England.'

'And what would you propose that I say to Lady Rochford?' Richard asked.

Norfolk waved his hand dismissively. 'All kings have mistresses, and do you fondly imagine that you were the Lady Jane's first roll outside the marital bed?'

'Assuming for one moment that what you propose is of interest to me,' Richard said, 'what do you require of me? I cannot imagine myself at the head of an army, I am no diplomat or statesman, and I have no money to fund an uprising.'

'You are well placed to bring down Henry Tudor,' Norfolk told him with what looked like a straight face.

'And how might that be?'

'He relies too heavily on only a handful of advisers. His father had the same inclination, but he was better served. Foxe and Wolsey were far more worthy opponents than Cromwell or Seymour. He also has no ideas of his own, and no notion how a nation should be governed. Should his advisers desert his service, or should they feed him bad advice, he would not survive long.'

'You wish me to somehow persuade Cromwell to desert the King's service?' Richard asked disbelievingly.

Norfolk shook his head. 'No. I wish you to work behind the scenes so as to ensure that the advice given to Henry by Cromwell is bad. The nation is close enough to uproar as it is, with a series of poor harvests, the Church in disarray, and one Queen after another gracing the royal bed.'

'But there is hope for the future, with the birth of Edward,' Richard argued.

'He is not yet six months old, and he is entrusted to that weakling Edward Seymour. While it might have been better to make our move during the scandals created by my whore of a niece, there is yet time. Once Henry is gone, Edward is a mere infant with a country oaf for a protector.'

'I was correct in my first understanding of why you are here,' Richard scowled back at Norfolk. 'The only task you have set me is to play Cromwell false in some way; this is really all about the enmity between the two of you, is it not? You pretend to offer me the crown of England in the hope that you can use me in your scheme to bring down my master.'

'There is much more to it than that,' Norfolk assured him. 'In the immediate future you would certainly be cutting one diseased arm from the rotting corpse, but in the longer term you would be seizing the throne in the name of your long-honoured ancestors, and restoring England to greatness. I must leave you now, in order to begin my long ride back to Whitehall on the morrow. I shall send word to you through your chosen bedfellow, and do you likewise.'

He strode out of the hall calling for his horse to be brought to the front door, without taking his leave of Jane Rochford, and Richard wandered out into the garden. It was approaching the middle of the day, and although it was now well into winter, the sun was hot in the clear sky, and the frost had retreated from its glare, leaving the lawn glistening with its memory.

Richard walked slowly to the small arbour and sat on the rustic bench inside, deep in conflicting thoughts. On the one hand he was being offered a dream of glory, a promise of rising beyond what even his wildest speculations as a youth had imagined possible. The throne of England, a noble born wife, all the riches of the Treasury, and a place among the princes of Europe. All that was required of him was something that appealed to a twisted side of his nature that had been born when Cromwell double-crossed him and bought his son a bride who Richard had dearly wanted for himself. It would be nice to be able to demonstrate to that snake of a man that he had trained Richard all too well in deviousness and treachery.

On the other hand, the mere prospect of lending even his name and lineage to something that would undoubtedly end on the scaffold if it misfired sent a churning through Richard's bowels. He had never witnessed an execution, and for traitors the chosen means of conducting one was the most hideous imaginable. And how could he, with his simple, workmanlike honesty, lead Cromwell into making an error in policy sufficiently grievous to ensure his downfall?

He would have to somehow make a commitment one way or the other, and communicate his decision to Norfolk before much more time passed. And what if he said no? Hadn't Norfolk gone too far in his disclosure of his disloyalty to Henry to allow Richard to live if he declined to go along with it? Richard urgently needed either some very sage advice, or a sign from God as to which road his feet should be travelling.

He looked up as Jane appeared in the entrance with a worried expression.

'Why did Uncle Norfolk dismiss me so abruptly, and why did he not say goodbye before galloping off like that?'

Richard reached out a hand to guide her to the seat next to his. 'Don't worry, my sweet. It was really only Court business between my master and him. Nothing for you to concern yourself about.'

They sat for a moment or two, hand in hand, with their faces upturned to the hot winter sun, then Richard felt compelled to say something. 'How would it be if I were King of England?'

'So long as it didn't damage your cock, I'd have no objection,' she giggled.

'But what if I were to take a queen to sit on the throne beside me?'

'If you were King, would I not be your Queen?

'And you'd require me not to take mistresses?'

'Of course. Particularly not now.'

'Why do you say "now"?'

'Because I'm carrying your child.'

XXII

Richard's conscious mind was so focused on the momentous news of his impending fatherhood that he remained oblivious to his surroundings as his horse trotted patiently through the wetlands of South Norfolk, the flat dry pastures of Suffolk, the tidal reaches of the Thames as he grew closer to London, and even the familiar clamour, smells and squalor of the settlements on the northern approaches into the city, and Austin Friars.

Cromwell had left word that Richard was to be summoned to wherever he was the moment that he returned, and it was in his master's upstairs study that Richard found him, surrounded by vellum, scrolls piled upon scrolls on the table, and with his faithful hound Bofus acting as a panting paperweight for the additional mountain of records lying on the bare wooden floorboards.

'I trust you had a restful and refreshing time away from those things that matter?' Cromwell enquired sarcastically as he looked up upon Richard's entry into the chamber, already illuminated by candles against the gloom of a drizzly October late afternoon.

'I'm going to be a father,' Richard told him, unable to hold back the news any longer, and having met no-one with whom he could share it during his five day ride south.

'Assuming that you didn't go to it with some wench employed in a wayside alehouse, isn't Jane Rochford a bit old for childbirth?'

'She's only in her forty-second year,' Richard replied. 'Women have been known to give birth at that age.'

'They certainly have,' Cromwell conceded, 'but not their first. She has no other children, of which I'm aware anyway.'

'And you'd be the first to know, of course,' Richard replied. 'A sparrow is not allowed to fart on a Thames-side rooftop without the news is relayed to Thomas Cromwell.'

'Talking of news,' Cromwell replied with a smile, 'there is much to impart, and much though it grieves me to have to admit it, I've missed your presence here.'

'You have other clerks,' Richard reminded him, 'and if I am to be a proper father, I must needs be absent more often. Grimston is five days' ride from here.'

'You forget that when Henry marries again, the Court will be resummoned, and your lady will then resume her duties as a Queen's Lady.'

'Assuming that she wishes to,' Richard reminded him. 'It may be that motherhood will absorb all her interest.'

'We are talking about Jane Rochford, remember,' Cromwell sneered. 'Court etiquette runs through her veins, and the child, when born, will find that it is slurping the latest scandal through her nipple. Do you hope for a boy or a girl?'

'I hadn't really thought that far ahead — it's probably not going to be born until next May.'

'Boys are the most trouble, in my experience,' Cromwell reflected reminiscently, 'but girls pull more at your heartstrings, and therefore finish up wheedling more favours out of fathers. If you haven't even thought ahead as to its sex, presumably it's too much to hope that you have names in mind?'

'Funnily enough, I have,' Richard smiled. 'I cannot think beyond "Thomas" if it's a boy.'

'Do you seek to flatter me, or have you, out of a total absence of imagination, lighted upon the most common name in England these days?'

'You would not object?'

'Why should I? It was also the Cardinal's name. Regrettably, it is also the name that was granted to Norfolk in the days when somebody loved him. I find it hard to conjure up any image in my mind of Thomas Howard as a helpless mewling infant wrapped in a shawl.'

'My other request is more delicate,' Richard ventured while the atmosphere between them was still civil. 'For a girl, I cannot get my mind beyond "Grace". It's the most beautiful name I've ever heard, but I know that you had a daughter of that name, and I would not wish to offend.'

Cromwell appeared momentarily stunned, then recovered himself. 'Should you wish to avoid incurring my displeasure, you may take this draft over to the other table and begin copying it. I have to present it to Council in two days' time, and it has seen so many changes in wording that even I can barely follow it.'

'What is it?'

'My latest proposals for the abolition of holy shrines. They are idolatrous, and if we are to ban statues of the Virgin in our churches, we should at least take steps to prevent pilgrims being seduced into throwing money into wishing wells, or wasting their hard-earned wages on altar candles and keepsakes that purport to be holy relics, but were created in monks' cells only the previous day.'

'There is such a shrine not far from Grimston. It is said to be the place where the Virgin appeared to the lady of the manor.'

'Walsingham,' Cromwell muttered in distaste. 'It's the first on my list, since even monarchs have been known to be lured there. It is also well within Norfolk's bailiwick, so it must go.'

'You made mention of the King's remarriage,' Richard reminded him. 'Is there talk of such at Court?'

'Not at Court, as such,' Cromwell replied, 'but of late I have been obliged to consider little else. My doorstep is all but worn smooth by the boots of Ambassadors seeking to urge upon me the merits of this princess, or that widowed Countess. Even, in Chapuys's case, a Spanish prince whose ambitions are such that he would bed the Lady Mary.'

'Has Henry shown any interest in these proposals?' Richard asked.

'I have not put any of them to him, as yet. He seems content to wallow in his misery following the death of Queen Jane, and it is probably safer for England's soul if I let it remain that way.'

'How?'

Cromwell looked disappointed by the question. 'I will assume that all this distraction of impending fatherhood has quite emptied your brain of any diplomatic sense. Chapuys speaks for Charles of Spain, who has Europe's greatest collection of ugly female cousins, while Francis of France has foolishly consigned his interests into the clammy hand of Jean de Dinterville, who when not constantly complaining of our weather, and dripping snot into his embroidered kerchief, is seeking to persuade Henry to dip his prick into some elderly aunt of the House of Valois.'

'Apart from the ugliness of these ladies — and let us remember that despite the undoubted talents of Master Holbein, Henry is hardly any longer the romantic troubadour — why should an alliance with either Spain or France not suit England's interests?'

Cromwell stared at him. 'I cannot believe that you have worked alongside me all this time, and still have to ask such a question. What religion do they continue to follow in Spain and France?'

'They are Catholic, I assume,' Richard replied humbly.

Cromwell slapped his hand against his forehead in a gesture of despair. 'You *assume*? They are as Catholic as a Requiem Mass, or salvation through the confessional. Charles and Francis each have a hand inside the Pope's vestments, and they are currently allied with each other. They wish to draw Henry into their net at the behest of the Pope, who has yet to accept that England is lost to him forever. Should Henry seek another bride from a royal stables, it will need to be in Germany or the Low Countries, where the Pope is no longer welcome either, and where Reformist policies are not regarded as treasonous.'

'And are there any suitable royal princesses to be found there?'

'A few, but I have yet to delve deeper into such matters. It may be that in due course I shall be obliged to squelch through the bogs of the Low Countries in search of same, but for the moment I would wish to create a flutter of diplomatic unease in Guelders. It is a wealthy principality which has long been a bone of contention between France, Spain and Germany. If the current alliance between Charles and Francis can be split like a walnut shell, it may be through their dispute over the territory. At present, the most likely to come between them is William of Cleves, who seeks France's aid to enforce his claim to Guelders against Charles of Spain, who jealously guards what he believes to be his ongoing entitlements in the Low Countries.'

'This is all above my head, but I take from it that you seek a bride for Henry in the Low Countries, so let us leave it at that. But you say that Henry is not for marrying at present?'

'Indeed not,' Cromwell confirmed. 'Instead he seems content to regard himself as a man cursed by God, which of course does not assist my attempts to push through further reforms in the Church.'

'At least he now has his male heir,' Richard pointed out, 'so in what way does he regard himself as cursed?'

'The loss of Jane, who, or so it would seem from his genuine grief, he truly loved. As for the infant Edward, he is stifled, smothered and cosseted by that insufferable prattler Margaret Bryant, who was aunt to the late Queen Anne, and had charge of the Lady Elizabeth until the birth of the heir. Before that she wiped puke from the infant garments of Henry Fitzroy. She is another Howard who has been allowed too close to the throne for my liking.'

'I received a visit from Norfolk during my stay at Grimston,' Richard said uneasily.

Cromwell looked up sharply. 'What did he want?'

'It seems that he has been talking to the Countess Margaret Pole, and she revealed to him that I am of the line of York. It also seems that the Howards were historically aligned with York.'

'The Howards would align themselves with Satan himself, if it would advance their interests,' Cromwell snarled. 'Do not be misled by anything you may be promised by a Howard. They might seek to place you on the throne for long enough to remind you that they put you there, and that henceforth you must do their bidding. Thomas Howard sees himself as another Warwick.'

'Who?'

'No matter. See to that copying before supper.'

XXIII

The next morning, fully rested, Richard was up and about early, with a healthy appetite. The bread was freshly baked, and the cheeses were still moist, while the small beer that he swilled them both down with made him glad to be English. He could hear birdsong from the gardens outside, and the sun had reappeared for the first time in days. All in all, life seemed somehow more enjoyable, and of course he could now look forward to holding his own infant in his arms once next spring gave way to summer.

Cromwell stumbled to the breakfast table like a man in the grip of a nightmare and took the bench on the opposite side from Richard. The two of them sat in uneasy silence, until Cromwell revealed the source of his discomfort.

'I have not slept, thanks to you.'

'I am aware of your eagerness to blame me for every misfortune that befalls you,' Richard snapped, 'but how did I disturb your slumber?'

'It was your talk of Grace,' Cromwell replied dully. 'She was my favourite, as you may know, and even now there are cupboards and storerooms here at Austin Friars that all but myself are prohibited from entering because they contain things that were hers. Her schoolbooks, in which she wrote in such a fair hand. Her Christmas guise costumes, in which she was wont to prefer the role of angel, with gossamer wings and wax halo.' His voice began to crack, and his lips trembled as a harbinger of tears. 'She came to me last night, and I fear that it was not in a dream,' he continued in a trembling voice. 'There she was, my lovely Grace, as I remember her. She begged me, if I loved her, to allow her name to live on in your daughter's name. "*If* I loved her"? Dear God, she was my world!'

He choked, and his shoulders heaved. Instinctively Richard reached out and placed a hand over Cromwell's two trembling ones interlaced on the table between them. Cromwell bowed his head on Richard's hand and began to weep like a child — choking, unashamed sobs that racked his entire body.

Richard sat looking at his bowed head, embarrassment mingled with compassion, until the sobs subsided, and Cromwell looked up at him through bleary reddened eyes. He wiped the mucus from his nose with the back of his hand and stared Richard in the eye.

'I have gone about showing it in the most unlikely of ways, but you have been like a second son to me. Gregory is of my flesh, obviously, but I have provided for him at your expense, and it plucks at my conscience. Before Grace left me, she enfolded herself in my arms and begged me, as a final token of the love we shared, to provide for the girl that will perpetuate her name. She was cold as ice as we embraced, but I have no doubt that it was no mere dream, and that Jane will be delivered of a girl.'

'And it will give me a great awareness of the honour you do me, to be allowed to perpetuate her memory,' Richard replied through welling tears of his own. 'I am sorry that on occasions in the past, harsh words have passed between us, but have no doubt that the respect I have for you borders upon that due by a son to a father. Let us be reconciled.'

'There must be more than that,' Cromwell insisted. 'You are held back for lack of an estate, and I have many such at my disposal, as the abbeys and monasteries fall into my pockets. Before Grace faded from my sight, there was another standing in the corner of the chamber, smiling that smile of his, his red robes shining clear in the moonlight from the open shutter.'

'The Cardinal?'

'The very same. I held him in the same regard that you assure me you hold for me, so this gift that I shall make to you will be all the more fitting.'

'Gift?'

'Of land. One of the larger houses that I have been obliged to dissolve of late has been the old Abbey of Leicester. It had already begun to fall into ruin, and local desecrators have taken to removing the stonework for their own houses. It is only a matter of time before they loot the graves.'

'And?'

'One of those graves is that of the Cardinal. I always intended to cover it with a suitable memorial, but the time was never auspicious. Now it would probably be adjudged hypocrisy on my part, given my opposition to shrines, but the grave itself must be kept from desecration, and that task I entrust to you.'

'Willingly, but how does this involve an estate?'

'The Abbey has several estates that over the years have been added to its rental rolls, and of these the finest was — and still is — the one at Knighton, slightly to the north of Leicester itself, which I am pleased to grant to you, for your convenience as you see to the preservation of Wolsey's final resting place. It brings in several hundred a year, if properly stewarded, and there is still an old manor house, according to the latest return I had from the abbot. Also on the land is a small house of Benedictine nuns that was endowed by the late Queen Katherine; they are believed to be no more than four in number, but I would be greatly obliged if you would allow them to remain, out of respect for the memory of that most pious lady. She was a good friend to the Cardinal, and it sore grieved him that he was obliged by Henry to pursue the annulment.'

'It was said that he shrank from doing so, and that this was the cause of his downfall.'

Cromwell's eyes flashed. 'Be in no doubt that the cause of the Cardinal's downfall was the malevolence of the Boleyn witch and her evil uncle. The Cardinal was a true servant of Henry's, and would have secured the annulment if he could. That did not prevent his big heart from lamenting the grief that it caused Katherine, however.'

Richard reached for the wine jug that was still covered by a cloth, uncovered it, and poured some of it for Cromwell, which he drank with a pale smile of thanks.

'You have given me much to think about,' Richard assured him, 'and of course I shall be ever grateful of your generosity, but when will it be convenient for you for me to return to Jane, to see how she fares, and bring her the glad tidings?'

Cromwell glanced up at the high window and smiled. 'The weather appears to be set fair again, and who knows how long this might last at this time of the year? Perhaps you should set off without further delay.'

'But I returned only yesterday. Do you not need me here?'

'Indeed I do, but as you yourself advised me, I have other clerks. I have only one man I can trust to preserve the Cardinal's grave, and only one father of a girl called Grace who has yet to be born.'

'Thank you — Thomas,' Richard replied as he addressed Cromwell by his first name for the very first time, and reached across the table to grip his hand.

'Before you journey to Leicester, you might wish to know something of your neighbours. To the north of your lands in

Knighton, less than half a day's ride, lies the Bradgate estate of Henry Grey, Marquess of Dorset. His great-grandmother was the fabled Elizabeth Woodville, wife of King Edward IV, your great-grandfather. Before Elizabeth married Edward she was wed to Sir John Grey. Henry Grey's wife is Lady Frances Brandon, the daughter of our current Duke of Suffolk, Charles Brandon, and his then wife the late Princess Mary, the current Henry's sister. You had best write all this down.'

'Why?'

'Because they will be your nearest ennobled neighbours, and Lady Frances has recently given birth to a daughter they have named Jane. Your daughter Grace will require a playmate during her childhood, and better that she play with someone of noble birth than the offspring of your local blacksmith or butcher.'

'Someone other than Thomas Wolsey, son of a butcher, or Thomas Cromwell, son of a blacksmith, you mean?' Richard grinned in reply.

Cromwell couldn't prevent the chuckle leaving his throat. 'I have taught you too well, and you have learned too readily. Be on your way, before I find some boring monastic charter for you to decipher for its hidden wealth.'

Jane rushed out of the modest manor house at Grimston into the thinly swirling flakes of the first snowfall of winter. Richard had barely dismounted and was about to lead the horse into the shelter of the stables when she threw herself into his arms and hugged him warmly.

'Back so soon! Baby must have known, for I felt him stirring inside me!'

'It's a girl,' Richard told her as he smiled down at her eager face and kissed the snowflakes off her lips. 'And she, like you, would be better off inside, by the fire. I hope there's mulled wine.'

There was indeed, and while Richard helped himself as they sat with their legs extended towards the log fire in the centre of the room, betraying the house's Saxon origins, Jane demanded to know why he was back so soon after his departure.

'Cromwell has sent me on a mission to preserve the Cardinal's grave from the plunderers of Leicester Abbey.'

'If the grave is in Leicester, why are you in Grimston?'

'Leicester is two days' ride to the west of here, and we leave once this snow stops falling.'

'We?'

'Yes — you and I. My new role as tenderer of Wolsey's grave brings with it an estate I can finally call my own.'

'For as long as you do Cromwell's bidding, presumably?' Jane asked suspiciously.

'He and I are reconciled, and he has given his blessing for us to call our daughter Grace,' Richard told her with a beaming smile.

'But now we will be dependent on Cromwell's good will to abide on our new estate? I have seen how Cromwell's good will can turn into an evil gale in a matter of hours. You forget that he had me summoned to his rooms in Whitehall, and that he questioned me without relenting until he had the information he needed against Anne.'

'Information that you gave both freely and gleefully, as he tells it,' Richard reminded her. 'Now, are you content to journey to Leicester without delay?'

XXIV

The snow abated with nightfall, and by the following morning there was no evidence that it had ever fallen, as Richard and Jane pointed their mounts with their backs to the brightly rising sun. They struck across verdant acreages and pleasant wooded vales until the ramparts and towers of Leicester Castle came into view, and they passed through the town in the late afternoon of the second day, chasing the setting sun to their destination on their new estate.

'Is this it?' Jane enquired disconsolately as they rode through the old moss-covered gate that was hanging from its hinges.

Richard gazed forlornly at the cluster of broken-down buildings. One was larger than the rest, and appeared to have retained most of its roof, although chickens ran squawking from its gloomy interior as they approached. From a barn of sorts came the mournful lowing of a cow, and two donkeys were grazing listlessly outside the front door of the third building, little more than a squat tower, from which came bustling a middle-aged woman wearing the black habit and white cowl of a nun of the Order of St Benedict. She looked up, smiled, and walked across as she wiped her hands down the side of her habit.

'Good afternoon, and welcome to the Convent of Knighton, a Benedictine house. You are seeking a night's sanctuary? If so, you should know that we poor sisters live strictly by the code laid down by the founder of our order, and can offer only the roof above your head, and the barest of potage to line your stomachs. I'm Sister Maria Magdalena, and since the recent promotion of Mother Boniface to the right hand of God, I am the one responsible for what transpires in this house, of which there are only two more sisters, apart from myself.'

Richard smiled benevolently down at her from his horse's back. 'You do not fear that even the remaining three of you will be obliged to renounce your vows following the great purge of holy houses?'

Maria smiled up at him with a confident beam in her warm brown eyes. 'We have nothing to fear from the heretic and blasphemer Cromwell, since we live our lives in simple purity. Even should our house be taken from us, we shall continue to do God's work, safe in the knowledge that He will provide.'

'Your faith and purity do you credit, Sister Maria. I shall be sure to commend both to my master — the heretic and blasphemer Cromwell.'

If she was shocked by this revelation, there was no evidence of it in her face as she invited them to dismount. As Richard helped Jane from her side saddle, Maria's eyes widened slightly at the sight of Jane's somewhat protruding midriff when her riding cloak fell away to reveal her rich gown.

'You are with child, my daughter? Come, lose no time in entering our humble hospitium, and resting your stomach. Sister Hortense will bring you food and drink, and the rushes are fresh. It is to be regretted that we have no bolster on which you may sleep, but Christ himself entered this life in a stable, so we are told.'

An hour later, Sister Maria ducked back into their accommodation and enquired whether or not they had been fed, and if there was anything else that they required which could be provided 'within the means of this humble house.' Jane shook her head, and smiled her thanks for what they had already received, but Richard was seeking more information.

'I am advised that this house was endowed by the late Queen Katherine.'

Maria crossed herself and muttered some blessing in Latin before answering. 'Indeed, she was most pious and devout. Since her death, the Devil has been able to wreak his evil throughout the nation. And, I have to say, mainly through the hand of the man you serve. I have no doubt, as you indicated earlier, that this house will soon fall by his hand, and we shall all be back in the wicked world that we sought to escape from into the loving arms of God, whom we serve.'

'That's precisely the point, though, isn't it?' Richard argued. 'Because you have withdrawn from the world, and make no contribution to the community by which you are surrounded, it is too easy for men like Cromwell to accuse you of idleness, and thereby justify the closure of your houses.'

For once Sister Maria was not smiling. 'You accuse us of withdrawing from the community, and yet, were you to ask the people who seek to survive in this locality, they would tell you of our good works. Of the food we supply in times of poor harvest. Of the divine blessings we can bring during sickness. When the last outbreak of the Plague visited the village just down the road, it was myself and my sisters who ministered to the dying when no-one else would venture near them, for fear of contracting the pestilence themselves. And not just in times of sickness — were you living here, for example, I would be available to assist in the delivery of the baby that your wife is expecting.'

'Actually, we're not...' Jane began, until silenced by a look from Richard, who smiled back at Sister Maria.

'You were not to know, Sister, but we *shall* be living here. This estate has been granted to us by my master, Thomas Cromwell, and we are your new lord and lady of the manor.'

'*Deo gratias*,' Maria mumbled as she once again made the sign of the cross. 'You seem to be honest Christian people, so perhaps this humble house may be allowed to remain for a little while longer?'

'Your wish is to continue to do the work of God?' Richard enquired.

Maria nodded.

'Is there any reason why you need to do so under holy orders?' was Richard's next question.

Maria thought deeply before replying. 'Of course not, but even were I to cast off this humble mantle and resume the clothes I wore before taking my vows, I would continue to honour them, both in my heart and in my deeds.'

'The two other Sisters,' Richard replied, 'what work do they do?'

'Sister Hortense is our farmer, tending the plants and beasts that you see all around you. It is through her good deeds that we are fed daily. Sister Catherine is our builder, and in company with some of the local men she ensures that the fabric of our buildings remains such that we can continue to be protected from the elements.'

'And yourself?'

'As I have already advised you, my particular calling is toward nursing the sick.'

Richard thought for a moment, then smiled back up at Sister Maria from where he was resting in the rushes. 'So if you were allowed to remain here, even if not under holy orders in a convent, you would continue to serve this local community under the inspiration of God?'

'Have I not already said so?'

'Not in so many words. I take it that the sad hovel in which we are currently accommodated was once the manor house?'

'Yes, but it has not been occupied by a lord since it came under the overlordship of the Abbey at Leicester, which itself is shortly to be closed.'

'And your Sister — Catherine, I believe she is called — could supervise local tradesmen to restore it to what it once was?'

'If we are to remain here,' Maria replied, 'it would be the least we could do by way of thanks.'

'And Sister Hortense would see to the tending of crops and the raising of animals?'

'As I said.'

'You yourself would continue to nurse the sick, and deliver children into this world?'

'That is my vocation, under God's holy guidance.'

'Then there remains only the matter of how you are dressed, and how you are named. There can be no objection to your remaining here, and continuing your work, provided that you do not flaunt your vestments and continue to call yourself a convent. You would be officially closed, but quietly going about the work you have always done.'

Maria knelt on one knee, fingered the cross that hung around her neck, intoned a string of joyful Latin, then raised her hand in a blessing to them both before scuttling out in floods of tears.

'You are actually intent on living in this shithole?' Jane asked as soon as Maria was out of earshot.

Richard smiled. 'It will not be a shithole for much longer,' he assured her. 'The Holy Sisters will be so grateful to be allowed to remain as they were that they will restore the manor to what it presumably once was. And it shall be *our* manor, not one that can be taken from us any day that King Henry wakes to a sick stomach or a toothache.'

'I'm not lying in these disgusting rushes for more than one night,' Jane insisted with a firm set to her jaw.

'You will not have to. Tomorrow I honour my undertaking to secure the grave of Cardinal Wolsey, and then we shall impose upon our neighbours to the north.'

They found Wolsey's grave with the guidance of Abbot Joseph, who was loading a donkey with his few possessions prior to returning to his home village of Clifton, on the banks of the Trent a day's ride north. The grave itself had not been violated in any way, but it was weed strewn, and the humble marker at its head was drooping at a perilous angle before Richard placed it back upright and hammered it back in with a stone. Then he stood back and surveyed the simple mound.

'He was once the second most powerful man in the realm, and this is all that remains of him,' Richard mused sadly.

Jane rested against him, her hand through the crook of his arm. 'Cromwell may well finish up the same way — and sooner than he imagines.'

'What makes you say that?'

'Wolsey fell foul of the King, did he not? You forget that I once served Queen Anne, and I heard the lies she poured into Henry's ear regarding Wolsey's efforts with Rome. Henry believed that Wolsey was in league with Rome because Anne and her uncle Norfolk persuaded him that he was. Norfolk need only pour similar poison into Henry's ear regarding Cromwell, and he will be a mere memory.'

'Thomas Cromwell is a stronger man than Wolsey ever was. And stronger than Norfolk.'

'Pray God that it never comes to the test. Now, where do you propose that we rest tonight?'

They were admitted to the large house at the south end of Bradgate Park the moment that Richard mentioned the magic name of Cromwell, and were met in the main hall by Henry Grey, Marquess of Dorset.

'You are both most welcome, Sir Richard. And of course, Viscountess Rochford. I trust that the purpose of your visit is purely of a social nature, and you do not carry your master's commission to close us down?'

'Not at all,' Richard assured him. 'In fact, we call in the capacity of near neighbours, since I have recently taken over the lordship of Knighton, to the south of you. Our own humble house is undergoing repair at present, and we have need to cast ourselves upon your hospitality while those repairs are completed. In the fullness of time I would hope to repay the favour, although even when completed our humble manor house will have nothing of the splendour of Bradgate House.'

'It shall be our pleasure,' Henry Grey assured him in a cringing tone that was almost embarrassing. 'Any friend of Thomas Cromwell is a welcome guest in this house. Come into the Hall and meet my wife and daughter.'

Over supper, Henry began to enquire after their business at Knighton, and Richard was at pains to set his mind at rest.

'As you know, the Abbey at Leicester is in the process of closing down, and my master has honoured me with the task of preserving the grave of the late Cardinal Wolsey.'

'Your master was in Wolsey's service, was he not?'

'Indeed, and he still honours his memory, although it would seem that others do not.'

'My parents had much to thank him for,' Lady Frances chimed in. 'They were wed in secret, and my late mother being a royal princess, Henry was all for having my father's head until the Cardinal talked him round. So in that sense I owe him my very existence, and of course the existence of my new-born daughter Jane.'

She had introduced the topic, so Richard felt entitled to pursue it.

'Lady Jane is herself with child, as you may observe. If it is a girl, we would be most obliged if you would permit the two girls to be companions through their childhoods.'

'We would be most content for that,' Henry Grey assured them, 'since there would seem to be few of any suitable lineage in this part of the country who would make a suitable companion for our own dear daughter.'

'Talking of lineage,' Richard replied, scarcely able to believe how easily these matters were arising in general conversation, 'my master advises me that you can trace yours back to Elizabeth Woodville.'

'Indeed,' Henry confirmed with an air of self-satisfaction as he reached for the wine jug. 'This was of course before she became Queen. Prior to her marriage to the late King Edward, she was wed to my great-grandfather, Sir John Grey.'

'So King Edward would have been your grandfather's step-father, if you can carry that concept in your head?'

'Indeed, and somewhere in an upper chamber here we have the family tree drawn up. You may inspect it on the morrow, should you be so minded.'

'I would take great pleasure in doing so,' Richard confirmed, 'but sufficient to say that the children born to Edward — most notably the two boys Edward and Richard — would have been cousins of sorts to your grandfather?'

'That's correct, but of course they were murdered in the Tower.'

'So it is said,' Richard replied quietly.

Henry raised an eyebrow. 'You doubt that?'

'I have good reason to do so,' Richard replied with a smile, 'but we may discuss this on the morrow.'

That night Richard told Jane all he learned about his true history and the real fate of the Princes in the tower,

'That explains why Uncle Norfolk came to see you,' Jane murmured as she took it all in. 'When I was married to George, Norfolk was forever muttering about how "the old order" had been pushed aside in favour of what he calls "undeserving incomers". If he means Henry, then that makes his words treasonous, doesn't it? Can't Cromwell use that against him?'

'I think you'll find that his references to "undeserving incomers" were aimed at Cromwell himself, and before him Wolsey,' Richard explained. 'It began with Wolsey, as you yourself recall. The two were sworn enemies, and Cromwell has replaced the Cardinal as Norfolk's latest target. Cromwell was trained by Wolsey, and has remained loyal to his memory — hence our new estate — while, to make it worse, Cromwell is even more low born than Wolsey was.'

'But if you're serving Cromwell, doesn't that also make you a target for Norfolk?' Jane asked in a voice tinged with fear.

'No,' Richard assured her, 'because of who I am, and who my grandfather was. Norfolk will certainly seek to make use of me, to undermine Cromwell, and even bring him down totally, but at the same time he hopes to make use of my Yorkist ancestry in some way. I need to visit Margaret Pole, in order to find out how heavily the Howards were committed to the Yorkist cause.'

'Where is her estate?'

'Bisham, in Berkshire. I can be there in two days of hard riding, I think.'

'Are you planning on leaving me here, among all these strangers?'

'Only briefly. On my return journey I can see how far our own manor house has progressed, and if it is suitable we can move back in time for the Christmas celebrations. Then you can remain there until the time of your lying in, under the care of Sister Maria.'

XXV

Three days later, having excused himself from the company of the Grey family by claiming that he had urgent matters to attend to in Leicester, Richard was admitted to the Great Hall at Bisham, where a familiar figure rose to greet him with a broad smile.

'If I were to believe in omens,' Norfolk boomed in welcome, 'then this would be both a good one and a timely one. What brings you to this hotbed of Yorkists — are you perhaps in search of a throne? And why have you not yet been in communication with me regarding what we discussed during our last meeting?'

'Leave the young man alone, Thomas, and how dare you welcome him into *my* house?' Margaret Pole chided Norfolk from the chair in which she was seated in front of the fireplace. 'Come and join me by the fire, Richard. Allow me to introduce my son Geoffrey.' She indicated the man sitting to her right.

Richard accepted the seat on her other side, leaving Norfolk to lurk near the table in the centre of the hall, helping himself from time to time from the wine jug in its centre. Richard explained the events of recent months that had led to his taking occupation of his Knighton estate, and the forthcoming birth of his child by Jane Rochford.

'Excellent,' Geoffrey responded. 'An heir for an heir.'

'Geoffrey is in communication with his brother, and my son, Reginald,' Margaret explained, 'who is now a Cardinal in the Church of Rome, and currently living in Italy. Reginald is close with the Emperor Charles, and between them, with the blessing of his Holiness, they are planning a trade embargo on

England that will finally deprive Henry of any remaining support from the merchants. Geoffrey and Norfolk will then raise an army, together with my other son, Lord Montagu, who is in communication, through his Ambassador, with Francis of France, who has promised additional troops. It wants only a figurehead, and we had originally thought in terms of the Lady Mary. But, as Norfolk has already observed, your unexpected arrival may be the sign we needed from God.'

Richard was stunned, and his head spun with the suddenness of it all. 'You intend to set me up as King of England?'

Norfolk stepped across towards the fireplace and placed a heavily mailed gloved hand on his shoulder. 'If you refuse, after all that has just been revealed to you, I might be obliged to run you through.'

'Thomas!' Margaret Pole upbraided him. 'Give the young man time to think the matter through at least. You are asking him to place his head on the block should we fail, and then what chance the Yorkist cause, even if Jane Rochford gives birth to a boy?'

'If you insist,' Norfolk grumbled, 'but he's Cromwell's man, and you've already revealed more of our plans than was wise before we knew whether or not he is with us.'

'Who would not wish to be King?' Margaret queried.

'I'm not sure I would, after all I have learned this past two years,' Richard blurted out without thinking, then looked anxiously back at Norfolk. 'But I would not betray you, on that you may rely. I simply wish to be allowed to live in peace with my woman and family, perhaps with a little more in the way of an estate, but no more. It does not matter to me who is King of England.'

'Then it should!' Norfolk thundered, before turning to Margaret. 'Let me finish him now, and be done with it!'

'You will do no such thing in my house!' Margaret commanded him. 'And you forget yourself — *he* is the one with Plantagenet blood in his veins, not you. You lay one hand on him and I will see to it that when the House of York is finally restored you will pay for that with your life!'

Norfolk threw himself angrily back onto his seat by the table and poured himself yet more wine, while Margaret placed a gentle hand on Richard's shoulder.

'You must take time to consider your position, clearly, and I am happy to offer you the hospitality of my house while you do so. You have my word that Norfolk here will make no attempt on your person while you are under my roof, but you must carefully consider the consequences of refusing what we offer. Without us you are a lowly clerical servant of the son of an innkeeper from the streets of Putney. Join with us, and you will be King of England, with an heir to the throne already born. Is that really a choice that any sensible ambitious man would need to consider for more than a moment?'

'You do me great honour, Countess,' Richard replied as humbly as he could, already calculating his best means of escaping alive from this den of traitors, 'but there is much to consider. I have seen enough of life at Court to know that a king cannot do whatsoever his heart desires, but must act in the best interests of his people. While I do not lack education, it was not of the finest, and I have no skill or training with the sword. Does England not deserve someone more fitting at its head?'

'Don't waste your breath, Margaret,' Norfolk snarled from his seat at the table, 'he's Cromwell's man, and if we set him free to roam the country, he'll betray us!'

'Richard is our guest, Thomas,' Margaret replied, 'and we shall talk with him more in the morning, when your brain is clear of all the wine you have consumed. Richard, please join us for supper after you have rested for a while in the chamber to which my Steward will direct you.'

Richard bowed from her presence, his mind whirling with ideas of how he might escape the dreadful situation in which he had unwittingly placed himself. Escaping from the house itself ought to be a simple enough matter, and he had not yet unsaddled his horse, which he had seen being led into the only stable. Once out of the house, he could ride like the wind, but where to? Should he rush back under Cromwell's protection in Austin Friars? But what would happen to Jane and her unborn child? Would Norfolk seek her out?

He eventually resolved on a compromise as he lay on the bolster in the guest chamber, whose door he had locked on the inside in case Norfolk got any drunker, and opted to ignore Margaret's insistence that there was to be no action against Richard's life in her house. He reasoned that first and foremost he needed to return to Jane at Bradgate, secure her immediate safety, then send word to Cromwell of what he had learned, and his need for protection.

He lay counting the minutes in his head until he heard the unmistakable sounds of trestles being erected for supper in the hall below, and the chatter of pages and serving wenches as they laid the trenchers in place on damask table coverings. Then he sauntered casually into the hall, as if hungry, and joined Countess Margaret and her son as they chatted away about nothing in particular.

He waited until Norfolk had joined them, glaring at Richard with eyes that threatened death as he rapidly got drunker and drunker. When he deemed the moment appropriate, Richard kept his voice light and casual as he announced that he had clean forgotten the main reason for his visit to Bisham, which was to make a gift to the Countess Margaret of a family tree that his grandmother had commissioned some years previously, which he had left in his saddlebag, and he sought leave to retrieve it from the stables.

Margaret graciously granted leave, and with one final look at Norfolk, who was slumped over the supper table, Richard strode casually to the front door, resisting the urge to break into a run. Less than five minutes later he was pushing his horse north from Bisham through deepening snow, praying that the latest fall would not persist, and that the tracks to the north would be passable.

He had no memory other than of howling icy wind, a stumbling horse, road signs obscured by drifting snow hanging off them, and wayside inns locked and shuttered firmly against the elements until he was being revived by stable grooms who had seen him fall exhausted from his saddle a few yards short of the front door to Bradgate House. He lay in delirium for two days until, on the third day, he opened his eyes and looked into the tear-streaked face of Jane Rochford, and beside her the physician who was anxiously preparing to pour some potion down his throat.

'A foxglove simple,' Richard was advised as the physician pulled open his mouth and poured it in, both without Richard's leave. 'It stimulates the heart.'

Richard had the presence of mind to turn on his side and expel most of it from his mouth before dismissing the physician. He looked quizzically back at Jane, who was now grinning and crying, both at the same time.

'God be praised that you are back among us,' she murmured as she leaned down and hugged him. 'Where in God's name have you been, and what led you to return in that fashion?'

As Richard's memory of recent events began to return, he made a supreme effort to rise from the bolster, but fell back when his strength failed him. He looked up at Jane with urgency written all over his face. 'I must speak with our host without delay! You and I — and our unborn child — will be in great danger if word is not sent immediately to my master!'

'In good time,' Jane assured him. 'For the moment you must rest and regain your strength.'

'There is no time to spare!' Richard all but shrieked. 'Word must be sent to Cromwell that there is a plot against Henry's throne by Norfolk and the Countess of Salisbury. It was revealed to me only days ago, and there may still be time to suppress it, but you and I, and our child, are in danger from Norfolk. We must send to Cromwell for protection!'

'And what makes you think that Henry Grey is incapable of protecting guests in his own house?' came a commanding voice from the doorway, as the man in question stepped into view and looked down at Richard with a smile. 'How are you faring? They say you were labouring in delirium when they brought you into the house. Is this talk of a plot against the throne part of it?'

'It is as real as you or I,' Richard persisted, 'and now that I know of it, my life, and the lives of those dear to me, are at risk.'

'From Norfolk, did I hear you say?'

'Norfolk, and those associated with him in this plot. The Countess of Salisbury and her sons, in league with Spain and France, and urged on by the Pope, no less!'

'The King should learn of this without delay,' Grey observed.

Richard shook his head. 'It would be my word against Norfolk's. But we must advise my master Cromwell immediately, since he will know how best to use the knowledge. He must be told before I am sought out by Norfolk and done to death!'

Jane gave a squeak of horror, and hugged Richard to her bosom, but Grey simply smiled.

'You forget that my wife is the daughter of Suffolk and the royal Princess Mary. Suffolk and Henry were brought up in the same nursery, and my father-in-law has ever looked upon Norfolk and his like as usurpers of the royal favour.'

'But Suffolk has no love for Cromwell, or his servants,' Richard argued, only to be silenced by a hand gesture from Grey.

'He loves Norfolk even less, and would not stand by and watch his armed bullies invade his daughter's house in order to harm one of her guests. You and your lady must remain here for your own safety, while I send for a force from Suffolk's own standing army to form a steel ring around Bradgate.'

'We would be prevailing unbearably on your hospitality,' Richard protested, 'and we had hoped for our child to be born at Knighton, where there is a Holy Sister skilled in childbirth duties.'

'You have seen our daughter Jane?' Grey enquired, and when both Richard and Jane nodded, Grey continued, 'And do you see aught wrong with her?' They both shook their heads, and Grey smiled. 'Clearly, we have those available here who can safely deliver children. And if our daughter is to have your offspring — boy or girl — as a childhood companion, is it not fitting that they should be delivered by the same skilled midwife?'

'He speaks sense, Richard,' Jane urged him, 'and Norfolk can do little while this weather persists. Were we to attempt to move back to Knighton, we would expire from the cold, and we would be even more exposed to Norfolk. Best to remain here, at least until the spring, and then we may decide where our child is to be born.'

'If you are adamant,' Richard told Grey, 'then we shall be eternally in your debt, and perhaps may one day be in a position to repay it. As things are at present, we would seem to have little choice. But once the foul weather lifts, can you arrange to have a letter from me delivered to Cromwell at Austin Friars in London?'

'Of course,' Grey assured him. 'We have regular communication between Suffolk's family and our own, and no-one would suspect an additional communication finding its way to Master Secretary, who must have messengers coming and going at all hours.'

Two days later, Richard was able to venture downstairs to the fireplace, where he sat, regaining his strength with bowl after bowl of beef tea, supplemented with mulled wine, Jane holding his hand and listening with horror to the tale that Richard told to first her, and then Henry Grey, of what had been unwisely disclosed to him at Bisham. As soon as he could sit for any length of time at the table, Richard was supplied with vellum, pens and ink, and wrote a long account of his experiences for Cromwell's benefit. The letter was sealed with the Grey family seal and sent by messenger a week prior to Christmas.

The New Year of 1538 was brought in at Bradgate with much merriment, fine food, good wine and expressions of pleasure at new-found friendships.

As Richard stood at their chamber window, gazing down at the moonlit frost-hardened front lawns of Bradgate House, he allowed himself an unaccustomed prayer for the safety of the growing child in Jane's womb, and the success of Cromwell in thwarting Norfolk's evil schemes.

XXVI

When Cromwell finally opened Richard's letter in the pile that had remained with their seals unbroken while his household forced him into Christmas and New Year celebrations, his first reaction was to curse so loudly that Bofus scuttled, head down, into a corner of the chamber, and rested with his head on his front paws, looking up apprehensively at his master with doleful brown eyes. Then plans formed themselves inside Thomas's scheming head, and he gazed into the corner in which the late Cardinal had materialised months previously.

'Justice is best enjoyed as a cold dish, so they say,' he gloated, then returned to his fifth attempt at the wording of the succession document that Henry had commanded, and which required the most minute care in drafting. Cromwell was due at his first royal audience of the year the following day and given the delicacy of the matter there could be no mistake, particularly since Henry had chosen to proceed in these matters by Act of Parliament.

The first of these, four years previously, had bastardised the Lady Mary and excluded her from any prospect of succeeding Henry to the throne of England. This had followed the annulment of Henry's marriage to Katherine, and a second Act two years later, and almost identically worded, had disentitled the little Elizabeth following the execution of her mother Anne. It had done so by confirming the illegitimate status of both royal princesses, and clearing the way for any child born to Jane Seymour following her marriage to Henry. It was now a matter of adding Prince Edward, the three-month-old Duke of Cornwall and Earl of Chester, to the succession, with a proviso that should he die without issue, the crown of England would devolve first upon Mary and her heirs, and then upon Elizabeth and her heirs.

The sticking point was whether or not, and if so under what circumstances, Henry might nominate another successor entirely under his will. This point was not merely academic, even at this point in Henry's life, since there were some who were championing the cause of children of Henry's two sisters, Margaret and Mary. Margaret had married King James IV of Scotland, and that marriage had produced the reigning monarch of that country James V. Much though he was regarded as unsuitable, and however bitter the ongoing border squabbles between the two nations, James of Scotland could raise a legitimate claim to the English crown, no doubt asserted by armed invasion, if the succession were not organised in such a way as to exclude him completely.

Less horrifying to English minds was the possibility of the royal line descending through the second of Henry's sisters, Mary, the late wife of Charles Brandon, Duke of Suffolk. Mary had died some years previously, and Suffolk had since remarried, but their daughter Frances was now wed to Henry Grey, Marquess of Dorset, and could be regarded as having a legitimate claim to succeed her Uncle Henry. Failing her, there was now another Dorset claimant in the recently born Lady Jane Grey.

This was not a good time for Cromwell to be pushing through more Church reforms, as Henry was becoming increasingly convinced that he had invoked more of God's curse by installing himself as the head of the English Church.

At Bradgate, Jane was nearing the time of her confinement behind a ring of armed defences that gave any outside observer the distinct impression that the tranquil park, with its well-appointed brick manor house, was preparing for a lengthy siege. Some of those who had been sent north by Suffolk were allocated personal bodyguard duties on the several occasions upon which Richard had made the half-day journey south in order to review progress at Knighton.

The original house had been carefully restored to a watertight condition by the seemingly inexhaustible former Sister Catherine, who had dutifully reverted to her birth name of Catherine Beddingworth, while her senior colleague Sister Maria Magdelena was now simply Mary Calthorpe. She stood proudly alongside Richard during his latest tour of inspection.

'You have all done very well,' Richard told her, 'but our return must now wait upon the birth of our child, which is due at any time.'

'The mistress is well cared for in Bradgate?' she asked.

Richard nodded. 'As far as a mere man such as I can tell. A mere man, what is more, who has neither knowledge nor experience of such matters.'

'She has a midwife in attendance?'

'Not as yet, but I am assured by our host that such will be summoned when needed.'

There was a slight pause before Mary came to the point. 'I would deem it a further great honour and favour were you to take me back with you, to attend day and night on the mistress to whom we owe so much. I have both experience and skill in such matters, and she should be attended well before the birth itself, to ensure that no infection or bad humours are allowed into her chamber. Also, since I assume that you are no longer attending her at night, she might welcome a companion ahead of that joyous moment when her waters break.'

Richard grimaced. 'I have no knowledge of what you refer to, but I would concede that a friendly and skilled lady in attendance at such a time — particularly one so imbued with God's grace — would be most welcome. Prepare yourself for the ride north — perhaps on one of these donkeys, since we have no spare horse.'

Mary smiled. 'Since our Lord Jesus Christ entered Jerusalem on a donkey, there would be no disgrace in that — only honour to be following his example.'

Two weeks later, in the third week of May, Richard's distraught pacing up and down the main hall as he heard the shrieks and pleas for mercy from the upper chamber was brought to an end by a final scream, followed by a brief silence, the sound of a protesting infant squawk, and the voice of Mary Calthorpe calling out praises to God.

Richard was on his fifth mug of wine when Mary brought down the infant wrapped in a shawl.

'The mistress is sleeping, and all the afterbirth is out, so there is no risk of infection. You have a daughter, and I am advised by its mother that she is to be called Grace. It is a most fitting name for someone so blessed by God to be given life through the loins of a woman so advanced in her years. There should perhaps be no more, since her time was difficult, but that is a matter for the two of you. In the meantime, hold your daughter in your arms and give thanks to God.'

XXVII

'Your subjects would expect it, Sire,' Cromwell urged upon Henry as he worked his way through yet another tedious daily audience dominated by Henry's obsession with God's curse upon him, and his image among the crowned heads of Europe.

'A fourth wife, and so soon after the death of my dear Jane?' Henry quibbled.

Cromwell sighed inaudibly and tried again. 'It's been almost a year now, Sire, and now that Spain and France are at peace, you would be well served seeking a foreign bride in one of the Low Countries, or perhaps Germany.'

'I already have an heir,' Henry argued petulantly, 'so what need have we of another one, even assuming that my increasingly weary frame could be prevailed upon to sire such? And you forget that we are now even further from God's grace, since this latest angry gesture from the Bishop of Rome.'

Cromwell winced inwardly when reminded that his success in persuading Council to allow the destruction of the saintly memorial at Canterbury had finally provoked the Pope into excommunicating Henry, and tried to divert the conversation. 'It was indeed fortunate for England that when your brother Arthur died, your father had bequeathed you to the nation as his worthy successor, so would it not be a matter of caution to ensure that there is another royal prince available should ought befall Prince Edward?'

'He is in robust health, or so I am constantly advised by Lady Troy, who currently has responsibility for his welfare. He is tall for his age, as was I at that time in my life, and even now, despite my widening gut. Who are you proposing I should marry?'

'It is a matter both of religion and diplomacy, Sire,' Cromwell assured him. 'France and Spain being still unrepentantly under the thumb of Rome, any alliance by marriage with either of those nations would be bound to lead to more pressure from Pope Paul. The Low Countries, by comparison, are ruled by princes whose religious policies accord more closely with yours, and they are no friends of either Spain or France. A marriage alliance with one of those would strengthen us against any joint incursion from across the Channel by either Charles or Francis, alone or in league with each other. There is also the matter of our many trading links with the likes of Antwerp and Bruges.'

'And are there any available princesses who you might have in mind, Thomas?'

'None as yet, Sire. There are known to be several, but I would not wish to lead you astray regarding their comeliness and suitability to grace your bed. I must first journey over there and assess them for myself.'

Henry's face set in sour distaste. 'You make yourself sound like some breeder of horseflesh seeking out a suitable mare, Thomas. Find me one who is not so repulsive that my cock will shrink at the task being assigned to it, and she will suffice. Take Master Holbein with you, and should you find one who you think will be suitable, have him paint her portrait and bring it back to me, that I may decide for myself.'

'It shall be as you wish, Sire,' Cromwell mumbled as he bowed his way out.

Earlier that week, Cromwell's patience had been rewarded with the acquisition of correspondence from Cardinal Reginald Pole in Padua, to the Spanish Ambassador in London,

Eustache Chapuys, seeking his good offices with the Emperor for the implementation of a trade embargo on England. Also enclosed was a separate despatch under seal to his brother Geoffrey, urging him to have his army mustered and held in readiness for the uprising in London that any diminution in trade would provoke. There was no direct reference to Norfolk, although it was hinted that 'others in our enterprise' were in regular contact with the French Ambassador, and that French troops were slowly and circumspectly being assembled on the outskirts of the Pale of Calais, the traditional extent of English holdings in Northern France, ready for a full scale attack.

This was as good an opportunity as any, if Cromwell was to nip this treachery in the bud, and expose the entire plot. The ultimate prize would of course be the implication of Norfolk in all this, but experience had taught Cromwell that in order to catch mackerels it was necessary to begin with the sprats, and he ordered the arrest of Geoffrey Pole, and his transfer to the Tower, on suspicion of treason.

The Constable was instructed that the timid Geoffrey was first to be shown the various instruments of torture, in the hope that the mere sight of them would loosen his tongue, failing which Cromwell would leave it to the discretion of those more skilled in such matters in what order the practical functioning of those devices was to be demonstrated. Above all, Geoffrey Pole was to be kept alive — perhaps blinded by the knotted rope twisted into his eyeballs, but alive anyway. Then Cromwell turned his mind to his planned trip to the Low Countries.

Back in Bradgate, two little girls were getting to know each other. Jane Grey was now over a year old, tottering around on wobbly legs and learning her first words. Mary Calthorpe, following the birth of Richard and Jane's child Grace, had been invited to remain as the nurse for both girls.

As for Richard and Jane, they occupied their time in either watching with pride as their daughter began to learn her first essential lessons in life, or journeying under armed escort to their more humble estate at Knighton.

Richard and Cromwell continued to communicate by regular exchanges of letters, and from these Richard learned that Cromwell was on a diplomatic mission to secure another bride for the King. Richard experienced frequent pangs of guilt regarding his absence from his duties clerking for Cromwell, but it had been agreed that it was not safe for him to reappear so soon in London, and Cromwell assured him that it would be sufficient for Richard to continue to guard and tend Wolsey's grave in the grounds of Leicester Abbey while Cromwell sought out the evidence he required of the plot against the throne in order to bring Norfolk down.

XXVIII

Cromwell, in company with Hans Holbein, arrived in the Duchy of Cleves, which sat in wealthy splendour with Holland on its northern border, in February of 1539, as the winter snows were beginning to recede, making the roads just passable with care. They made their way to the ancient castle of Schloss-Berg in Solingen. Cromwell had sent letters ahead of their arrival, advising the ducal court that Henry of England was in search of a bride.

A royal match with a lady of Cleves was perfect for Cromwell's plans for England. There were three sisters, two of whom remained unmarried, while their brother William, the recently installed Duke, following the death of their father, was a staunch Lutheran, despite his mother's Catholic loyalties. The oldest of the three sisters, Sybille, was married to the Elector John-Frederick of Saxony, and he was regarded as the driving force behind the Church Reform movement in Europe.

The entire family had been engaged for some years in a dispute with Emperor Charles of Spain over suzerainty of the neighbouring Gelderland, and this kept Charles focused to his east, while at the same time holding down his captured territories in Italy, and while he was thus engaged on two fronts, his alliance with Francis of France could not blossom into a joint campaign against England. England would gain much, in Cromwell's estimation, by being linked by marriage to Cleves, but it all depended upon whether or not one of the unmarried ladies of the ducal court could be rendered acceptable to Henry.

The two men were afforded a warm welcome, and Holbein lost no time in discharging his two commissions. His first sitting subject was the younger of the two remaining ladies, Amalia, and he and Cromwell argued long and loudly over Holbein's preferred practice of painting what he saw, rather than what his sitters wanted him to imagine. Although Holbein always took the trouble to include the good features, nothing would persuade him to omit the less favourable ones, and his completed portrait of Amalia, although it captured to perfection her delicate oval face, left her looking somewhat nun-like, despite the fashionable bonnet she wore for the preliminary sketches, and hardly someone who would appeal as a bed-mate for the sated appetite of an ageing monarch who had formerly taken his pick of the painted Palace whores.

Amalia's older sister Anna was, if anything, even plainer, since she had a decidedly masculine set to her face, which was in no way softened by the French hood that Cromwell forced onto her head for the occasion. Holbein agreed to incorporate her generous bosom into his final portrait, and tried to reflect, in her face, something of the docility and quiet virtue that Henry had admired in Jane Seymour. But Cromwell was still concerned that there was nothing in the appearance of either girl that would appeal to Henry's tastes, insofar as he understood them.

Then towards the end of their second week in Schloss-Berg, the oldest sister Sybille arrived on a family visit, and Cromwell was taken immediately with her long, free-flowing golden red hair, her almond-shaped eyes, her doe-like peaceful countenance and her inviting mouth. He ordered Holbein to paint her portrait also, and when he had done so to create a copy. The original was presented to Sybille and her husband with many expressions of goodwill and hopes for a stronger and more formal alliance between the Houses of Tudor and Cleves, while the copy made the journey back across the Channel in Cromwell's saddlebag.

Back at Austin Friars, Cromwell ordered the framing of all three, with those of Amalia and Anna in a plain setting, while Sybille's was surrounded by gilt. Two days after his return he sought an audience with Henry, and pulled off the covers that had been protecting the paintings during their journey upriver.

Henry stood staring at them briefly, then asked, 'They are sisters, say you? I find one to be much more comely than the other.'

'Which pleases you more, Sire?'

'It must be obvious, Thomas, even to a man such as yourself who, rumour has it, has not ventured between a woman's thighs since the death of your late wife. Which is the one with the flowing red hair?'

'That is Anna, Sire,' Cromwell lied, 'while the other is her sister Amalia.'

'And they are both unmarried, with no prior understandings?'

'So I am advised, Sire.'

Henry gave a low chuckle. 'If you assure me that the nation so expects it, Thomas, then I would have the more comely of the two. "Anna", is that her name?'

'Yes, Sire, but perhaps "Anne", if she is to become Queen of England.'

'That is perhaps too close to the former witch who betrayed me, but if you insist. Proceed with the negotiations, before she is snapped up elsewhere.'

Cromwell lost no time in returning to Cleves with the proposal, and spent most of the remainder of that year on horseback, carrying one draft of the marriage agreement after another until its final terms were hammered out, and arrangements were being made for the reception onto English shores of 'Anne of Cleves', as she was to be known prior to the nuptials.

In the meantime, the incarceration of Geoffrey Pole had produced results with only minimal need for the royal torturers to demonstrate their skills. Word was relayed to Cromwell that Geoffrey had implicated not only his mother Margaret, Countess of Salisbury, but also his brothers Henry, Baron Montagu, and Reginald, Cardinal of Rome. Reginald was regarded as untouchable for reasons other than pure geography, but Margaret and Henry were arrested on Cromwell's order and conveyed to the Tower, along with Henry Courtenay, Marquess of Exeter, a cousin of the Pole family who was alleged to have pledged troops to the cause. None of them was subjected to torture, but none of them had, at that stage, breathed so much as a word against Norfolk, and Cromwell was becoming more frustrated by the week. He therefore gave word that Geoffrey Pole was to be given closer attention.

XXIX

Shortly before the Christmas celebrations of 1539, Cromwell turned up unannounced at Bradgate, ostensibly on a pilgrimage of sorts to the tomb of Wolsey. But he was fooling neither Richard nor Jane, and as they sat on a viewing bench surveying the ornamental garden to the rear of the house, Richard tackled him regarding the true reason for his journey north.

'You are renowned for your aversion to shrines,' Richard reminded him suspiciously, 'so what is your real reason for being here?'

'Perhaps, as a doting grandfather myself, I came to see how my late daughter's namesake is faring. Grace is a beautiful child, and you have just cause to be proud of her.'

'You are a grandfather?' Jane queried.

Cromwell nodded. 'Gregory and Bess had a boy named Henry, a month before the birth of Grace.'

'But I suspect that business involving another Henry brings you here under pretence of family matters,' Richard persisted. 'You are no more famed for family sentiment than you are for idolatry.'

Cromwell sighed. 'You would have made an astute diplomat, but such matters are these days entrusted to me, and my true reasons for being here are two-fold.'

'At last we reach the nub of it,' Richard said, but Cromwell was not smiling.

'Despite all my efforts, and despite having consigned most of the Pole family to the Tower, I am no nearer naming Norfolk in the conspiracy against the throne.'

'Your torturers have lost their appetites?' Richard demanded cynically, at which Jane grew pale and turned her face away.

'Those who are ennobled may not, by law, be tortured,' Cromwell told them, 'and left unmolested they are standing firm. Except for Geoffrey, who is reported to be losing his reason under the harsh conditions in which he is confined, but even he remains silent beyond condemning his own family. I have ordered that he be questioned again. However, there is another way in which I might reach out and seize Norfolk.'

'That being?' Richard asked.

Cromwell smiled back in that infuriatingly knowing way of his that Richard had come to despise. 'Who else was present during that meeting at Bisham, when all was revealed?'

'You already have them all, save myself and Norfolk.'

'Take Norfolk from the list, and who remains?'

Jane gave a sharp intake of breath, while Richard glared at Cromwell.

'You cannot be serious? Who would believe my word against Norfolk's?'

'It may come to it, and I merely wish, at this stage, to enquire as to your willingness to speak, should it be demanded of you?'

'By whom?'

'Perhaps Henry himself? But we have not reached that stage.'

Richard thought only briefly, then waved both hands in an expansive gesture that indicated the extensive grounds of Bradgate Park. 'We are confined here because of Norfolk's malice. If I could free my family to return to Knighton, where we truly belong, by speaking out against Norfolk, then you need only ask. But surely, given my birthright, my motives would be suspect?'

'Indeed,' Cromwell nodded, 'your royal lineage has become something of a handicap, although it does explain why Norfolk chose to take you into his confidence.'

'But you do not require Richard for this hazardous task at present?' Jane asked, seeking reassurance.

'No, as I explained,' Cromwell replied.

'Then proceed to your *second* reason for being here,' Jane demanded.

Cromwell smiled. 'Your days of Court intrigue have clearly honed your appreciation of such matters,' he flattered her, 'and it is in that capacity that I seek your return to London with me.'

Both Richard and Jane opened their mouths in protest, but Cromwell pressed home his point.

'Clearly, you would be loath to leave Grace here while she is so young. But, being merely months into this life, she will not notice your absence as much as she might were she, for example, five years old. And you would seem to have an excellent nurse in that former nun.'

'But if there is no Queen,' Jane argued, 'why should a Queen's Lady be required? Or did you have something more devious in mind?'

'I wish you to journey to Dover shortly after Christmas, to accompany the Lady Anne, from Cleves in Germany, who is to be the new Queen. She has her own Ladies coming over with her, obviously, but it would nice for her to have available someone who can guide her in the etiquette of the Court here in England.'

'Does she speak English?' Jane asked doubtfully.

Cromwell shook his head. 'Not at this stage, it would seem, but she is accompanied by those who do, and it will be their task to educate her in such matters after the wedding, which is likely to be in the first week of January, at Greenwich, with Cranmer officiating, since she is more comfortable with the Protestant form.'

'You would take a mother away from her child during its first Christmas?' Richard objected. 'You have often recounted to me, when overcome by the splendour of your own wine cellar, how much you enjoyed your own family Christmases at Austin Friars. Is that to be denied to others, now that they are no longer available to you?'

'You judge harshly,' Cromwell replied with a darkening face. 'And you also forget that I shall be obliged to forego my first Christmas with my grandchild.'

'Could I not remain here at least for the main festivity, on the day itself, then lose no speed in joining you in London?' Jane asked.

Cromwell thought briefly before nodding. 'That should be possible. If you bring your own escort from among Suffolk's men here at Bradgate, you may join the main progress as it crosses London Bridge on its way south.'

'Am I to remain here?' Richard asked.

Cromwell nodded. 'Yes, Norfolk may still be seeking to silence you, although of late he has more to fear from those in the Tower.'

'I thought you said that they were remaining silent,' Richard reminded him.

It fell ominously quiet before Cromwell looked him squarely in the eyes and replied, 'The Tower can have a strange and unpredictable effect on those within its cheerless walls.'

XXX

The preparations for Christmas at Bradgate were the more subdued for the knowledge that once the main celebrations were over on the first day, Jane would be heading south under escort for a period of time that could not be estimated, determined as it was by whatever events might transpire following the royal wedding.

Richard and Jane sat holding hands like star-crossed lovers as the mimes and masques were duly performed by household staff who had spent many weeks rehearsing and perfecting them, and the two little girls giggled and screamed as the various characters in costume came and went. Then it was on to the roast fowl and plum pudding, and Richard was curious to see Grace being encouraged to eat from a spoon held invitingly to her face by a young woman he had not seen before. He called Mary over with a beckoning gesture.

'Who is that girl seeking to feed Grace her first plum pudding?' he asked her.

Mary smiled. 'By your leave, that's my niece Kate, my brother's daughter. He passed away some years since, and Kate foreswore taking her vows while she looked after her mother, who passed from us only last week. The poor mite had nowhere else to go, and of course she will not now be able to enter our holy house. If you'd be so kind, master, I've taken her into my care, and she shows considerable skill as a child's nurse, so I'd like to keep her on to assist me while the mistress is away in London. I have to tend to the Lady Jane as well, of course, so I would deem it a favour should you allow Kate to remain with us. She will cost only what she eats, and can lodge with me in my room under the roof.'

'Of course she may remain,' Jane replied without even consulting Richard, 'since Grace so obviously finds her presence comforting, and I have no way of knowing how long I shall be away.'

'God bless you both,' Mary muttered as she slipped away to give Kate the glad tidings.

The journey to Dover proved uneventful, and Cromwell had persuaded Henry to award, to the Duke of Suffolk, the honour of escorting Lady Anne from Dover to London, so that Jane's personal escort had blended in perfectly with their former colleagues as they trotted south in a long line over London Bridge in a waving sea of Brandon livery, with Jane riding alongside Cromwell and several clerks and grooms in the centre of the progress.

At Dover Castle she made her first acquaintance with Anne, and although distanced somewhat by the need for an elderly retainer from Anne's party to translate between them, they seemed to form a natural bond at their first meeting, and as the combined party set off back north through the Kent countryside, rendered crisp by the New Year frosts, the two of them rode alongside each other, exchanging pleasantries that passed in each direction through the interpreter who rode immediately behind them, Cromwell by his side with a contented smile on his sleek face.

Their pace was so sedate that overnight stops were required, first at Canterbury, then at Faversham, before, on the late afternoon of the third day, they clomped through the gateway of Rochester Abbey and took thankfully to their allotted chambers for a rest before supper. For Jane it was a brief respite before an usher announced the entry of Master Secretary.

Jane gave him the benefit of a wry grin. 'Do you not fear for your reputation, visiting a lady in her chamber in this fashion? I recall a previous meeting between us when you accused me of whoredom — do you not apprehend that your reputation might suffer by association?'

'Save your honeyed words for Richard,' Cromwell replied curtly. 'The King is here in Rochester, and wishes to indulge in one of his foolish charades. I wish you to be at Lady Anne's side when he does so, for they are both about to receive an unpleasant surprise.'

'In what way?'

'Anne has not been prepared for how gross Henry has become during his widowerhood, and Henry has been led to believe that Anne is more comely than she is, particularly after three days on the road.'

'Led to believe by whom?'

'Never mind for the moment. Just ensure that you are there, along with that little German who speaks English, when Henry prances in like some lovelorn troubadour. And for God's sake don't burst out laughing, else it will mean *both* our heads.'

Jane scurried off to Anne's chamber, on the pretence that she was enquiring after her comfort, and the suitability of her overnight accommodation. She made excuse after excuse to remain there, thus detaining Anne's visibly annoyed translator, who was anxious to rest before the formalities of the evening, which the King was said to be attending. Eventually there was a knock on the chamber door, and the page who opened it engaged in a brief but stunned conversation with the two men outside in the corridor. Then Jane had to turn her head away, for fear of exploding into helpless laughter at the spectacle that presented itself.

Cromwell entered, accompanied by a hugely obese man decked out in so much greenery that he resembled a walking forest. Even under it all, and after so many months, Jane was able to recognise King Henry, but he remained stern faced as he walked into the presence slightly behind Cromwell, and bearing a large box in his hand.

'Lady Anne,' Cromwell announced in his best German, before the interpreter could beat him to it, 'here is a gentleman of the royal forest, bearing you a gift from your loving intended bridegroom, Henry of England.'

Anne turned to regard the bearer of the gift with a disapproving stare, as her eyes took in the huge bulk, the red face with the drooling lips, the quivering mass of foliage, and the pronounced limp as he moved forward, palm outstretched. It was obvious to anyone who knew him that he was far from impressed by what he was approaching, and he bowed his head as he grew close to Anne.

'My master would have you accept this as but a small token of his loving regard, and his joyous anticipation of your impending wedding,' Cromwell told Anne.

Anne inclined her head graciously, took the box from Henry and opened it, giving a gasp of surprise as her eyes lit upon the richly studded gold necklace encrusted with precious stones. She replied, and it was Cromwell who urgently and tactfully supplied the translation for Henry's benefit.

'She is most pleased with the gift, and is eager to meet he who sent it,' he told Henry.

'Perhaps we should withdraw at this stage, Sire,' Cromwell whispered, and Henry nodded, his slack mouth still open in horrified disbelief as he took in Anne's height, her masculine face, her drooping over-large bosom and the intimidating glare of her eyes.

The two men bowed from the presence, and had just regained the privacy of the corridor, the chamber door reclosed behind them, when Henry grabbed Cromwell by the collar of his tunic and pinned him up against the wall.

'Who the fuck was that, Cromwell? My intended bride, or her washer woman?'

'That was indeed the Lady Anne of Cleves, Sire.'

'And you expect me to bed *that*? Not even for England, Thomas — not even for England. You have fucked up badly this time, and you may well pay for it with your head.'

XXXI

Jane sighed softly to herself, as she thought wistfully of the precious child two days' hard ride to the north, and the loving man who never failed to give her the affectionate devotion and sexual satisfaction that was so important in her life. And here she was, stuck in Greenwich as lady-in-waiting to a Queen of England who spoke no English, and whose irritating little pooch of a translator trailed behind them wherever they went. She would dearly love to be elsewhere, but Cromwell demanded her loyalty, and she had everything dear to her dependent upon his continued goodwill.

Jane had held Anne's train at her marriage to Henry two weeks previously in the chapel at Greenwich Palace, wondering in her own mind whether or not her precious Grace was fully walking yet, in order to blank out the drone from Thomas Cranmer as he plodded his way through the order of service. Jane had then shown Anne's other Ladies how their mistress was to be prepared for her wedding night, and had retired, wondering which of the happy couple she felt the most sorry for. They had now been married for almost three weeks, but there was nothing to be gained from the inscrutable face of her mistress to indicate how she was faring under the groping sweaty hand of the fattest man at Court.

Henry, however, never missed an opportunity to berate a wincing Cromwell regarding his experience of newly married life.

'Could *you* get it up a fat cow with a face like a man, and sagging tits that resemble over-full wine gourds?' he demanded.

'She smells so bad that I would rather fuck yesterday's cold venison.'

Cromwell was already taxing his brain with strategies to extricate both himself and Henry from the diplomatic mire that he had got them into. An annulment might be the best way forward, even after so short a period, but it would be beyond embarrassing for the King of England to admit that the marriage had not been consummated because of his already widely suspected sexual inadequacy.

Cromwell had dispatched three of his best interrogators back to Cleves to seek other grounds, but it was difficult to believe that someone so plain — and, in Henry's eyes, repulsive — could have lost her maidenhead to anyone with functioning eyesight, or, if Henry was to be believed, a half-developed sense of smell.

Jane was making her way back from the laundry at which she had deposited yet more of her Queen's sweat-stained shifts when Norfolk stepped out of an alcove to block her way down the hallway.

'Viscountess Rochford. Or is it "Mistress Ashton" these days? How goes your daughter — still learning the lessons of life amidst the greenery of Bradgate?'

'Spare me the shit — what do you want?'

'If we are to descend immediately into matters of detail, I wish you to introduce my niece to Court, and secure her a position as a Queen's Lady.'

'And if I am not so minded?' Jane asked with more defiance that she felt.

Norfolk smiled horribly. 'Then a few idle and bored men-at-arms lounging around a field in Leicestershire may not prove adequate for the protection of either an infant girl, or her father, who has aspirations to acquire the throne of England by armed rebellion.'

Jane looked anxiously around to ensure that their conversation was not being overheard. 'That is all you desire — that a niece be made a Queen's Lady, just like the last one?'

'That is all — for the moment. Her name is Catherine Howard. Another Howard, but with less venom than the last one.'

'The last one who was executed?' Jane fired back.

Norfolk smiled. 'If this one goes to the block, rest assured that you will accompany her, along with your traitorous lover. Both he and your daughter Grace will remain safe from harm, if Catherine Howard becomes a Lady-in-Waiting by, shall we say, the beginning of March?'

'You may safely rely upon me,' Jane whispered. 'But can I depend upon your word?'

'The word of a Howard? Do not insult me, my lady. And so good day.'

Catherine Howard became a sparkling, lively and bewitching member of Queen Anne's otherwise sombre retinue within days, and Henry soon had his eye on the new addition to Court.

XXXII

'She is beautiful, both in her looks and her nature, and she is a great credit to her parents,' Kate Calthorpe said as she lifted Grace onto her knee and smiled at Richard. 'Would you like to hold her?'

Richard nodded, then breathed in heavily as Kate leaned across to hand him his daughter. He had learned that Kate had the most delicious and arousing aroma about her person, and he shamelessly took a deep draft while negotiating Grace onto his knee, where she sat gazing up at him with adoring eyes that melted his heart.

'She clearly knows her father,' Kate said as her long fair hair fell gently back onto her light blue mantle. 'Not every child in this wicked world has that blessing bestowed upon them.'

'You were intended for a convent?' Richard asked.

Kate blushed unexpectedly. 'Indeed I was, master, but as events have transpired I count myself fortunate that I was prevented from so doing before I learned that I would much prefer to be wed, and to have children of my own. Little Grace here has taught me that.'

'How can a small child have such an effect?' Richard asked, surprised and somehow elated by her reply.

'You are not a woman,' she smiled back at him through clear eyes the colour of cornflowers in full bloom. 'It is a feeling you get in a certain part of you that God did not create in men. A craving, it might be called. When does the mistress return?'

'She writes that she is likely to be gone for some time,' Richard told her. 'England has a new Queen, and Jane is one of her Ladies.'

'She was one such before, or so I am told,' Kate replied.

'She was indeed. To Queen Jane, and before her Queen Anne.'

'It must be a wonderful opening for a woman, to attend upon a Queen,' Kate speculated out loud. 'So much opportunity to appear at one's best, with fine clothes and rich perfumes — and, of course, the chance to catch the eye of a gentleman such as yourself.'

Something about the way she said it caused a stirring inside Richard's hose, and he found himself urging Jane, in his mind, to return without delay, before matters drifted in a way that would not be good for any of them, and Kate least of all.

Things were not progressing well in Council, and Cromwell was aware of the hostile atmosphere that surrounded him from those around the table, even Cranmer, who seemed concerned to avoid provoking those who were loudly advocating a move back to greater orthodoxy in Church liturgy and practice.

Norfolk had judged the time appropriate to call for an end to any further forays into reform, and to table a series of proposals designed to return the Church, even in its English manifestation, to observances with which the more traditional, God-fearing and downright superstitious felt more comfortable. Transubstantiation would return in order to convert the eucharist into the actual body and blood of Christ, while salvation might once again be sought through the confessional. Finally, all priests were to revert to celibacy, and any marriages entered into during the laxer previous few years were to be annulled by Act of Parliament.

Throughout all the vituperative debate, and most notably that between Cromwell and Norfolk, Henry seemed restless and distracted, except when Norfolk began to push for his final proposal, that any form of heresy should be deemed treasonous. The King was nodding sagely to this formal recognition of his position at the head of matters religious as well as secular when Cromwell could stand it no longer.

'These reforms upon which you are insisting are not for the good of the nation,' he snapped across the table at Norfolk, 'but to prop up your waning support among the bucolic fossils who still stomp around the more isolated counties of the realm. And you propose that anyone who does not abide by these new laws of your making shall be deemed to be traitors. Are you not in danger of setting yourself up against His Majesty?'

There was silence as the two men locked glares. Finally Norfolk broke the tension.

'Master Secretary would of course know all about treason, given the evil schemes of his Senior Clerk.'

This time the silence was almost palpable, and all eyes turned to Cromwell in anticipation of one of his stinging rejoinders. Instead he gathered up his papers and rose from the table. 'If Your Majesty would permit, I have more important matters to attend to across the Channel.'

'Going to inspect your army?' Norfolk called after him, immediately before Cromwell slammed the door on his way out.

'To what was Norfolk alluding?' Henry asked Cromwell the following morning.

Cromwell had enjoyed the advantage of a whole sleepless night in which to prepare his reply. 'I had hoped to be in possession of much more proof than I have at present, Sire, but as you may have been advised, I have several members of the Pole family currently confined within the Tower, and they are slowly revealing details of a plot to challenge your throne.'

'You have had them tortured?' Henry asked, aghast. 'They are ennobled, and it will sit ill with my reputation should they have been harmed.'

'No, Sire, you may rest assured on that score. Although I am bound to observe that the common folk of England, with whom your reputation must best be preserved, would not care too greatly were I to rack a member of the nobility.'

'This challenge to my throne,' Henry persisted, 'was Norfolk correct in his claim that it is being led by one of your clerks?'

Cromwell laughed for effect, then explained. 'On the contrary, Sire, it was one of my clerks who discovered it, and Norfolk seeks simply to divert attention from what this same clerk learned about Norfolk's own role in it.'

Henry looked stunned. 'You say that Norfolk is plotting against my throne?'

'I cannot say so without further evidence upon which I may have him arrested and conveyed to the Tower, which is why I have thus far not made Your Majesty aware of the full extent of the treachery. At present it is only the word of my clerk against that of Norfolk, but you may rest assured that those who were to be its main actors are safely in the Tower.'

'You are planning another journey to Cleves, as you advised Council? Is there ought to suggest that this treason may be traced back to there?'

'Would that it could, Sire, since that would be an end to another difficulty that we must confront.'

'It is *I* who have the difficulty, Thomas, thanks to your incompetence. I must own that the Lady Anne at present seems content for me simply to fumble with her duckies and kiss her goodnight, but should word leak out of my inability to do the deed with her, I shall be a laughing stock. Thank God that she still speaks no English, but leave her Ladies in no doubt that I will have their heads if one of them so much as hints that the hairy furrow from Cleves has not yet been ploughed by me.'

'We cannot therefore plead non-consummation,' Cromwell mused out loud, 'but yet there is hope. I journey again to Cleves to test for myself a rumour brought back by one of my interrogators that Anne was formerly betrothed to Francis of Lorraine.'

'Did he bed her? If so, he must have been in the throes of desperation.'

'The arrangement was called off before either of them was fifteen, and without them meeting,' Cromwell explained, 'but under our law — which Your Majesty may need to amend for that purpose — it may be that this is sufficient prior contract to justify an annulment, particularly if the lady can be bought off.'

'It is to be hoped that she can, Thomas, if you are to make proper amends to me. Put shortly, you dropped us into this pile of shit, and you must dig us out. On another, but perhaps related, matter, have you seen the new Lady at Court?'

'I regret that my duties for Your Majesty are currently so onerous that I have little opportunity for social occasions. To whom do you refer?'

'Her name is Catherine, and she is Norfolk's niece.'

'God preserve us, not another Boleyn?'

'No, a Howard this time. A lovely little piece, quite sporting and lively. A pleasant diversion from the German misery. Would that you had brought me Catherine Howard instead of her.'

'Perhaps if the lady from Cleves can be persuaded to relinquish any hopes of the Crown?'

'She may as well, since she most certainly won't be realising any hopes of my cock. Catherine Howard, on the other hand... See to it, Thomas — and shortly.'

Cromwell wasted no time in summoning Jane to his suite of rooms on the ground floor of Placentia Palace, and seating her in front of him at his desk. 'You have a new Lady at Court? Catherine Howard?'

Jane sniffed her disapproval. 'A flighty baggage insisted on by Norfolk, under threat of proceeding against Richard and Grace, despite the guard at Bradgate. She seems artless and frivolous, but what of her?'

'Henry is lusting after her already,' Cromwell confided. 'First he must be rid of the Flanders Mare. How go matters between her and the King, so far as you have been advised?'

Jane screwed her face in contemptuous disgust. 'She speaks only of fumblings beneath the sheets, and seems to think that this is sufficient behaviour between husband and wife, if accompanied by a kiss morning and night. When may I return to Bradgate?'

'Not yet, if we are to see this through. I am currently seeking the means to annul the marriage with the current lady of the royal bedchamber, but then you may find yourself in the service of another Howard niece.'

'Is there to be no end to this? How many wives does Henry intend to have?'

'If I knew that, I would be on firmer ground. But until I have the evidence against Norfolk, I must continue to walk on eggs. As must you.'

'If only life could be much simpler,' Jane complained. 'I never imagined, when I first came to Court, that I would be drawn into such intrigue and back-stabbing.'

'It is the price we pay to be guaranteed food in our bellies and tiles over our heads,' Cromwell reminded her. 'Now go and attend on your lady, and see what else she can tell us of the secrets of her bedchamber.'

Less than a week later Cromwell had received the reassuring confirmation from Cleves, and had begun negotiations with one of its ducal daughters for her to submit to annulment proceedings in return for a lavish pay-out that included Richmond Palace, where Henry had spent much of his youth, and which had been his father's favourite residence. Another gift, more ironic, was that of Hever Castle, where Henry had courted Anne Boleyn and which had been forfeited by her family upon her execution. There were other regal properties besides, plus a promise that Anne would henceforth be treated with the highest respect and regard and would always be welcome at Court as 'Our Beloved Sister', and with precedence over anyone bar any subsequent Queen and the royal daughters Mary and Elizabeth.

To show his gratitude for this solution, Henry gifted Cromwell the vacant titles of Earl of Essex and Earl of Oxford, to be assumed when their current incumbents died.

XXXIII

Richard had received a letter from Jane, expressing her sadness at the fact that she was obliged to remain at Court, but advising him that as a result Richard and Grace had been promised continued immunity from any threat to their lives from Norfolk.

In reliance on this, he had begun making more regular trips to Knighton, along with Kate, who supervised Grace while she demonstrated her new-found mobility by racing up and down the recently scythed lawns at the front of the house, calling for 'Dada' and 'Atey' to admire her antics. Then when she had tired herself out she was put to sleep in a new cot purchased in Leicester, and Richard and Kate politely declined any offer of food from Hester Cudworth in their enthusiasm to prepare their own meals.

Once night fell, Kate insisted upon sleeping, with Grace at her side, in the former cell occupied by her Aunt Mary in her days as a nun, and from Richard's perspective this was perhaps as well.

They had been at Knighton for three days, supervising the new tapestries that would further protect the main hall from any draughts caused by slight imperfections in the plasterwork. They had sent their small escort back to Bradgate, following Jane's written assurance that they faced no immediate threat from Norfolk, so they looked up and exchanged puzzled looks when they heard the sound of horsemen thudding through the main entrance gate. Richard stepped outside, with Kate behind him carrying Grace in her arms, just as the apparent commander of ten armed men, all bearing the Norfolk livery, dismounted carrying a small scroll of vellum.

'Sir Richard Ashton?'

'I am he.'

'I have here a warrant for your arrest on a count of treason. I am to convey you forthwith to the Tower.'

'On whose authority?'

'My Lord of Norfolk.'

'I have committed no treason — unlike he who has ordered my arrest.'

'Tell that to the Constable of the Tower. My orders are merely to convey you there.'

Richard looked round helplessly at Kate. 'See to Grace, and ensure that Sir Henry is informed without delay.'

His last vision of Kate was of tears streaming down her face as she assured him that she would take care of Grace 'as if she were my own, because that is how she feels to me', then he assured the captain of his escort that he would give them no trouble if he might be allowed to make the journey to the Tower on his own horse.

Four days later he was installed in a tiny chamber in the Bell Tower, cold, hungry, and terrified by stories he had heard of what they did to prisoners in this awful place. He could only hope that Cromwell had been informed.

'You go too far!' Cromwell yelled at Norfolk as he burst past the two guards on the entrance door to his suite of rooms in Whitehall Palace. 'You have ordered the arrest of my Senior Clerk Sir Richard Ashton on a charge of treason for which you have no evidence. And for that matter, no authority!'

'I had the authority of Lord High Steward when I presided over the trial of my own niece for treason,' Norfolk sneered back at him. 'So far as I am aware, that title has not been withdrawn since, and if it is sufficient for one count of treason, why not another, by some lowly clerk who is far lower in status than Queen of England, as Anne was when she went to the Tower?'

'Where is your evidence?' Cromwell demanded.

'Also in the Tower. Geoffrey Pole required only one turn of the rack screw to loosen his tongue, and he was more than happy to subscribe his name to a confession of his own treason, on an evening when Sir Richard Ashton was in attendance, in his capacity as the pretended long-lost Yorkist heir to the throne. You would be well advised to seek another clerk, Master Secretary.'

'The King shall hear of this!'

'He has already heard of it, and what is more he has commended my loyal and timely action. He is now left wondering how such a traitor came to be in service so close to the throne, and naturally I was obliged to advise him that Ashton came into your service with no prior experience of such duties, plucked — as it were — from obscurity and made to believe that he was the rightful King of England.'

'If you have him tortured, I swear to God that I will run you through personally!' Cromwell yelled.

Norfolk smirked yet again as he turned to the usher who had been standing in the corner of the chamber. 'You presumably heard that? Threatening death to the loyal servant of the King who has but lately unearthed a plot against the throne. I would imagine that such a threat would merely confirm the man's own complicity in the matter.'

'Damn you, Norfolk — you have overreached yourself this time!' Cromwell thundered as he swept out of the chamber and down the hallway to the royal apartments, where he demanded to be admitted.

'Sire,' he announced as he bent down on one knee, and nodded brusquely at the dark haired beauty who sat at a window seat in the corner, 'please pardon this unscheduled intrusion, but there is a matter of grave urgency with which I must speak with you. In strict privacy,' he added, as he made an informed guess as to who the lady in the window seat might be.

Henry turned to the woman and smiled lovingly. 'Catherine, my sweet, you will appreciate that being King of England brings with it certain duties that cannot be avoided. Pray leave us and return to your chamber, where I will send word for your return without delay, once this business had been disposed of.'

Once Catherine Howard had withdrawn with a kiss blown in Henry's direction, and with a dark stare at Cromwell, Henry took the initiative. 'I presume that you are here in an attempt to save the skin of your traitorous clerk?'

'He is no traitor, Sire. Quite the opposite — he was offered the opportunity to make a bid for the throne, to which in the circumstances he might be thought to be entitled, but far from seizing that chance, he lost no time in reporting it to me.'

'He was meeting with Margaret Pole and her tribe of ungrateful traitors, as Norfolk so advises me?'

'He came upon it by accident, Sire. He was merely visiting his great aunt.'

'He is related to Margaret Pole?' Henry asked. 'If that be so, then surely that alone proves his guilt. The entire family has been plotting in the Yorkist camp for generations, and have only survived to this day because of the mercy of first my father, and now me.'

'Hear me out please, Sire,' Cromwell pleaded. 'You mention your father's reign — the Henry Tudor who left you the crown of England. You will recall that my former master the Cardinal served him faithfully, as indeed he did you in your early years.'

'Yes, of course. His death was most unfortunate.'

'Tragic, Sire. He was the most loyal servant any king could wish for, and he was betrayed by treachery close to the throne.'

'I need not be reminded of that, Cromwell,' Henry glowered with a facial expression that those who knew him recognised as the first rumbling before the volcano blew. 'What is the point to all this?'

'Before his death, as the result of two deathbed confessions by men who had been involved, my master learned that the man hung by your father as a pretender — Perkin Warbeck — was indeed the rightful Richard, Duke of York, and the remaining Yorkist heir to the throne.'

'Wolsey breached the sanctity of the confessional? Perhaps it was God's punishment that he died when he did.'

'He kept silent all his life in order to protect you, Sire, since those behind the murder of the older brother Edward were paid by your grandmother. But the Cardinal's own conscience compelled him to disclose these matters to me, shortly before his death in Leicester.'

'Even if I believe this fairy tale,' Henry objected, 'surely, since Warbeck has been dead these many years, there can be no ongoing threat.'

'His grandson lives on, Sire.'

'And where might he be now?'

'In the Tower, on the order of Norfolk.'

The light of understanding lit up Henry's face. 'Your clerk? Ashton?'

'The very same, Sire.'

226

'Surely, then, Norfolk was correct to have him arrested? He shall be deprived of his head without further delay! And how can I be sure that you did not encourage his plot against me? After all, you were the one who introduced him to Court.'

'If I were guilty of such treason, would I stand here and admit it?' Cromwell challenged him.

Henry smiled. 'Indeed not, you are too wily for that, Thomas. But why should I condemn Norfolk's actions in having Ashton removed to a place where he can be of no further danger?'

'In this, Sire. Ashton was offered the opportunity to claim the throne as the figurehead of an uprising being planned by Margaret Pole and her family. But not only did he refuse, he escaped at the first opportunity, and at considerable risk to his own life he revealed the plot to his then host, Sir Henry Grey, Marquess of Dorset, at Bradgate. Dorset, in turn, advised Suffolk, and Suffolk advised me.'

'So Charles Brandon knew of it as well?'

'Indeed, Sire, but on my counsel he remained silent, in the hope that the entire nest of conspirators could be emptied all at the one time. But one of them — the real leader — remains not only at large, but as close to the throne as I am.'

'Whom do you accuse?'

'Norfolk, Sire.'

Henry's jaw dropped, then he burst out laughing. 'It is well known that you and Norfolk have no love for each other, but surely this takes your feverish fantasies too far? Norfolk has ever been a loyal subject, and I shall shortly be marrying his niece.'

Cromwell swallowed hard. 'Please forgive me, Sire, but I am bound to remind you of your previous misfortune in marrying a former niece of Norfolk.'

Henry turned bright crimson, and gripped the arm of the chair in which he was seated. Then he took several deep breaths and looked back at Cromwell as his natural colour returned. 'By God, Thomas, you took a grave risk in reminding me of my own folly in bedding *that* witch! This matter must be of considerable importance to you, that you were prepared to hazard your neck in that fashion.'

'I have ever served you loyally, Sire, and if England is to be saved at the expense of my neck, so be it. But I also wish to preserve the neck of an innocent man who has risked his own life this past year by holding into himself his knowledge of Norfolk's true treachery. And that is why Norfolk has had Ashton consigned to the Tower — he knows too much.'

Henry sat deep in thought, during which Cromwell held his breath and prayed, searching the King's face for any sign of how his thoughts might be inclining. Eventually Henry looked up with a pained smile.

'Take yourself off to the Tower, Thomas, and convey my personal command that no harm is to befall Ashton, but that he must be kept under constant guard. In the meantime I will summon Suffolk, and perhaps also Dorset. If they confirm your story, Ashton will be transferred, under close arrest, back to Bradgate under the personal guard of Henry Grey. If he removes himself from there, I shall know the truth of it, and both of you will pay with your heads. Now leave me, and send word to Lady Catherine to re-join me here.'

A week later, Richard looked up with a pang of fear as the door to his cell opened, and his jailor Bedingfield stuck his grimy head round the door.

'Yer free ter go, yer miserable shit. Yer can thank Master Secretary fer that, but afore yer goes ter thank 'im, I suggest yer 'as a good wash.'

Three days before Grace's first birthday Richard was delivered back to Bradgate under an armed escort led by Henry Grey. As Richard dismounted by the stable door, he heard the urgent scurrying of light feet behind him, and turned in time to see Kate Calthorpe standing, and visibly trembling, her face dripping tears of joy. Their eyes met, and as they walked instinctively towards each other Kate was the first to speak, in a voice shaking with emotion.

'Thank God! I have prayed three times daily for your safe return. You may wish to go into the house and embrace your daughter. But before you do that, in God's mercy embrace *me* as well!'

XXXIV

For the second time in a month, Cromwell presented himself at the lodgings of the Constable of the Tower, Sir William Kingston, but this time he asked to speak personally to Amos Bedingfield, the most senior of Kingston's staff, and the most experienced in the administration of 'the question', as various appalling forms of torture were euphemistically described. Bedingfield presented himself with an apprehensive look on his face, and Cromwell blanched as he stared, transfixed, at the leather apron around the man's ample gut, signifying that he had been summoned part way through a process involving hot irons. Cromwell handed him a jingling bag of coins, and man's face relaxed in a sooty smile.

'What d'yer want ter know, Master Secretary?'

'You racked a prisoner called Geoffrey Pole some time ago?'

'Yeah, but 'e weren't no fun. Give in after only one turn.'

'What did he tell you?'

'What I wanted to 'ear, same as they all does, why?'

'He gave you names?'

'Sure did — never fails.'

'Did you suggest any names to him in advance?'

Bedingfield's face fell. 'Only the one I were asked ter get.'

'Richard Ashton?'

'Yeah, that were 'im.'

'And who asked you to secure that name?'

'Norfolk.'

'Presumably he paid you for that little service?'

'O' course — just like you just did.'

'Quite. But what I just paid you for was any *other* name that Pole might have mentioned in his enthusiasm to stop the cogs turning.'

'Only Norfolk 'isself, but by then 'e were singing art all sorts o' names — mostly folk what 'e were related ter.'

'He definitely named The Duke of Norfolk when asked who had been at that meeting in Bisham?'

'I were only told ter ask fer names, not places. But 'e definitely mentioned Norfolk — that were just afore 'e shit 'isself.'

'Thank you *very* much, Master Bedingfield,' Cromwell replied, 'you've been most helpful. And of considerable service to England.'

Cromwell walked back across Tower Green with a broad smile and wondered whether to disclose what he knew before or after the royal wedding to which he had been invited.

'What do you want *this* time?' Jane demanded as 'Uncle Norfolk' was announced. 'And when may I be reunited with my daughter?'

'All in good time,' Norfolk smiled unpleasantly. 'I may see my way to having her brought down here, since I am advised that Queens' Ladies may accommodate their own families here in Whitehall. Unfortunately your boy lover is under house arrest at Bradgate, by order of the King, but even that might be modified should you agree to my proposal.'

'Just get to the point.'

'The Queen Anne, whom you formerly served, spoke with you regarding her doings with the King in bed?'

'She did, but in confidence, as I always understood.'

'The time for confidences is over, I regret. The matter of the annulment is to be debated in Council, and I wish to be able to present it with a testimonial from you that confirms Anne's own words to you that she and Henry were never, shall we say, "carnally coupled"?'

'If you mean did Henry fuck her, then the answer is no,' Jane said bluntly.

'Excellent,' Norfolk replied, 'although we might express that in terms more suited to the royal bed.'

'A fuck is a fuck, whoever is engaging in it,' Jane retorted. 'Perhaps someone should have instructed your late nephew that it is normally conducted between two adults.'

'Quite, but you have since increased your own experience of such matters with that snivelling little clerk of Cromwell's, have you not?'

'If you mean Sir Richard, I am proud to admit that I have,' Jane said sarcastically, 'and I burn to do so again. So once again I ask — when may I leave the Queen's service?'

'That rather depends upon which Queen you have in mind,' Norfolk replied. 'You will of course be aware that my niece Catherine will soon become your next mistress?'

'Indeed, and by all accounts she knows more about fucking than her cousin George ever did,' Jane replied tartly. 'What hold do you have over me, now that Richard and Grace are officially under the protection of Dorset?'

'Test my patience just once more, and you will have that question answered, to your considerable cost,' Norfolk replied threateningly. 'Your next task will be to serve Queen Catherine, and keep her from her more dangerous inclinations. She is given to carnal lapses with quite the wrong people, which has at least given her the skills to keep Henry's cock pointing in her direction, and in a rigid state. If she steps from the path of marital virtue just once, she will take us all down with her.'

'You alone, surely?' Jane suggested, to which Norfolk replied with a wry grin.

'Trust me, *niece*, when the Howards go down, you go down with them.'

'I'm *so* sorry,' Kate sobbed as she lay across Richard's naked chest in his bedchamber, her long blonde hair spread across it like ripening wheat in an autumn stack. 'I have never behaved like that before, and should you choose to dismiss me from your service, I will of course leave without whimper or accusation. It was pure lust, I imagine, for which I will penance myself horribly, but nothing could be a worse penance than being dismissed from the presence of you and the child I adore equally.'

'Hush,' Richard comforted her as he stroked her head and regained his breath from the most devastating experience of his life. 'It takes two to behave like that, and if I am honest I have often dreamed of how it might be with you. But the experience was more beautiful than even the fantasy of it.'

'What of my mistress?'

'We are not married, as you know, and have only ever been drawn together for the convenient quenching of those natural lusts that build up after some time of abstinence. But with you it was like — oh, I just don't know how to describe it. You love Grace as well?'

'With all my heart, but that is perhaps because she has come partly from you. If I fall into motherhood as the result of what we have done today, I'll be even happier — if that's possible. But you have to think of Jane Rochford.'

'How can I, after this? And, in any case, she is lost to me, while she is at Court, and I am imprisoned here at Bradgate. For all I know she's already found another lover — she cannot survive too long without going to it, as I discovered. I was just another one that she made use of — as I did of her, of course.'

'So — no love either way?'

'Not on my part, anyway. Just lust, but nothing like that will satisfy me ever again after what we just did. I must have you forever, dearest Kate. Will you consent to marry me?'

He was a little concerned when he felt her entire body shaking, and realised that his chest was beginning to soak from her tears. She replied in a choking whisper, and he gently lifted her head to gaze at her red, tear-drenched cheeks.

'Was that a yes?' he asked nervously, and she nodded vigorously, then collapsed back onto his chest with what sounded like groans and shrieks of sheer joy.

XXXV

Cromwell looked down the Council table in surprise as he breezed in late as usual and noticed the absence of Henry in his usual seat at the head, and several gaps still existing further down. There was usually a mad scramble for seats around the table itself, and Cromwell, often one of the last to arrive, had spent many a Council meeting with one arse cheek perched on a window ledge. He sat down and arranged his papers, then realised that there was not the usual distracting chatter among Council members.

'What has happened to Norfolk?' he asked. 'Did he indicate his intended absence? And where is His Majesty?'

It fell ominously silent, until Suffolk took pity on him and told him, 'You'll see Norfolk soon enough.'

Cromwell looked across enquiringly at Cranmer, and his blood froze when his customary ally could not look him in the eye, but dropped his glance to the table as the colour drained from his face. Then the door burst open, and Norfolk stormed in, accompanied by four men at arms in the Tudor livery. He strode purposefully towards Cromwell, who rose to meet him, and with a gleeful smirk Norfolk reached out and ripped the medallion of St George from the ribbon on which it had been suspended around Cromwell's neck.

Cromwell's mind flashed back to a similar scene when Norfolk had snatched the Lord Chancellor's seal from the Cardinal, and with a sinking feeling of history repeating itself he dimly heard the words, 'You are under arrest on a charge of high treason, and my orders are to convey you to the Tower.'

There were no gasps of surprise around the Council table, and suddenly the earlier uneasy silence was explained.

Cromwell glared back at Norfolk defiantly. 'Where is your evidence?'

'It lies in an alleyway off Thames Street, where an officer of the Tower was hacked to death last night, as he left a low whorehouse. The men responsible were said to be wearing Cromwell livery, and Sir William Kingston testifies that you visited the man yesterday and gave him money.'

'Bedingfield?' Cromwell demanded disbelievingly, as he remembered how the last witness he had found to an act of treachery by Norfolk — on that occasion the man who had forged the papers that led to the Cardinal's final ruin — had ended his days face down in the Thames.

Norfolk sneered as he looked round triumphantly at the remaining members of Council who had also heard Cromwell identify the victim. 'You see? He can name the man. The man he had silenced because he could reveal more regarding his plot to seize the crown using his young dupe Ashton.'

'Bedingfield had just given me *your* name as the person behind that plot!' Cromwell yelled back at him. 'Kingston was present when he did so!'

'Kingston has already been closely questioned, and claims only that Bedingfield named you. Take him away!'

Hours later, confined in the same cell within the Bell Tower that he had once visited in order to take advantage of the terrified and naive Mark Smeaton, Cromwell realised the full extent of his isolation. Kingston had presumably been bribed or threatened out of telling the truth, Bedingfield had been assassinated on Norfolk's order, and King Henry was refusing all Cromwell's pleas for an audience in which he might clear his name.

When, a week later, Cromwell learned that he was under a bill of attainder that avoided any possibility of a trial, he also surmised that the latest royal fancy, Catherine Howard, must have prevailed upon Henry in the same way that a former queen had brought Wolsey low. History was indeed repeating itself, but this time the victim was the man who had sought vengeance against the Boleyn whore, and would now pay the price for his skills in deviousness and betrayal.

Cromwell knelt in his cell and prayed to God that the end would be merciful, at the same time seeking His absolution for any offence he may have committed in His eyes by removing the Pope, and all that he represented, from English religious life.

XXXVI

Jane Rochford gently combed Catherine Howard's hair into the specially designed wedding veil.

'Do you miss your daughter?' Catherine asked.

Jane nodded. 'Indeed I do, my Lady, and perhaps you might give leave for her to be brought to Court once you are Queen?'

'It shall be my pleasure,' Catherine cooed back reassuringly, then looked down reflectively. 'It is strange, is it not, how some women either crave motherhood, or take to it lovingly once a child is born? For myself, I have always feared that I would fall into motherhood before I was able to complete my progress through the Court.'

Jane looked down in embarrassment, but Catherine seemed determined to revel in the details of her promiscuous past.

'Do not be shocked, dearest Jane — you must know how it is for women like ourselves, who burn for a man inside us. I hope that Henry proves a robust and eager lover, as he has thus far promised to be.'

At almost exactly the same time, on the same day, a noisy baying crowd cheered the humble procession onto Tower Hill and gathered as closely as the guards would allow to the block stained with years of dried aristocratic blood.

Cromwell made the customary short speech commending King Henry to his subjects — the price of not being hanged, drawn and quartered — said his final prayer, then lay his head sideways on the evil smelling block, whose ominous brown stains probably commemorated the memories of men he had sent there. Innocent men, like Mark Smeaton, Harry Norris and Francis Weston.

His last thought was of the Cardinal, as the executioner grunted with the effort of lifting the axe he had sharpened only that morning. The blade flashed, the crowd roared their appreciation, and Cromwell's campaign for his perception of justice was at an end.

The news was brought to Henry as he sat with the other guests at the wedding banquet at Baynards Castle, which brought back memories, for him, of playing the child host at the wedding of his fifteen-year-old brother Arthur to the Infanta Katarina. He nodded at the news and remembered his regret when the tidings had been brought to him of the death of Cardinal Thomas Wolsey, and how angry Thomas Cromwell had been when conveying them. For a brief moment he wondered if he would ever regret ordering Cromwell's execution, then became diverted when his new bride leaned to one side and kissed his cheek.

'Will I be allowed my own household, as you promised, my sweet?' she asked seductively, and on that day of all days Henry would have granted her anything.

And so before very long it became obvious to Jane that her main function was to act as a decoy, guide, messenger and liar for her new Queen, as night after night Catherine played host to former and current lovers after slipping from Henry's side, following another failed attempt at coitus. He was probably now too fat, but he seemed also to have no bone left in his shaft, and he would roll off her with a grunted apology and a request that she complete with her hand what he was unable to achieve in her cunny. But there was no shortage of reserves, and she took care to always be back by Henry's side when he awoke and made his usual noisy progress across the bedchamber to his close stool.

Then there was Thomas Culpepper, one of Henry's favourite Gentlemen of the King's Privy Chamber. He was in regular attendance during Queen Catherine's afternoon audiences, and Jane was reminded of how Richard Ashton had suddenly appeared from nowhere, in the service of the now dead Master Secretary, and how easy it had been to seduce him.

Before long Jane was being required by her mistress to pass notes back and forth between Catherine and Thomas Culpepper. She never read them, nor was she ever advised of their contents, but there could be little doubt that they were lewd. But although the likes of Mannox and Dereham came and went in the small hours, there was no sign of Thomas Culpepper creeping up the back stairs for as long as the King was in residence.

Then came the day when the Archbishop of Canterbury was announced as Jane sat in her private room at Whitehall Palace, embroidering a small gown that she hoped would fit Grace, insofar as she could picture in her mind how much her beloved child might have grown during their separation.

Thomas Cranmer bowed perfunctorily, and Jane indicated for him to take a seat.

'Have I become religious without knowing it?' Jane asked sarcastically, and Cranmer bowed his head once again.

'I can only hope for that happy day, my lady, but I come to ask if you have retained any fond memory of Master Secretary.'

Jane snorted quietly. 'He went the same way as the man whose memory he was seeking to restore in the King's eyes. He failed to appreciate the extent of Henry's lust, and the inconstancy of his loyalties.'

'Were I to repeat those words, you would be his next victim. But I come instead to seek confirmation of information that has come into my hands regarding the prior behaviour of our new Queen.'

'And why would that be of interest to a man of the cloth?'

Cranmer smiled in embarrassment. 'I seem to have caught the disease of my former confidante Master Cromwell. I seek justice for his death.'

'Against Henry? That would indeed be a dangerous road to tread, as Cromwell's death and Richard Ashton's confinement at Bradgate can attest.'

'Not Henry — Catherine and Norfolk.'

'I would have no qualms about ridding myself of Uncle Norfolk, but you are asking me to betray my mistress?'

'Merely to confirm what others have alluded to. I have reason to be suspicious of the tales they tell, since they themselves speak out of revenge, because when Catherine became Queen they did not secure the preferment they hoped for, having served her in her previous residences. They speak in particular of Henry Mannox, her former music tutor, and Francis Dereham, former Secretary to the Dowager Duchess, both of whom have joined her at Court.'

'What gain is there to me, should I confirm these tales?'

'If Catherine goes the same way as Henry's other wives, Norfolk's undoubted hold over you and Richard Ashton would be at an end, and you could be reunited with both him and your daughter. And not before time, I am sad to relate — it seems that Sir Richard has taken up with your daughter's nurse of late.'

'Kate? That inconsequential piece of servitude? If she has become his whore, so much the better. While he is going to it with her, he is not being ensnared by someone more worthy of his rank.'

'But do you wish to remain in servitude yourself, to Salome reincarnate?'

'Of course not. And if it will gladden your heart, and suit whatever devious purpose you pursue, I can confirm that Queen Catherine has more than once confided in me — although it sounded more like a boast — that she had allowed both the men that you mentioned the benefit of her favours. Does that satisfy you?'

'Indeed,' Cranmer confirmed with a grateful smile, 'although it may prove to be only the start. A prior carnal relationship is hardly something that Henry himself can deny, and not always within the sanctity of marriage. It may be that she can explain those away simply as the irresponsible and largely uncontrollable bodily urges of youth. But if these intrigues are ongoing...'

'They are, my Lord Archbishop, be in no doubt of that. She creeps from Henry's bed almost nightly in order to have to do with either Mannox or Dereham, but most usually Dereham. But she aims higher, I believe.'

'How high?' Cranmer asked eagerly.

'To the Privy Chamber, no less. Thomas Culpepper.'

Cranmer's eyes widened slightly as he nodded. 'If you could but bring me evidence of transgressions between the Queen and Culpepper, that would most certainly be an end to her.'

'And Culpepper, no doubt.'

'Most certainly.'

'Leave it with me, my lord Archbishop, and I shall send you word when I have the necessary evidence.'

Fate played into all their hands when Henry decided to take a trip to Dover, leaving Catherine behind at Hampton Court. The entire Queen's Court remained with her, and when Thomas Culpepper excused himself from journeying south with Henry, and appeared at the next afternoon audience, Catherine slid a small note from her bodice and handed it to Jane with a whispered instruction. 'See that Master Culpepper receives this ere the afternoon is out.'

An hour later Culpepper rose to leave, and Jane accompanied him to the doors. Then, as she had once done with Richard Ashton, she guided him a few yards down the hallway and handed him the note.

As he read it his eyes lit up and his smile broadened. 'Tell your mistress eleven of the clock.'

He had just signed his own death warrant.

XXXVII

Henry rose from his first morning prayers since his return to his private chapel inside Hampton Court and finally noticed the note left on the prayer stool in front of his own. It was addressed to him, and therefore he opened it, and remained on his knees as, spellbound, he read its lengthy contents. Then with a howl of rage he shot to his feet and stormed out of the chapel and into his Audience Chamber to the side, yelling to an usher to summon the Duke of Suffolk.

Charles Brandon entered the presence cautiously, since he had been able to hear the raving and shouting halfway down the hall on his approach. He was barely through the door when Henry, his face incandescent with rage, bellowed a curt instruction. 'Arrest Norfolk and bring him to me — by the bollocks if necessary!'

Ten minutes later, as Norfolk stood with his head bowed and surrounded by royal guards bearing halberds, trying not to look at Henry's face twisted in a horrible combination of rage and grief, his worst fears were realised.

'Do you breed nothing but whores in your family, Norfolk?'

'Majesty?'

'Don't "Majesty" me, you lump of whore-mastering slime! Just read that, and then be prepared to argue as to why you deserve to retain your head!'

Henry handed over the note, and there seemed to be little point in Norfolk commenting that he recognised the delicate hand of Archbishop Cranmer. In any case, its contents were enough to make his stomach lurch.

It was all there. The prior carnal relationships with Mannox and Dereham, and now the latest betrayal with Culpepper, all dating back almost to the date of Catherine's wedding to Henry. Enough to guarantee his niece's appointment with the headsman, along with several others, but they were now lost anyway, and his best hope was to plead total ignorance.

'This is to be regretted, Sire...' he began, before being shouted down.

'*Regretted?!*' Henry screamed. 'It is to be more than "regretted", Thomas Howard! You knew that your niece was such a whore, and yet you led her to my bed nevertheless?'

'Not I, Sire,' Norfolk wheedled as he sank to his knees. 'If these rumours be true, then the fault surely lies with those responsible for her supervision.'

'And why should she need "supervision", as you term it? If she was as pure and maidenly as was pretended to me, then she should have been allowed her freedom without other whores as her jailers! You knew, did you not?'

'No, Sire, I swear I did not! She was strictly supervised by the Dowager Duchess before ere she came to Court, and since then I had assumed that the attendance upon her of certain experienced Queen's Ladies would be sufficient, since of course she was most nights with Your Majesty.'

'Not for the *whole* night, it would seem!' Henry spat back. 'On my order, Culpepper has been arrested, and his chamber is being searched. Should these vile accusations be proved, I shall be keeping my headsman very busy in the coming weeks, and it behoves you to tell me *now* which of the Queen's Ladies was responsible for her "supervision", as you choose to call it.'

'That would be Jane Rochford, Sire.'

Henry seemed to calm down somewhat on hearing this, and his face set in a sneer. 'That would make a great deal of sense, since she was also attending upon the former Queen Anne when she betrayed me with Smeaton and all the others.' He turned to address the guards. 'Pass on the order for the arrest of Viscountess Rochford. Then she can be escorted to the Tower along with Culpepper, Mannox and Dereham. As for you, Norfolk, you would be as well quitting my sight while you still retain your head. But do not grow too attached to it while this matter is being fully investigated.'

Six months later, in March of 1542, news was relayed to Bradgate that Richard and Kate could now make plans for their wedding without fear of recrimination. Jane Rochford had gone to the same block, on the same day, as her former mistress, and former Queen, Catherine Howard. Dereham and Culpepper had suffered death in the manner of common criminals, at Tyburn, where a jeering mob had watched as Culpepper's head flew into the dirt following its severance on a block, while Dereham suffered the traitor's death of being hung, drawn and quartered. Two months later Catherine and Jane Rochford had been executed, one after the other, by an axe blow on Tower Green, and Jane had been obliged to lay her head on a block still smeared with the gore of the mistress she had served only too well.

Richard walked out of the house after receiving the news from his host Henry Grey, who had it by letter from his father-in-law Suffolk. It was a clear cold day in early spring, and as Richard's eye fell on the daffodils that had bravely poked their stems out of the grass to announce their impending yellow blooming, he took it as a symbol of new life generally, and his in particular.

It was reported that Norfolk was in virtual hiding, penning one cringing letter after another to a still irate Henry, seeking to convince his monarch that he had been as badly duped by Catherine as had Henry. There was therefore unlikely to be any further risk from him, but Richard was still apprehensive that in his desperation to save his own neck Norfolk would seek to implicate Richard further in his alleged ambition to seize the throne to which he was entitled by birth. However, Suffolk had also suggested that Richard's best option might be to play the innocent that he was, and resume his occupation of his estate at Knighton, thereby signifying that he had nothing to hide.

He had certainly gained nothing by being the great-grandson of the last Yorkist king, and indeed it had brought nothing but death and hardship to almost all of those associated with him. Cromwell had succeeded in taking his revenge on Queen Anne for the death of the Cardinal, but had reached too far in seeking to bring down that most devious, duplicitous and black-hearted villain Norfolk, who still survived to wreak more havoc throughout the realm in his vicious continued grip on power. Richard himself now had his own estate, and had been knighted by the King, but was he much further advanced for all the deaths that he had witnessed? What did he have to show for being removed from a more humble estate in Wiltshire six years ago?

He heard a small voice behind him calling 'Dadda!', and he turned to smile at the little girl who ran down the slope towards him, arms flailing and feet stumbling slightly on the uneven grass. She was being hastily followed by the smiling woman she had taken to calling 'Momma', the woman who had been the closest to a mother she had ever known, who loved her as her own, and would no doubt love her no less when in a few months' time she gave birth to the burgeoning lump inside her own belly.

Surely this answered his question? Despite the many deaths he had witnessed — most of them unjust — there was hope for his own future, if he kept well away from Courtly politics. There was no future in seeking to claim a lost crown in which he had no interest anyway.

All that he wanted from life was heading down the slope towards him, and there was a lot to be said for being a virtual nobody in this world.

A NOTE TO THE READER

Dear Reader,

Thank you for joining me in this romp through the bawdy tumultuous middle years of the reign of Henry VIII.

As Henry lurched from one wife to another, rivals for power fought between themselves behind his throne, but even these senior Courtiers seem to have eluded the searchlights that subsequent historians and novelists focused on the leading players. This makes the middle Tudor period a fertile land for writers like myself, seeking to delve more deeply into this whirlwind period of English history.

There can be little doubt that Anne Boleyn was the architect of her own downfall, allowing rumours of her infidelity to be employed against her when Henry grew tired of her shrill tongue. The first blush of lust and romance had faded to a mere memory by the time that the more docile Jane Seymour caught Henry's eye, and it's a matter of historical record that the largely false charges against Anne proved highly convenient for the husband who was seeking to put her aside.

But rumours require willing distributors, and what could be more feasible than the suggestion that the most eager of these should be the man devoted to the memory of his mentor Cardinal Thomas Wolsey? It had been largely Anne, with the active encouragement of her uncle the Duke of Norfolk, who had hounded Wolsey to his death by pouring falsehoods into Henry's ear, and it was poetic justice for Anne to fall by the same sword when Thomas Cromwell sensed that the time was ripe for revenge. I am by no means the first to spot his hand on the scabbard.

But whereas Anne was laughably easy to dispose of, her uncle proved to be altogether a different challenge. He was more devious than Cromwell, and in many important ways better connected, and he hadn't survived for all of his sixty odd years in the clash of battle and the intrigue of Privy Council only to be brought down by an upstart public servant whose father had been a blacksmith in an obscure London suburb.

Thomas Howard, Third Duke of Norfolk, was an 'old school' Catholic who was not only appalled when Henry led the Church of England away from Rome, but was well connected to the last remaining vestiges of Yorkist pretensions to the throne of England, the Pole family. His grandfather and father had fought for Richard of Gloucester, and not even the mercy shown to them by the incoming Henry VII had sufficed to sweeten their bitterness against Tudor rule. Again it's a matter of recorded history that the Pole family were behind a last-ditch attempt to put a scion of York where Henry VIII was now seated, but not so obvious who that person was intended to be.

The fictitious Richard Ashton who dominates much of this novel is on the one hand the figment of my imagination, but on the other a suggested solution to the age old mystery of the Princes in the Tower. The first Tudor had his doubts when Perkin Warbeck was produced at his Court, and even though Warbeck was put to death by false rumour of his intended escape, by then his wife Catherine Gordon was safely installed in the service of Queen Elizabeth of York, who would have been Warbeck's sister had he indeed been the long-lost Richard, Duke of York, as he asserted at the time.

Catherine is known to have had a son by Warbeck, but little to nothing is known of his subsequent fate. It's not beyond the bounds of credulity that he also sired a son — the Richard

Ashton of this novel — who would therefore be the last remaining legitimate York descendant of Edward IV.

To Cromwell, Ashton is simply a means of acquiring inside intelligence of the loose talk and bawdy innuendo surrounding Anne Boleyn, but to Norfolk and the Poles he is the icon around which they might create a credible challenge to the current Tudor. The stage is set for flights of imagination in a new 'take' on this well worked period of English history that does not sacrifice or misrepresent a known fact unearthed by serious historians of that era.

I cannot let Richard Ashton rest on his laurels, and he is a main character in the next novel in the series, *The Uneasy Crown*, in which his daughter Grace becomes the lifelong friend and companion of the doomed Lady Jane Grey.

As ever, I look forward to receiving feedback from you, whether in the form of a review on **Amazon** or **Goodreads**. Or, of course, you can try the more personal approach on my website, and my Facebook page: **DavidFieldAuthor**.

Happy reading!

David

davidfieldauthor.com

Sapere Books is an exciting new publisher of brilliant fiction and popular history.

To find out more about our latest releases and our monthly bargain books visit our website:
saperebooks.com

Printed in Great Britain
by Amazon